MW00964045

It couldn't be true. The woman was dead. Wasn't she?

"But who could possibly want me now, who is even left other than you two that know my secret?" Levi asked.

"Lady Grustmiener," Aura said. "Or at least her sympathizers. Amaline told us there is an army building. She came here to warn us, to help us."

He had killed Lady Grustmiener. He knew he had killed her. He felt the power build in his body and release toward her, a feeling he'd never experienced before. There was no way she, or anyone, could have lived through that. He was certain of it.

"No," he said, "that's impossible. I killed her. She is dead. I saw her dead body."

It couldn't be true, he told himself. It was a huge mistake. Theirra thought she heard something, Amaline thought she heard something, and at any moment Emily would walk through the door. A misunderstanding, that's all this was. Emily got lost. No one took her. Lady Grustmiener was dead, everyone was safe, and he could go back home.

"We are still confirming this fact," Aura said, "but it may be true. We need to prepare ourselves for the possibility that she may be back, and she may have Emily."

Aura's voice sounded a thousand miles away. Levi sat. The weight of the last several years crashed down upon him.

He looked out the windows of her office, but where there was once sunlight, now only darkness poured in.

Four years after his adventures in Esotera, Levi's life is unrecognizable. Now an accomplished author for his "fantasy" story *Saving Esotera*, a visit from someone he never expected to see again has put his new future in jeopardy. Esotera again needs his help. Familiar faces, along with some new ones, greet him upon his return, but it's not all happy homecomings. A threat from their past is rising to power.

Will Levi, Aura, and the rest of our heroes be able to defeat their enemies once and for all? Or will it not just be Esotera at stake, this time, but the world as well?

KUDOS for *Two Worlds*

In *Two Worlds* by Kristin Durfee, we are reunited with Aura, Theirra, Levi, and Emily, as well as meeting some brand new characters, several of whom are products of both Levi's world and Aura's—born of Earth mothers and Four Corners fathers. Once again, the Kingdom of Esotera is in danger from Lady Grustmiener's army, and Levi is called upon to help. At first, he doesn't believe it's true, sure that he killed her in their last battle. Will he now have to face her again? The story is well-written with a very unexpected ending. I certainly hope there is another book coming as I can't wait to find out what happens next. ~ *Taylor Jones, Reviewer*

Two Worlds by Kristin Durfee is the second book in her *Four Corners* series. In this book, our hero Levi has finally gotten his act together. He's written a best-selling novel about his adventures during the first book and is now a famous author. In fact, he is on a book tour when Theirra, the queen of Esotera's aide, comes to a signing to recruit his help for another war. It seems that our evil villain, Lady Grustmiener, isn't dead after all, and she is once again causing havoc in the Four Corners world. But this time, she wants more than dominion over her own world. She wants dominion over Earth, too. And the only thing standing in her way is Levi and Queen Aura's army of soldiers, peasants, and animals. Oh, and don't forget the dragons. *Two Worlds* is a clever and well-written tale of ordinary people being thrown into dangerous situations and doing extraordinary things when they have to. It's an entertaining read that paranormal fans of all ages will love. ~ *Regan Murphy, Reviewer*

ACKNOWLEDGEMENTS

"No man is an island," the saying goes. I think writers can adopt this as well. The support that both myself and my work has received since the release of *Four Corners* has been awe-inspiring.

I was welcomed into an incredible community of writers and readers in humbling amounts. While my gratitude could fill its own book, I have limited space, so I will say this: if I've met you at a writing event, school visit, or through social media, you've had an impact on my life, and I thank you graciously.

I would be remiss, however, if I didn't highlight some particulars. To the Orlando Indie Authors group, the Winter Park Writers group, and the lovely crew at Writer's Atelier—especially guru extraordinaire Racquel Henry—my deepest and sincerest thanks. You have all helped inspire me, taught me, and most importantly made me laugh (squirrel!).

Erin, Jessie, and Amy. Thank you for reading early drafts of this story. Your enthusiasm and suggestions helped me find my way on several occasions when I'd gotten myself quite lost.

Christina Benjamin, an accomplished and award-winning writer, didn't hesitate to take me under her wing and show me the in's and out's of this business. Your success brings me such joy. Thanks for having such an open heart.

To the team at Black Opal Books: Lauri, Faith, and Jack and the amazing fellow authors I am proud to be on the same team as, especially Tonya Royston. Your support and guidance continues to make me a better writer.

Matt C, again you have blown me away with your artistic skills. I provide a rough idea and you bring my vision to life. I, and my books, are blessed to have you on our team.

And as always, to my amazing family and friends. I wouldn't be here without you. For attending my events and asking for updates, I am humbled by your love.

I hope this was worth the wait. Enjoy and, as always, happy reading, happy life.

A Black Opal Books
Signature Edition
4 of 60

Two

Worlds

Laura—
What world do you
belong to? ♡ Kristin Durfee
Thanks for your
support!

Kristin Durfee

A Black Opal Books Publication

Black Opal Books
BECAUSE SOME STORIES JUST HAVE TO BE TOLD

GENRE: YA/NA/PARANORMAL ROMANTIC THRILLER

This is a work of fiction. Names, places, characters and incidents are either the product of the author's imagination or are used fictitiously, and any resemblance to any actual persons, living or dead, businesses, organizations, events or locales is entirely coincidental. All trademarks, service marks, registered trademarks, and registered service marks are the property of their respective owners and are used herein for identification purposes only. The publisher does not have any control over or assume any responsibility for author or third-party websites or their contents.

TWO WORLDS
Copyright © 2016 by Kristin Durfee
Cover Design by Matt Conway
All cover art copyright © 2016
All Rights Reserved
Print ISBN: 978-1-626945-17-3

First Publication: AUGUST 2016

All rights reserved under the International and Pan-American Copyright Conventions. No part of this book may be reproduced or transmitted in any form or by any means, electronic or mechanical, including photocopying, recording, or by any information storage and retrieval system, without permission in writing from the publisher.

WARNING: The unauthorized reproduction or distribution of this copyrighted work is illegal. Criminal copyright infringement, including infringement without monetary gain, is investigated by the FBI and is punishable by up to 5 years in federal prison and a fine of $250,000. Anyone pirating our ebooks will be prosecuted to the fullest extent of the law and may be liable for each individual download resulting therefrom.

ABOUT THE PRINT VERSION: If you purchased a print version of this book without a cover, you should be aware that the book is stolen property. It was reported as "unsold and destroyed" to the publisher, and neither the author nor the publisher has received any payment for this "stripped book."

IF YOU FIND AN EBOOK OR PRINT VERSION OF THIS BOOK BEING SOLD OR SHARED ILLEGALLY, PLEASE REPORT IT TO: lpn@blackopalbooks.com

Published by Black Opal Books **http://www.blackopalbooks.com**

DEDICATION

To my mom and dad, for everything

Quemadmodum gladius neminem occidit,
occidentis telum est.
(A sword itself does not slay;
it is merely the weapon used by the slayer.)

~ Seneca the Younger *Letter to Lucilius*

Prologue

Nikolas was a few feet ahead of Emily as she jogged to catch up. The air that poured into her lungs felt sharp and burned. She was not sure how much longer she would be able to keep up. Several brambles and thorns tried to catch her clothes. They slowed her down and increased the gap between the two of them even farther. She could hear Nikolas's high, clear laughter in her ears and laughed to herself, unable to fully give in for lack of breath. The small boy jutted to a stop and looked back at his mother, his smile frozen on his face.

Emily pulled up sharply, hands on her knees, and gasped much needed oxygen back into her body. Her legs trembled from the exertion of chasing Nikolas around the forest all day. It had taken some convincing of her husband to let them go on an outing with just the two of them. Milskar didn't like when they strayed far from the castle, but she insisted upon their safety and promised that they would stay close and return well before darkness set in. He reluctantly agreed and kissed her passionately while their young son burst into a fit of giggles and protested, as he did every time his parents showed affection toward one another.

They'd set off along some of the same trails Emily had traveled on almost seven years prior when she was charged with keeping the young and old inhabitants of Esotera safe from the approaching Grustmiener army. It was a task that put her in more danger then if she had stayed to fight.

Her cousin, Levi, who was her whole reason for coming to this world all those years ago, had been kidnapped soon after entering Esotera. It had been an intense and confusing time in Emily's life. She had to come to terms with the fact that this person she'd known her whole life was really the heir to a magical world, parallel to the one they had both grown up in.

She'd agreed to accompany him on a whim, terrified to let him travel with alone with the band of misfits who came to get him. Yet almost as soon as they arrived, he was taken and Emily found herself lost and trapped in this foreign land. Lost, that was, until the point at which she fell in love with Milskar.

Milskar had been part of the team of people, led by Queen Aura of Esotera, tasked with the mission of bringing Levi back to her kingdom. Emily knew her aunt and uncle had adopted Levi, yet she was amazed and shocked to learn that his ancestors came not just from a different land, but an entirely different world. A world that needed his help. Stubborn Emily had foolishly followed them and soon was all alone in this strange land. It was not until she and Milskar began to grow closer that she started to feel at home in this place.

Their courtship had been short and intense, yet it had been the realest thing she'd ever felt. Once the war was won and Aura was victorious in protecting her future, Emily and Levi were scheduled to return to their home, but at the last minute Emily persuaded the Queen to permit her to stay and be with Milskar while Levi traveled back to their world without her. Emily and Milskar were quickly married, though it was difficult to explain to her parents about her sudden absence. They were furious at her and Levi for disappearing for so long, but were excited to hear that she had met someone and fallen in love.

One time Emily and Milskar made the trip back to her parent's house. While it was a pleasant visit, it solidified in Emily's mind that she had made the right decision. This place no longer felt like home to her. They wrote and kept in touch, though it had become more difficult with the arrival of her son, Nikolas. His name had dual meanings. Nick was her father's name and Kolas was the name of their dear friend who was killed during the Great Battle. She felt it fitting to honor both men with this new life.

Now Nikolas stood in front of her as the smile faded from his pudgy five-year-old face. She was about to ask him what the matter was when strong arms grabbed her tightly from behind. A scream caught in her throat and the last thing she saw was the face of her terrified son before a powerful blow hit the back of her head and plunged her into darkness.

Chapter 1

After

It had been almost seven years since the Great Battle, as those in the kingdoms of Esotera and Grustmiener called it, and yet for Theirra it felt as though no time had passed. Those who said time healed all wounds were lying, or never had any real wounds in the first place. The hole in her heart that Kolas occupied was still as raw as it had been when he was ripped from her.

They had met on a journey to the other world, a journey that should have been a simple recovery mission for one person, and turned into the greatest—and frankly only—battle her world had ever seen. Kolas helped Esotera's new Queen Aura form an army. Theirra had a concept of war, but having never experienced it herself, she had no basis to know what it would entail. As those around her died and were hurt, a hard knot formed in her stomach, a ball of fear like a cramp around her organs which stayed with her throughout the years.

The battle wore on and it appeared like Esotera had the upper hand. The Grustmiener army seemed poised for defeat and Theirra had begun to relax. For a moment she thought that maybe all those she cared about would be able to walk away safely in victory. On the second day, though, Aura, her friend since they were young—the pair bonded so strongly they didn't always need words to communicate—came to her. Theirra took one look at her face and knew. Kolas was dead.

It was as if the oxygen was sucked out of the air and she was breathing ice. Her lungs ached with the effort to pull air in and sent shooting pain throughout her entire body. She feared at one point that she may implode if she didn't physically hold on to herself. Somehow though, she survived. There were points when she didn't think it would be possible. Points where she thought that she would die from the pain of it all, but the human body is resilient, even when the mind and heart stay weak and brittle.

After the battle, life went on somewhat normally again. Grustmiener became under the rule of Esotera with Omire, the defector from that land, at the helm. Other than a change in leadership, no real differences were felt around the kingdom.

The lives that were lost were honored, and speeches about the sacrifices that were made happened at the anniversary each year. Anyone who walked away relatively unscathed and without the loss of someone close moved on successfully with their lives, but what about the rest of the Esoterans? Those who suffered a great loss either to their own bodies or those of someone they loved walked around the village and kingdom in a kind of ghost-like trance. People would stay away from them, like how on instinct animals will avoid something close to death. An invisible force seemed to surround these people and made them instantly recognizable to everyone.

Most of these broken people left the village that surrounded the castle and chose instead to live on the outskirts of Esotera, in an effort to escape the memories that haunted them. Whether they were successful, Theirra never knew, as they tended not to return. She hoped they were able to find some peace in their remaining days.

There were times when she longed for that kind of avoidance. That ability to escape memories and feelings, but she knew that was not an option for her. Her loyalties to her queen and kingdom were stronger than any pain, so she learned to live with it in the only way she knew how. Theirra threw herself into her work. No longer a royal stable worker, she'd become Aura's right hand person and confidant. She often dealt with important matters of the kingdom, which sometimes required her to travel throughout their lands. It was on one of these trips that she over-heard some news which disturbed her. She abandoned her assignment and rushed back to the castle to speak with Aura.

☙☙☙

Aura let out an exasperated sigh. "Theirra, slow down." She was used to Theirra's erratic behavior, from calm happiness to almost manic obsession, and took little concern to her changes in mood.

"She is back."

"She who?" Aura said, half listening as she looked through a stack of documents.

"Lady Grustmiener," Theirra said.

Aura looked up, a mixture of pity and concern on her face. Theirra was used to this look, like how you would view a child who was terrified of monsters under the bed. Placated amusement.

"Theirra—" Aura started, but was promptly cut off.

"I heard it. I heard it myself, in the woods of Grustmiener. There were people talking of her return."

"Theirra." Aura put her hand up when Theirra tried to interrupt her again. "It has been seven years. And I know those seven years have been very difficult for you, but it does not help to live in this fantasy land you have created for yourself. I am worried about you." Aura came around her massive desk and laid a hand on Theirra's shoulder, which her friend shook off.

"I am not crazy," Theirra said, her tone defensive. "I heard it. I think she may be alive. We never recovered her body."

"Only because her supporters, what few were left of them, recovered it first. She is dead Theirra. Levi—" She stopped, an image of him popped into her head and it was as if she had been transported back in time. The two of them so young, so foolish, yet so brave. She composed herself and continued. "Levi killed her himself. Do you not think that if she were still alive we would have heard something from her by now?"

"Not if it took her this long to recover," Theirra said.

"Theirra, I am very thankful for all your help and all you do for me in the kingdom, but maybe it would be a good idea for you to take a few relaxation days. Take a trip. You have been talking about wanting to visit Gilbert, have you not?"

"I am not sure if I am ready," Theirra said, her voice just louder than a whisper.

"We never are if we wait around for a moment when we *think* we are," Aura said.

"I will think about it," Theirra said and left Aura's office, mumbling to herself.

Milskar moved from his silent perch and stood across from Aura.

"Aura—"

She raised a hand. "I know. But I need to try something. I have tried listening to her, being sympathetic, giving her space, but she only retreats deeper within herself."

"And you think sending her away will do that?"

"I am willing to try anything. I think this may work. She will travel up north, see Gilbert, I hope that gives her some peace, and she can return here renewed."

"Lady Grustmiener?" He said her name as a question.

"She is confused. She has been confused before. There are only so many times we can search for a ghost before we determine that she's not coming back."

"Truth or wishful thinking?" Milskar asked.

"I hope it is the former."

ℰℬℰℬ

The idea popped into Theirra's head, as if it had been hiding out in the corners of her mind forever, just waiting for an excuse to show itself. Yes, it would be perfect. It would be the perfect alibi. It would give her plenty of time without any of the suspicions that kept her from do-ing it earlier. Her mind was made up.

She approached Aura later that evening to inform her that she would, in fact, take a trip. Aura embraced her and sent an aide to gather supplies for her journey. The hope in her friend's eyes made Theirra second-guess herself for a split second, but she pushed the negative thought away.

She knew to the core of her bones that this was the correct decision.

The next day, Theirra was on her way to Grustmiener when she heard the news of Emily's kidnapping. She knew in the deepest recesses of her body that Lady Grustmiener had something to do with it. She took care of what business she'd come for and then promptly set out on the second leg of her journey, more determined than ever.

Chapter 2

Tab

It was getting colder outside by the minute, but it didn't look like Tab's situation was going to change anytime soon. He'd tried the three shelters within walking distance of the park, but they already had lines longer than beds available. He cursed himself for not packing up sooner, but the afternoon sun, a rare treat this time of year, felt too good to turn his back on.

He knew he was better off on the streets than at his mom's house, but it took reminding sometimes. He'd run away before when he was younger, but his age made people pay attention to him, and he was always forced to return home. His mom would greet him at the door, fake hugs and kisses, and profusely thank whatever officer had dropped him off this time. She would usually invite that person in, drop her eyes, and allow her robe to open up just a bit, but mercifully they always declined.

As soon as they walked through the door of whatever crappy apartment he and his mom hadn't gotten kicked out of yet, she would unleash on him. "You dumb piece of crap!" she would yell while she slapped him around his face and shoulders. He would take it, hunch over, and cover his ears with his hands. She was the one person he could control himself around.

He often got into trouble in school and on the playground when other boys made fun of him. Tab never had the newest styles, most of the time his clothes weren't even clean, and even with his large size, he was often the butt of jokes and taunts. He tried to ignore them, really he tried to, but someone would take it just one step too far and, next thing he knew, a group of boys were pulling him off one who was lying on the ground in various stages of unconsciousness.

His one saving grace was that, for some reason they rarely, if ever, pointed him out as the culprit. They might be complete jerks, but they had some sort of moral code it seemed. That or they didn't want to seem like people who could pick fights and were unable to follow through.

He was a smart kid and could tell he frustrated his teachers. When they called on him, he always got the right answer and his test scores were often the best in the class, but he never turned in homework and never volunteered for anything.

"You have so much potential" should have been his name.

And his *name*. Ugh, what was his mother thinking? It was hard enough being one of the only Asian kids in his school. On top of that she had to name him after a soda? She assured him that he was named after some great warrior of folklore or something like that, but he believed she was just saying that in embarrassment for really naming him after a drink.

He'd met his dad one and a half times. Or maybe that should be, he'd seen his dad one and a half times. When he was maybe four or five, his mother packed him up and drove him across town. The houses got larger and farther apart the farther they got from their two bedroom place in the Vista Views. What the view was supposed to be, Tab could never figure out.

She held on to his hand a little too tight as she marched him up a long sidewalk to a gigantic two story red brick house in a sea of similar looking homes. The doorbell played an actual song when it was pressed. A small woman answered the door, took one look at his mother, and tried to shut it again in her face, but she wasn't quick enough, and his mom got her foot wedged in.

"I'm here to see him," she said.

"I don't know who you think you are coming here," the woman said, "but I am going to have to ask you to leave or I am calling the police."

"Stacey, who's there?" a male voice called from the top of the stairs.

Tab could just make out the man, handsome with black hair and features that Tab recognized as his own.

"No one," the woman said as she struggled with the door.

"No one, my foot!" his mother called. "Joshua, Joshua, come here and see your son. Your son!"

After much noise and whispered conversation, Tab's father appeared at the door. "It's okay, Stacey," he said over her loud protests. "I'll get rid of them. Go call the children for dinner."

"You can't avoid us forever," Tab's mother said when the three of them were alone.

Tab noticed that her foot was still the only thing holding the door open.

"There is no reason to avoid or not avoid you," he said. "You are nothing to me. This is not my son."

"Not your son! What kind of woman do you think I am?" she shrieked.

"The kind of woman who would come to a man's

house, a *married* man's house, and put her small child through something like this. I think it is time for you to go home now."

He began to push the door hard and Tab noticed that his mother was losing ground. She cried out as her foot got crushed by the closing door and, the next thing Tab knew, he'd broken his mother's hold and pushed back at the solid wood with all his might.

The door flew off the hinges and fell to a clatter on the floor along with his father. He knew this man was a liar. He knew his mother, even with all her faults, told the truth.

"Don't you ever hurt my mom," Tab said as the shaken man fumbled to get to his feet. Tab took his mom's hand and, this time, he led her away and to the car.

Ten years later, he saw the man on the street with a woman who was not his wife Stacey. His father did not see him, and Tab made no effort to get his attention. The man was arguing with this woman who proceeded to slap him full on the face. The crowds on the street clapped for her as she marched right by Tab. He and his father locked eyes for a split second, but Tab knew the man had no idea who he was, so Tab looked away. He felt a bit of satisfaction to know that, while his mother struggled with her own demons, his father's life wasn't so great without them, either.

It struck Tab as funny that you could have people in your life that you loved to the very core of your being, but that you could also not stand to be around them. He would always love his mother and would come if she needed him, really needed him, but for the most part he stayed away. They each had their own problems and issues, but also realized pretty early on they weren't going to be able to fix each other. It broke his heart a bit, so he often tried not to think about it.

As he wandered around the city he blew into his hands in a vain attempt to warm them. He ruled out trying to track his mom down for a chance at a place to crash. He'd try his luck in the park and hope the cops were giving everyone a break tonight because of the weather.

Though pretty soon, he was extra thankful that they didn't seem to be out.

It all started out innocently enough. He'd just laid down on a bench and was trying to get comfortable when he received a hard poke in the shoulder.

"You're lying on my bench," the voice barked.

Tab had this problem a few times, regulars seeming to think they had a monopoly on a particular place. Usually he relented without much fuss and moved on, but this bench was close to a heating vent and he didn't feel like moving.

"Bench was empty when I got here," Tab said. "Way I see it, if it was yours, you would've been in it." He shut his eyes and settled back down—an indication to the man Tab intended to stay.

The man said some colorful words under his breath then shoved Tab even harder, almost pushing him off and into the frozen ground. Tab just wasn't in the mood.

"Look," Tab said as he sat up. "You may have slept here every day for your whole life, but not tonight."

"All right, Jackie Chan," the man said.

Tab closed his eyes and balled his fists. People were so original. Tab wasn't even Chinese, yet he'd been called that name countless times, especially during or after a fight.

"Listen, man," Tab said. "I'm not dealing with this tonight. Just move along. Tomorrow, I promise, you can have the spot back, but not tonight."

"Are you kidding me with this?"

"I would listen to him," a woman's voice said from

the shadows.

It wasn't until Tab looked around that he realized how dark it'd gotten.

"What the heck is this?" the man asked.

"Like I said, I would listen to him and move on." She stepped out and into the light. She had dark skin and bright, clear eyes, and, while she was several years older than Tab, there was an innocence about her. It was almost as if she was seeing the world for the first time. The man didn't seem impressed.

"Why don't you get out of here before you regret getting involved?" he said as he took a step toward her.

Tab didn't wait to see what the man planned to do. In one swift move, he was behind the guy and, with a single punch, dropped him to the ground.

"Well," she said. "Now that that's taken care of, how about you and I go someplace warm?"

Tab grabbed his bag and, without a second thought, followed her into the darkness.

Chapter 3

Galina

Snow fell as Galina walked down the slick road toward her house. Though, in all truthfulness, house may have been a strong word. She lived in a two bedroom apartment with her parents and two sisters. Though, in all truthfulness, lived in would have may have been a strong word.

She was never much for labels or settling down. Even when she was a young girl of eleven or twelve, she always seemed to wander away from wherever they lived and returned only out of necessity. Her mother used to get worried, but after the millionth time calling the cops about her run-away daughter, they stopped looking and sent in social workers instead. In fear of losing her other, well-behaved children, Galina's mom let her do whatever she wanted. If she came back after five days gone, she was met with barely an acknowledgement of her return, much less her departure. Her sisters, though, were a different story.

Galina was almost ten years older than the other girls, and her sisters were fifteen months apart from each other. And again, in all truthfulness, her "father" wasn't really her father, but her mother's husband. So that also made her sisters her half-sisters, but she didn't like to dwell on such technicalities.

It was strange for it to snow this early in the year and, according to the weather reports, the next town over didn't report a single flurry. But the next town over didn't have a teenager who could control the weather and just got dumped by her boyfriend. He was a complete jerk, and she knew that. She told herself that, and all her friends told her that, too, but still, seeing it live in person almost made her lose her mind.

She crashed on his couch sometimes. He was three years older than her, had dropped out of college, and was working at some discount store. His apartment was crappy, crappier than even hers, but there were no adults there, just his two roommates and they weren't around that often. Sometimes, she would spend a week or more crashing on his couch, always his couch—she might not respect much, but she respected herself—and would return home after it got tiresome to just sit around and watch him play video games.

Sometimes, she went to school, but mostly she walked around town. It wasn't a big town and pretty much everyone knew everyone. This was probably another reason why her mother had called off her search dogs a few years ago. If anything had happened to Galina, you'd better believe it would get to her mom in about five seconds. Galina liked to pretend that this nosiness bothered her, but deep down she was comforted to know that help wouldn't be that far away. It made her feel less alone.

On this particular night, as her boots made soft crunching noises in the light dusting on the sidewalk, her boyfriend was probably still recovering from the ass-kicking she'd given him.

Earlier that day she'd walked into his apartment and

began to take off her coat when she heard noises from the bedroom. This wasn't a completely out-of-the-ordinary occurrence. He had roommates and those guys tended to bring girls home with them from the bar. But the trouble was it was only four-thirty in the afternoon, and she knew that they weren't supposed to be home. That was why she was there in the first place. She knew it was going to be empty, and she'd planned to surprise her boyfriend. Maybe she would take their relationship to the next level. She'd thought about it for the last few days.

She followed the noises and found a bedroom door half open. She couldn't be sure of everything that had happened, but when she looked down at her hands, she found several of the knuckles caked in dried blood, and her wrist ached. She remembered hearing screaming, but she thought it came from that girl. And not just any girl, but Abigail, her "best friend." It was difficult for Galina not to do something to her, too.

So here she was, walking in the snow. The cold air felt good on her aching fingers. That was why she'd even thought of snow in the first place. And now, the more she brooded over what happened, the heavier and thicker it fell. She heard a car in the distance spin its wheels and lose traction as it turned down a street and faded away into the night. There were few cars on these streets even on a bright summer day, and now, with the sudden storm, the place looked deserted.

Good, she thought, *a little discomfort for all of you.*

Soon she heard footsteps crunch behind her. She groaned. Was he seriously following her? What? Did he think that he could throw that good-for-nothing trash out of his bed and then come after her? That he could kiss her and tell her he was sorry, and her hate would melt like the snow around her? Fool. She whirled around to face him and was shocked to see a woman walk up to her. She was older than Galina and dressed in not enough clothes for the weather, but it didn't seem to affect her. White air puffed from the woman's mouth as she got closer.

"What do you want?" Galina asked.

She pushed out her chest and tried to look big. Her hand was killing her and she was afraid that, if cornered, it would be useless in a fight.

"That looks like it hurts," the woman said.

Galina took a step backward. "What's it to you?"

"Nothing really, I just figured if we were going to travel, you would probably want to be in good shape," the woman said as she rifled through a bag.

"Travel?"

Did this crazy person plan to kidnap her? Strange part was, Galina wasn't sure if she minded. What did she have to live for here? What was her life doing for her anyway?

"Ah, here," the woman said and produced a blue bottle filled with liquid. "May I?" she asked but, without waiting for an answer, unscrewed the bottle and splashed some of Galina's hand.

"Hey, what the—" Galina said and let a string of obscenities lose as the chemical burned her hand.

"It will only hurt for a moment, but I am sure it is not as bad as what caused the injury in the first place. Do you want to tell me what you did?"

"Tell you?" Galina said as she rubbed her hand. "Why would I tell you?"

"No reason, just curiosity on my part, I guess."

"Why would I tell you?" Galina repeated.

"Oh, my manners," the woman said with a smile and reached out her hand. "I am from somewhere far away that needs your help. I have been searching for someone like you to assist me. It is a pleasure to finally meet you. Now, if it is not too much trouble, do you think you can stop all this foolish snow?"

Galina looked at the woman's face and then down at her own hand grasped in the stranger's. Her handshake was firm. Galina's hand didn't hurt one bit. The snow instantly ceased.

Chapter 4

Julia

Julia sat by herself, as she always did, in the sparsely green field in front of the school. Her fellow classmates played on the various pieces of equipment that littered the grounds during their half-hour recess after lunch. There were twelve other fourteen-year-old girls that made up Ms. March's class, and Julia was unlucky number thirteen.

She played quietly by herself, a skill she had learned in the eight years since that terrible day. Julia was in kindergarten, learning her ABC's while her parents, who'd taken a rare day off to paint their living room after they'd talked about it for months, startled two robbers who didn't expect them to be home. Her mother's car was in the shop for an oil change, so the men assumed no one was there. After Julia arrived home from school and stumbled upon the scene, she called nine-one-one—just like her mother had taught her if there was ever an emergency—and waited, her pink backpack still on when the EMTs arrived. They did what they could, but it was too late. Her parents were already dead.

Both of them were only children, their own parents

having died before Julia was even born. She had no place to go. A ward of the state, she moved into an orphanage and waited to be adopted. She was hopeful at first, but it soon became clear that no one wanted the small girl with the sad, dark eyes. Eventually, she made it to her current home, Sister Margaret's Home for Troubled Girls. Here Julia would live and attend school until she was eighteen and declared no longer a burden to the state. She looked forward to and dreaded that day in equal parts.

For now, she was resigned to spend her days drifting through classes, field trips, and watching potential parents parade through the grounds. They always looked past her, as if there was something in the distance that caught their eye. She sat on the ground, removed from the other kids, their screams and laughter floating like butterflies around her head. The dirt around her legs was interspersed with patches of yellow-green grass. She picked up a rock, threw it up in the air, and caught it moments before it landed. It moved as if through Jell-O, a tick slower than it should have. She paid so much attention to what she was doing that she didn't notice that a girl had moved close to her to recover a ball which had been kicked too far.

"Freak."

The word startled Julia and caused the rock to fall out of the air and land with a thud. The girl laughed and ran away. Julia's face burned red hot.

She was about to retrieve the rock again when she caught sight of the headmistress out of the corner of her eye. With her was a young woman, thirty maybe, with dark skin and wearing all black clothing. There was something about her that gave Julia pause, like she almost didn't belong. The woman shifted from foot to foot, as if trying to reposition uncomfortable clothing.

"Julia," the headmistress said, addressing her.

Julia got up and brushed dead grass and dirt from the back of her legs.

"I would like you to meet someone." The headmistress beamed. Did Julia imagine it, or were her eyes glazed over? "This woman would like to adopt you."

Julia's heart skipped and stuttered in her chest. Adopt? Was this some kind of trick? She looked over at the older girls in the playground to see if they laughed with their hands over their mouths, but they played intently, not one pair of eyes focused on her.

"Julia," the strange woman said with a sweet, soft voice that didn't seem to go with her dark outfit and haunted eyes. "It is very nice to meet you. My name is Theirra."

Chapter 5

Revisited

Levi pinched the bridge of his nose—in an attempt to dissipate the headache that formed between his eyes—and paced the parking lot. No matter how many of these things he did, he still got nervous and found it difficult to stay still. It had begun to drizzle out and he prayed that it wasn't a sign. He hoped it wouldn't keep people away. It was hard for him to even imagine this situation, hard to picture that anyone would come anyway, but come they did.

A line had already formed outside of the Great Reads Bookstore and Levi wondered how he would even enter. As he thought this, Kailly, the person who was making all this possible, stepped forward and held on to his arm. She pushed them through the crowd, as if he was some kind of pop star. None of the people who waited screamed—that would hopefully come later—but there was a kind of frenzy in the air. It was just around the edges, but it could clearly be felt, like when snow was right around the corner, hanging crisp and clear in the sky.

Levi walked in with his head down and nodded at those he passed. He moved along the perimeter, made his way to a large mahogany table near the center of the store, and sat down. He remembered coming into similar stores in his youth and running his hands along the spines of the hundreds of books housed inside like a temple of great thought. He never imagined that he would be among those who had published works. That his book held a place on a shelf where people could run their hands over it, buy it, take it home, and fall in love with it.

It happened slowly at first, but *Saving Esotera* had climbed to the top of the best sellers lists where it had remained for the past six weeks. Levi had been catapulted to instant celebrity and was currently on a grueling book tour that he was told was paramount to keep his book in the number one spot. He couldn't remember what city he was in and was about to ask Kailly when the first person came up to the table.

The crowds were steady throughout the evening, and Levi's hand began to ache. He soaked the hand each night in an ice bath and took more aspirin at one time than was suggested in an entire day, but it did little to quell the pain. He kept that to himself, though. He didn't want to seem like he was complaining about stardom, which he'd longed for since his return four years ago from Esotera.

It had been hard for him to adjust back to normal life. His parents had been furious upon his return. They'd been terrified for his life after his uncle found his apartment in shambles. He made up a story that he'd already left and that the place had been broken into while he was gone. They didn't seem to believe him, but wanted to so badly, they let the topic drop, happy that he was home and safe. His uncle was another story, for it wasn't just Levi who left on the journey, under the pretense of finding his birth parents, but also his cousin Emily who went with him. When he returned home, he had some serious explaining to do. He made up a story that Emily had met someone while they searched for his birth parents. The two hit it off, he told them all, and she wanted to stick around for a bit to see how it the relationship would pan out. She was also thinking about maybe taking some college classes and moving to California, he told them. The story was partially true. She had met someone and did want to see where their relationship would go, but California was never an option. She'd stayed behind in Esotera.

Somehow Emily was able to get letters to her parents and spoke of this great love and their plans to move overseas. She said this man—she called him Mike, which Levi thought was close enough—was in the army and was going to be stationed overseas for several years and she had decided to go with him. This last part made Levi laugh a little, and he felt like she added it just as a wink for him. They came for a brief visit a few years ago, but stayed for such a short time, Levi didn't get to see her. He tried to send letters to the return address on her envelopes, but was never sure if they got to her.

Emily's parents were upset at their daughter's sudden abandonment of the family, but not having the financial means to come visit her in Europe prevented them from taking any immediate action, which Levi was sure was Emily's intention.

Levi shook his head to bring himself back to his current situation. A young woman stood in front of him, gushing about how much she loved his book and how she wished there was a real place like Esotera that she could go live in.

He nodded politely, like he always did, and signed the front inside cover. She was about to say something else when Kailly thanked her for coming and placed a hand on the woman's elbow. An employee of the bookstore escorted the woman to the counter to pay for her book.

This process continued and he barely looked up when the next person walked in front of his table. He just methodically moved another copy over from the stack that had slowly dwindled in the hour and a half he'd been signing pages.

"Whom can I make this out to?" he said with his pen poised over the paper.

"Levi?"

The voice was so soft, but he would have recognized it even in a room of a thousand screaming people. The blood in his veins went cold as he lifted his eyes. He nearly fell backward out of his chair as he sprang up.

"Th—Theirra?" he stammered. She looked much older than when he had seen her last, as if the years had not treated her kindly, and he imagined they had not. He said something to Kailly about how he needed a break and pulled Theirra into a back room of the store with him. "Theirra, what are you doing here?"

"I am so sorry to have come here. Queen Aura would be furious with me, but I felt that it was important that you be informed, that you would want to be informed. Sometimes she does not always know what is best for herself and her people." Theirra seemed shocked at herself for having spoken such words and closed her mouth with an audible snap.

"What news? What's going on?"

"It is Emily."

Levi felt what little color was left in his face drain away. "What about Emily?" he asked, afraid to hear the answer.

"She was taken several weeks ago. There was a massive search effort, but we were unable to locate her whereabouts or those who have taken her." Theirra said. "I have been keeping in touch with various people in Esotera and Grustmiener to keep abreast of what has been going on, but I am afraid to say there has been no good news."

"Taken? Emily, taken?" A hole in his chest he'd ignored for months began to pain him again. "What do you need from me?"

"Aura believes they are just gypsies or vagabonds, looking for some type of ransom, but I think this is just because she wishes to believe the best in all situations, to keep painful truths away from everyone, especially Milskar," Theirra added. The sadness in her voice was palpable.

"Milskar. How is he?"

"He is beside himself and sick with blame, but at least their son was safely found in the woods soon after."

"Their son? They had a son?" He didn't remember being told this the last time he saw his aunt and uncle. Words swam around Levi's head when a hard knock came on the door.

"Levi? Levi, stop being ridiculous. You have to come back out. People are waiting." Kailly's panicked voice came from the other side of the door. "Levi, answer me!"

"I'll be out in just a moment."

"Hurry up!" she hollered.

"But you don't think it was vagabonds, do you?" Levi asked.

"No."

"Theirra, can you stay for a little while longer? I need to finish with a few things here and put some affairs in order, but I want to figure this out with you. Maybe I'll come back with you, I don't know." Levi wasn't sure how he was going to explain this to his agent, but he knew he could figure something out. Family emergency, which technically wouldn't be a lie.

"Yes, of course. We have several hours before a portal near here opens, so we have time."

Moments later, he left the small room with Theirra still inside. Kailly called for him to hurry up the second he was within earshot, but he tuned her out. His words fell in a rush as he informed her that he had a family emergency and, after the people who remained, he would be out of town for a few days. He could tell she wanted to protest, but thought the better of it after she saw how upset he was.

It was difficult for him to focus, and he was relieved when, thirty minutes later, the store began to close and he could leave. He got Theirra, promised Kailly he would keep her posted on when he would return, and asked her to cancel any book signings in the meantime. As he and Theirra walked to his car, both silent and deep in thought, the skies opened and soaked them.

Chapter 6

Revelation

Emily's breath came rapid and shallow. Her arms and legs ached from walking for hours and now being held in tight restraints. A hand touched her, and she tried to scream, but found that something covered her mouth. Panic rose in her again as she pulled against whatever it was that held her down. She looked around wildly, but could see nothing. It was a moment before she realized that her eyes were covered as well.

"Pretty little scar you have here," a rough voice said and traced the line on her side with a rough finger.

It had been many years since that day in the woods that she had come upon Levi, crazed with whatever lies the Grustmiener side had fed him. He'd accidentally cut her, and while she willed the mark to leave her and remove the memory of that day, the raised pink portion of flesh remained, a contrast against her pale skin.

She tried desperately to process what had happened. She had, just moments ago it seemed, ran and played in the woods with her son. Her son! Was he okay? Did this terrible person take him as well? Again she tried to talk, to yell for him, but was unable to. Her body sagged, resigned to the fact that there was no escape from her current situation. Instead, she listened hard to what was around her. Holding her breath, she found it difficult to pick up any noises but the swoosh of blood as it pumped through her veins. She heard the ragged breath of the person in the room with her, but other than that, she could decipher no other noises. Not even birds or animals called to one another. Maybe Nikolas got away, she hoped. Maybe they never got their hands on him.

A door creaked to her right, and Emily's head tried to whip in that direction, but it was restricted somehow as well. So she was in some type of room. That would at least explain the lack of outside noises, but where could she be? It seemed as though she'd walked for miles, but being unsure of what direction, she didn't know if she was still in Esotera.

"So you got her," a gruff voice stated.

"Obviously."

"She will be very happy."

"I would hope so. I believe I fulfilled my obligation. Do you have what I need?"

There was a rustle and some type of heavy object was removed. Emily heard murmurs as hands passed over metal, and then the footfalls seemed to move away. The door was shut, the noise so loud it caused her to jump.

She released a mouthful of air in one push and tried to regain some semblance of consistent breathing, when the blow hit her. The shock of it got to her before any pain was able to register. Where had this come from? Hadn't she heard two sets of feet leave?

She tried to process what had happened, her thoughts abuzz, when she felt herself lifted back up again. At this moment, she also realized that whatever she sat on had fallen with her, so it could also be assumed that the chair she was on was attached to her too. Emily longed for her eyes. If she could just see, she felt like she could make some sense of the situation.

As if the person could read her mind, he ripped her blindfold off as he righted her. There was a single dull light source which came from the low ceiling in the room, but its brightness caused her to blink rapidly against it. Whatever was in her mouth was still tied and she found it difficult to swallow properly. Now with her sight, all she wished for was her voice.

"Emily of Esotera." The voice seemed to boom from all around the room and brought her back to the reality of the situation.

She tried to look up at him, but was only able to open her eyes into tiny slits against the light. What she could see, though, frightened her. The man looked about eight feet tall and close to 300 pounds. He looked relaxed, standing with his arms across his chest and one leg supporting his weight as the other bent in front of him, yet she could feel movement from him. Like a cat ready to pounce, perfectly still, yet buzzing with anticipation.

"Hmmphfm," she tried to say through the gag.

"Ahh, right," he said a little softer this time. "I suppose it is difficult to talk with that in your mouth. Shall we remove it?"

He ripped the rag with such force, Emily was sure the lower half of her jaw went along with it. Saliva poured back into her throat and almost burned when the liquid hit all the dry parts of her mouth. She swallowed hard and tried to wet her tongue enough to be able to talk.

"My—son," she choked out.

"Ahh, your son."

"Please." The words were like knives cutting her mouth and teeth as she pushed them out.

The man turned from her and started to walk toward the door. Panic again ran through her, stronger than blood, and filled her mouth with a metallic taste of terror.

"Please!" she screamed.

"I do not believe a boy arrived with you," he said. He left the room and shut the door behind him.

Emily crumpled against her restraints and sobbed. She leaned over and spit a glob of blood onto the floor. Perhaps it wasn't fear that she had tasted, but her own blood as she had bit through her cheek, sick with the anticipation of his answer.

Chapter 7

The Spy

It felt strange to Amaline to walk back through these parts again after so many years. Her life had changed in some profound ways, but what surprised her most was how similar it still was. She still trained and hunted each day in Grustmiener, but now she had students who learned from her. Amaline took great pride in her ability to pull talent out of those guards deemed hopeless cases by other officers.

Her fiery personality made up for her small stature, and she quickly made a name for herself as someone who must be listened to, and not just because of her close relationship with the new ruler of Grustmiener. There had been talk of renaming the kingdom, and while some residents supported the movement, King Omire decided against it. It took months of persuasion on Queen Aura's part, but Omire agreed to make his temporary status as ruler permanent about three years ago. While Esotera technically had rule over Grustmiener, Aura allowed them to govern themselves, though she was still an active member of their counsel. She came to them for their meetings, giving Amaline no cause to travel to Esotera.

The population of Grustmiener was considerably smaller than before the war. Death in battle had claimed many lives, but their loyalty to their fallen king caused many more to leave the city center once the fighting was over.

It was difficult, though, to determine how many resided in Grustmiener because of the way they lived. While lush and dense now from their rainy season, the second half of their year was marked by intense drought. Residents built their houses underground or partially obscured to help combat the intense heat that was sure to come and change the land around them to dust.

The low-lying houses also helped with the rain. They kept the residences warm and insulated while the waters ran downhill and filled the lakes and streams that crossed through to Esotera. While they weren't able to put an exact number on their inhabitants, lately it seemed as though the population had slowly trickled out from the castle and surrounding areas. Amaline was determined to find out why.

She'd tracked a group of four men and two women as they moved through the woods headed north. The bogs and marshes that made up most of Grustmiener helped conceal her and dampen the sound her sloshing footsteps made. The party she followed made no attempts at stealth and, several times, she was able to follow them based on their noise alone.

The air grew colder after several days and the damp earth began to harden under her feet. She became increasingly more careful about where she placed her steps. Any sharp, dry snap of a tree branch would reverberate in the forest and reveal her to the group.

In the last moments of light on the sixth day, the party vanished in front of Amaline's eyes. She looked around, frantic and fearful they might have caught on to her presence and were prepared to ambush her. She found some shrubbery and hid within the thick branches.

Amaline cursed herself for coming here with no plan or even support. She had packed some food and water, but she hadn't expected the journey to last as long as it had. As she thought back, she couldn't even remember if she told a single person where she would be going or what she would be doing. Preparation was one of the first things she taught her students and here she was, trapped in a bush with no escape plan.

As darkness moved in, strange animal noises echoed through the woods. The hairs on her arms and neck stood on end and sent a prickling sensation over her entire body. She was sure a large creature had brushed against her foot, and she fought not to scream.

Lights started to appear in patches around her. Through the glowing flames, Amaline could make out faces, hundreds of them. The breath in her lungs caught and froze, and she had to resist a primal urge to flee. She knew if she moved now, she risked certain capture. She pulled her arms close to her body and settled in for what was sure to be a sleepless night.

In the early hours of the morning, she awoke with a start to the sounds of movement around her. Two pairs of legs appeared directly in front of the foliage she hid in. She kept perfectly still and slowed her breathing as the two people started to talk.

"So now what do we do?" a woman asked.

"Wait, I suppose," the man answered.

"I talked to people who said they have been here for days with no sign of her."

"We knew we might have to wait. If the rumors are true, she is assembling forces from all around. I imagine that will take some time," the man said.

"I hope not. I cannot stand to be ruled by that murderer and her puppet Omire any longer," the woman said as she spat on the ground.

"Well, if Lady Grustmiener fulfills her promise, we will not have to wait for much longer."

The gasp that came from Amaline's mouth took her by such surprise, for a moment she wondered who uttered it. Then horror struck as she realized her mistake. She stayed absolutely still, afraid to even breathe.

"Did you hear that?" the man asked as Amaline tightened her grip on her knife, grateful she'd decided to at least bring a weapon.

"Probably more of those blasted iellas they have running around these parts. Stupid useless creatures," the woman said.

As if on cue, a large rat-like creature ran out from an adjoining bush and toward the two. Amaline heard the sound of an arrow being released, the soft sound of penetrated flesh, and a feeble squeak.

"Come," the man said, "Let us find the others. We will need to hunt soon, anyway. I cannot bear to eat one more of these things. Just leave it."

Amaline watched the legs disappear and, as quickly and soundlessly as she could manage, extracted herself from her hiding place. She ran back the way she had come until she collapsed, panting on the forest floor.

Her head swam with the terrible conversation that had just taken place in front of her. Lady Grustmiener? Back? Gathering an army? Theirra had had her suspicions. A few weeks ago, she'd even asked Amaline to look into it, but she hadn't taken Theirra seriously. Amaline had agreed to check it out, but hadn't planned on doing much about it. So even though she'd followed these people, it hadn't been at the forefront of her thoughts that this would be the root cause of the exodus.

She knew she had to get back and tell Omire, or

should she go straight to Esotera and inform Queen Aura?

She started to pick her way back home and tried to avoid the worn path she arrived on, in case other travelers used it as well.

One time, she came upon a group of three, but was able to hide in a tree until they passed. They didn't notice her eyes as she watched them from far above. While she was able to move faster on her own, it still took her four days to journey back to the castle.

It was dusk when she made the final turn toward the long road that led to the half-buried castle. She was exhausted, but knew she had to find Omire before she rested. This information was more important than her need for sleep.

Amaline stumbled through the front doors and was immediately and roughly stopped by two guards.

"Oh stop," she said in an exasperated tone. "I am Amaline, aide and head training guard of King Omire."

They released their grip and looked down at her with sheepish expressions.

"Amaline, we are terribly sorry. I did not recognize you," the one man said. "Is everything all right?"

"Yes, I am fine," she lied. She must have looked awful from her ten-days' journey to have these men not recognize her, especially since she had spent six months training the pair of them. "I need to speak with the king, where is he?"

"Gone," the other guard said. "He took a trip to some outlying farms in the far east, said something about new crops and rotations. I expect him to be back in a few days."

Amaline was crestfallen. The decision had been made for her and now she had to journey to Esotera. The trip would take just a day or two, but she was so tired. Still, she knew the information she held could not wait.

"Is there anything we can do for you?" the first guard asked.

"Yes," Amaline sighed, "I need a horse. I leave for Esotera immediately."

Chapter 8

The Pull Back

Levi opened the door of his hotel room—in Dallas, he'd later remembered—and shut it behind Theirra. The room was of a decent size and nice enough, though he longed for home. He'd been on the road for months as he tried to drive up excitement and sales of his book. Finally, it had done well enough that he was able to purchase a place of his own without help from his parents, yet he rarely ever got to see it.

The TV had been left on by the cleaning staff and Levi went to turn it off. The news showed the picture of a fifteen year-old boy who had gone missing from his group home.

It didn't matter what city Levi was in, each news station talked about a string of missing children. Levi thought he saw Theirra give a slight start and then relax when the image turned off.

"Talk," Levi said as they each settled on to one of the two double beds. They drove to the hotel in silence and he could take it no more.

"I already told you," Theirra said. "We need to go back and find Emily."

"And by we, you mean you, since Aura doesn't even know you are here."

"Something like that," she retorted.

Levi could still see the pain that swam behind her eyes. Time didn't always heal wounds or pull blankets over memories. He knew a thing or two about that, but Theirra looked as if she held onto the pain like it was a life raft, and she would drown without it. Drown in what, he wasn't sure.

His head spun. "Theirra, you can't just walk into a book store after four years and expect me to just follow you. Tell me what's going on."

"You followed us once before," she reminded him.

"Because I was an idiot and was scared and—t—this is d—different," he stammered. He was having second thoughts about agreeing to accompany her so quickly. After having some time to process it, the notion seemed insane and impossible.

"Yes, it is different. It is even more important because your cousin is involved, and I suspect other parties as well…" Her voice trailed off.

He leaned forward. "Other parties?"

"Aura does not share my same beliefs," she gushed, "but I believe there is only one person who can be behind this. I believe it is the start of something much bigger."

"Who? Who is behind it?

"Lady Grustmiener."

The silence hung in the air like a balloon. It bounced up and down. Her words punched him in the gut, and it took a second for him to find his voice again. "So you think," he stated, "that Lady Grustmiener somehow came back, took Emily, and now has some plot involving her, to what, take back Esotera?"

"Yes."

He laughed. It was all so ridiculous. "She's dead."

"No," Theirra said.

"How do you know? Did you see her? How do you know better than I do? Better than the person who killed her?"

"I just do," she said.

He didn't want to argue and sat back on the bed. "All right then." He sighed. "All right."

"Lady Grustmiener did not just lose Esotera that day. She lost her lands, her husband, her confidant Winester, as well as any potential for the power she so desperately wanted. I hold a grudge when someone does not thank me for getting them a glass of water..." Theirra trailed off again.

Levi chuckled and looked over at her. He could see something else in her eyes—past the grief, even deeper down. It seemed like a desperation hid in them. For what? It could not be just for Emily. Could they have gotten that close in the years since Levi had left? Revenge, he concluded. She wanted to get back at the person who took her love Kolas away. That had to be it. Emily was probably not even in any real danger. It probably was gypsies or whatever Aura had said, but Theirra wanted a war. Another war. A war for Kolas.

"Theirra—" he started, his voice low and soft, but she held up her hand.

"This has nothing to do with him," she said bitterly. "I know I am right. I know she has come back to power and will to try to take our lands again. I just need to convince Aura of it. If you come back with me, she will realize that I am correct and something needs to be done to protect not only Esotera, but the entire Four Corners."

He sighed again. Did he owe them all something? Did he owe Theirra anything? He walked into their life and battled to save a land he was, unbeknownst to him, the heir of. He came close to losing them that land as well.

He'd been kidnapped and brainwashed. Aura had almost lost everything, but he escaped and Emily found him. She found him and brought him back to his senses, and they were able to help save Esotera.

Levi came back home and wrote about his adventure, his true adventure, and audiences fell in love with the characters, as he had. They wept when Kolas died, as he'd wept. Did he owe it to them, the people who had enabled him to actually make something out of his life? He knew Lady Grustmiener was dead. He knew it. But Emily was still gone. Someone had taken her.

"I can give you one week," he said, "but then I must come back. I have a life here. I will do what I can to help find her, but then I must come back." He gathered his thoughts. "I need to know what makes you think we will be able to find Emily? And if we do, what hope will we have in getting her back safely? Someone clearly wants her for something. How can you assure me that we will be successful?"

A smile broke out on her face. "I will do better than that," she said, "I will show you."

Chapter 9

Aftermath

How are you holding up?"

Milskar raised his eyes to the steaming coffee cup that appeared before him. His gaze followed the dainty hand and wrist, past the pale blue lace sleeves and up to Aura's face. She was filled with concern for him. He moved his lips in what she could only assume was an attempt at a smile, but abandoned the effort and lowered his head back down. She moved into the seat next to him and placed a hand on his back. She hoped her firm touch would reassure him.

"Milskar, please, please tell me what else I can do," Aura said. She kept her voice low as if she talked to a frightened animal. "I have sent teams into the woods, into the other kingdoms, everywhere I can think of. Tell me what else to do."

He lifted his gaze back up to meet hers. It had been mere weeks that Emily had been taken, but it looked like he'd lived a million lifetimes.

"What if we cannot find her? What if—" He broke off.

"Do not think like that. We need to focus on what we can do," Aura said. "What can we do?"

"I do not know. Theirra?"

"She is still not back. A poor time to send her on a vacation," Aura said, her voice laced with regret.

She had hoped to reach Theirra in time to ask her to cancel the trip, but she missed her by minutes and had no clear idea where her dear friend had gone, so she had no easy way to contact her.

"What do we do about Emily's family?" Milskar asked. "She is in contact with them, sporadic, but enough that they might start to get worried if they do not hear from her soon."

"I do not know."

"Seems to be a lot of that going around, does it not?" His voice held no malice, which seemed to make it worse for Aura.

Silence hung around them like a heavy blanket. It suffocated the air and prevented either from being able to talk.

A burst of noise came through the door. They both looked in its direction, as Nikolas broke away from the woman who held his hand and sprinted up to them.

A reluctant smile broke across Milskar's face as he scooped up his small son up and pulled him to his chest. They stayed that way for a long time until Nikolas's squirmed too much for Milskar to hold him steady and he was forced to let him go.

The boy bounded off, ran to the counter in the main hall, and helped himself to a glass of milk that sat just within his reach. The sight of him filled Aura with equal amounts of love and sadness, each emotion jockeying for position.

Milskar sat back down as the woman mouthed her apology at them before she hurried after the boy.

Aura reached across the table and held Milskar's hand. "We will find her," she said.

He nodded, got up, and took Nikolas from the woman as he left the room.

Chapter 10

Truth & Lies

Lady Grustmiener walked down the hallway with such purpose, those who stood around leaped out of her way and proceeded to act busy so as not to be pulled into whatever new mission she was on. They averted their eyes and snuck glances at one another, but never at her. She paid them no mind.

Her focus was on a door at the end of the corridor. It had taken her years to get to this point. One could probably argue an entire lifetime, what with the rise and fall, crushing defeat and slow rebuilding. Those memories rattled around in the back of her mind, flies buzzing inside her scalp, but she paid them no attention. Today was too important. There would be time, there had been plenty of time already, to put forth effort into those thoughts, but not today.

The door opened seconds before she reached it and a man stepped out, about to close the heavy metal slab behind him when he saw her.

"You have made it."

"I have," she answered gruffly. She had no time for formalities with lowly staff.

"He came willingly enough, only some mild—" He paused. "—encouragement was needed."

"I believe I can take it from here, Lieal."

"Yes, my lady."

He moved aside and she brushed by him, her shoulder pushed his arm slightly. More people than she expected sat in the large space. Sure, she didn't think this man would travel alone, but a party of twenty was not what she'd anticipated. No matter. More witnesses for her to tell, more people for her to convince, as she knew she would. The man looked up at her, his eyes widened in shock and possibly some fear. She noted some of the men and women who surrounded him had minor cuts and bruises.

"So it is true?" he asked tentatively. "Lady Grustmiener, you live?"

"I would never dream of doing the opposite," she replied curtly.

"But the battle."

"Was an unfortunate setback for my kingdom and people, but that is why I brought you here today. I am sure you have heard many stories and rumors, but I am here to tell you the truth of what really happened and to establish your loyalty against Esotera."

A wrinkle formed on his forehead. "Against Esotera? I do not understand," the king said.

"Listen, King Theaus, listen, and I will tell you everything," she said. "What have you been told of the battle?"

"We have heard some. That the king, rest his soul, led a fight against Queen Aura, leading to his, and we thought your, death. Though the specifics, and how the war even became, were not reported to us. We were left, as always, somewhat in the dark, as they say."

"Yes," Lady Grustmiener smiled. His answer pleased her. "Yes, I am sure you were."

She moved across the room like a tiger pacing in a cage, eyes focused on her prey. "Do you know what started this battle, what made the king of my land, my late husband, enter the war? What ultimately led to his death?" Lady Grustmiener asked.

"I assume you shall tell me." It was clear that King Theaus was annoyed at the whole situation and not particularly interested in her explanations.

"We received information that an outlaw was hiding out in Esotera and might be planning on crossing into our borders. A very famous outlaw," she paused for effect. "Kolas. Your son's murderer."

What remained of the color in the man's face, already pale due to the dim lighting, left his cheeks. His mind raced back to that day all those years ago. His son, full of such promise, killed by a man who never saw justice. King Theaus's entire body seemed to collapse in on itself before he was able to recover some semblance of composure.

"Why was I not told? Why was I not brought in?" he asked, pain in his voice.

"There was no time. The information came to us and we had to act. And after—after the battle, I was not in a position to send information to anyone."

"And Kolas?" the king asked.

"Dead. Killed by the king himself," Lady Grustmiener said.

"And King Grustmiener? Who killed him?"

"Queen Aura," she said in a tone that suggested the words had sharp, painful edges.

Theaus sighed and the two sat in silence for some time.

"Giving me this information, while I appreciate it, cannot be the sole reason why you brought me to this place. You want revenge," he said, more a fact than a question.

"Yes, that is part of it. After the battle, I lost everything. Not just my husband, but my kingdom as well. It has taken me years to amass the small army that I have today, but I cannot hope to destroy Esotera alone. I need your help. You army's help. Together we can defeat her," Lady Grustmiener said. "You can help avenge the man who helped avenge your son."

"And what will I receive for my kingdom's assistance?"

"Esotera." The words danced in the air over them and filled the small room.

"You would give me control over those lands?" King Theaus asked skeptically.

"All I wish is for *my* lands back. You can have everything else. Think of how those forests can be used to help heat the homes in your kingdom. You can cut every last one of them down and burn them to ashes."

"While this all does sound good, the question of war remains. How was it even possible? How did this great battle even come to be?" he asked.

Lady Grustmiener smiled. She'd waited and hoped that he would ask her that question. "That brings me to the second bit I had to tell you," she said, the Cheshire cat smile spreading on her face. "Esotera, Queen Aura, had the Missing Link. And I believe he will return."

Stunned only began to describe the look on King Theaus's face.

Chapter 11

Journey

Theirra pulled her hood down to partially cover her eyes as they moved through the light rain. Levi felt a prickling sensation on his skin that made him wonder if the rain here was different than in his world.

It was strange coming back. While it had been years since he'd physically stepped foot in Esotera, in his head he'd never left. After he'd written about it and toured with the book, part of him felt like he'd never really been separated from it. Yet being here again felt completely out of place. Everything was greener, louder, and bigger than what he remembered. Nothing looked familiar and it disenchanted him, like when you walked into your childhood home and the furniture had been rearranged. You forgot life went on without you, a concept that, at times, seemed impossible.

Levi wasn't paying attention, and it took Theirra's rough grip on his arm for him to look around at his surroundings. He was about to ask her what was wrong when he saw it.

Nearly fifteen feet tall with deep blue scales, the dragon was massive. *Welcome back,* Levi thought.

Panic bubbled in the back of his throat. He wasn't sure if dragons were like bears where you shouldn't make a lot of noise and startle them. Or was it that you *should* make a lot of noise? "Will it hurt us?" he whispered.

"No, he will leave us alone. We should just stick to the path and move through as quickly as possible. We are almost there."

Levi hadn't noticed they were on a path until she mentioned it, but now he could make out the faintly-patted-down grass. They traveled along the perimeter of a large clearing, as he kept a watchful eye on the dragon, which seemed to take little notice of them. They went through another densely wooded area before it opened up to another smaller field.

The rain stopped and the sun broke through in beams that threw bands of light on the four tents haphazardly set up in a semi-circle. Several children wandered around a few campfires and cooked something that smelled both sweet and off putting. As he got closer, Levi recognized one of the boys. Recognized? The thought popped into his head before he noticed, but yes, he recognized this boy from somewhere. Possibly from the last time he was in Esotera? Just as suddenly as the hazy recognition hit him, so did the realization of who the boy was. The fifteen-year-old boy had been on the news in Levi's world. As he looked around the site, he realized that he recognized almost all the faces from the news. The feeling in the back of his throat intensified.

"Theirra," he said softly, as if she was a crazy person who held a gun and he had to talk her out of shooting him.

"I know," she said.

Now it was his turn to pull her roughly to the side. "You know? You know what? That you kidnapped these children? That their pictures are all over the news, and people have been looking for them for days? What are you doing with them?"

"No one will notice they are gone. They will quickly forget."

Levi was dumbstruck. "Forget?"

"They are orphans, homeless, unwanted," she said. Her voice grew stronger and she stood up straighter. "I did not take any child away from a home that they did not want to be removed from."

"It's not as simple as just saying, hey, I want this kid," he said. He remembered the stories his parents told of how long and hard they searched and fought for a child of their own. Paperwork and home visits were followed by years of waiting and held breath until, finally, Levi was placed in their arms twenty-three years before.

Theirra shrugged. "I spent some time with the witches in the North. I traveled there to speak with Resbuca. She was not there, but I was able to converse with some of them, especially after I told them I was a friend and what had happened to Winester. They never liked him, evidently. While I was there, I studied a bit under them. They are very skilled at mind control. Myself, not so much, but it seemed that any powers I was able to develop were strengthened when I entered your world."

"What the hell, Theirra?" He had no better response than that.

He allowed her arm to drop from his grasp and followed several steps behind her toward the fire. The children did look in good health and relatively happy, especially since they'd passed into a magical land and were surrounded by fire-breathing dragons. He thought he would have been happy too when he was their age, getting to enter this strange place. Scratch that—he *had* passed through here when he was their age and was scared, ultimately got kidnapped himself, almost killed his cousin, and almost doomed an entire kingdom. He ran several steps to catch up to her.

"Everyone," Theirra started, "this is my friend Levi I was telling you about. Much like you, he grew up in your world while having ties to this world."

She smiled at him and gestured. Was he supposed to make a speech or something?

"Umm, hi," was all he managed to squeak out.

The kids looked up at him with vague curiosity but, when they sensed that he had nothing more to say, went back to whatever mundane tasks they were doing before he interrupted them. One girl looked very young, maybe eleven or twelve. Levi glanced over at Theirra who seemed pleased with herself. Again, he grabbed her arm, excused themselves from the group—who didn't even look up—and dragged her back several yards out of earshot.

"Explain."

"Well—" She hesitated, as if she had rehearsed this speech a million times over in her head but was still afraid to say it out loud. "—these kids are hybrids."

It came out in such a rush it took Levi several seconds to figure out what she had said. Even with having all the words in order, he still didn't understand what she meant.

"Hybrids?" he asked.

"Products from a union of my world and yours."

"Yeah, I still don't get it."

She looked nervous. "There are people who travel from our world to yours. It is discouraged, in fact, many think it is illegal, but people do it, anyway. These children have one parent from my world and the other parent from yours. Often times they are born with some type of powers of varying degrees. Some are just very intelligent. They often run top companies or are celebrated inventors.

No one figured out how they know all they do, but some—" She looked over at the group. "—some have actual powers. Ones that cannot be explained in easy terms in your world. As I am sure you dealt with in your youth, they are often shunned or committed in one way or another."

Memories flooded back to Levi of countless trips to psychologists and doctors, specialists on every end of the spectrum who tried to "fix" him. He failed or got kicked out of schools, jobs, relationships, to the point where he actually started to believe everyone who said there was something wrong with him. He had powers, had them but didn't understand that he had them. It wasn't until Theirra and her crew, which included Queen Aura, informed him of who he was that his life started to make sense.

He empathized with this group and thought back to how frightened and alone he felt when he first arrived here, and that was before he was taken prisoner and was the catalyst for war.

"So you took them?" he asked, his voice kinder than before.

"Not all of them. I am technically fostering a few, but the others, yes I took them." She turned to him with a plea in her eyes. "Levi, you have to understand, we need them. Esotera needs them."

"But why?"

"Something terrible is going to happen. I know it. No one believes me but I know it, I am not crazy—" Her voice shook and broke. "There is going to be another war. While Aura is pretending that the danger has passed, I know it has not. We need to have something that can defeat the threats against Esotera and I know—I know it lies in these children."

She looked so different than Levi remembered her. Pain surrounded her like a bubble that he wished with every part of him he could pop, but it was as if it was made out of hardened steel. She looked desperate and crazed and seemed like she teetered on the brink. Of what, he was not sure. He was also not sure he wanted to find out.

"Okay," he said, against all better judgment. "What do you need me to do?"

Chapter 12

The Return

The going was slow, but after several days, Levi, Theirra, and the rag-tag bunch of youths arrived at the castle at Esotera. It looked exactly the same and completely different to Levi. It was surreal being back here after all these years. He thought he'd noticed several new buildings, or maybe he'd forgotten they'd been there. The castle was configured a little differently than he remembered and wrote about. It was strange to erase the pictures from his memory and replace them with the reality in front of him.

"It's been four years for me. How many have passed for you since I've been gone?" Levi asked.

"Seven years, I believe," she answered.

Levi noticed that faraway look streak across her face.

Seven years, he thought. He remembered that time moved differently here, but he hadn't given much thought as to how much.

A flash of a pretty face with red hair popped into his head and his stomach gave a slight flutter. He wondered how different she would look.

Theirra walked slower now and seemed a touch nervous at the prospect of entering the castle grounds. Levi wondered on what pretense she left here. Did Aura know she was going on a rescue/kidnapping mission?

The look on Aura's face said it all. She flew out of the front doors and stopped in her tracks, mid-stride, as if she had run into an invisible barrier. The shock, concern, and fear were clearly written on her face. The children looked from Theirra to Aura and then at one another. They hadn't expected such a greeting either.

"Theirra?" Aura asked as if she didn't recognize her.

Theirra sighed. "Please let me explain."

Aura looked over at Levi and her face grew even more strained. She looked so different from the last time he'd seen her. She had only been maybe sixteen, seventeen, a little younger than Levi had been. It was strange to see her so much older. He quickly did the math and realized that, due to how time moved differently in both their worlds, they were probably the same age.

A shyness came over him. He wished he could have hidden or given some profound explanation as to why he was there, but he didn't understand it either. He merely shrugged at Aura, a gesture he immediately regretted and wished he could take back. She whirled and went into the castle after Theirra. Levi hesitated for a moment, but decided not to follow.

⁊⁊

Aura and Theirra were already locked in a heated debate as they walked into her office. Aura shut the doors behind them.

"What you did was completely irresponsible," Aura said, exasperated.

Theirra didn't appear the least bit concerned at her queen's anger. "I did what needed to be done."

"Oh stop it, Theirra," Aura said. She sank into a large chair at the head of an oblong table. Theirra sat several seats away from her. "You knew perfectly well how I would feel about your little trip—a trip you lied to me about by the way."

"Not completely, I told you I was taking some time and I did," Theirra said with a hint of defensiveness in her voice.

"Some time?" Aura laughed, but it came out high-pitched and manic. "I think you would agree that this was hardly the relaxing excursion I intended for you."

"Aura," Theirra said as she got up and moved closer to her, "you need to listen to me. Esotera is in danger, real danger, and I know you do not want to hear it. I do not want it to be true either, but it is. It is and we need to prepare for the inevitable."

"The inevitable of what? Of war again? No one wants a war, no one wants another fight." Aura rubbed her forehead with her fingertips. Her composure seemed to leave her as she looked back up to Theirra. "What were you thinking?"

"Aura—" Theirra said.

"No," Aura firmly interrupted, seeming to finally remember that she was the one in charge. "I need you to answer some questions for me. Where did these children come from? Did you steal them away from their lives, from their parents, from wherever it was they came from? For what purpose did you bring them here? What were you thinking, Theirra?" Her voice lowered and concern laced her words.

"I took them from no one, they came willingly with me. We need them. We need them to fight."

"To fight?" Aura said, her voice rising again in pitch. "What is this mythical force that you are so determined to conjure up? Why can you not believe that it is over, all this fighting is over, and we are free to live in peace? Theirra, I know you lost a great deal—" She softened her tone and placed her hand on her friend's shoulder. "—but it is time that you realized that is in the past. No more fighting. You have to return these children to where they came from."

Theirra shrugged her off. "No."

"No?"

"They are needed here."

"It was not a question Theirra. I am ordering it."

Theirra shook her head. "No."

"I am your queen!" Aura yelled at her. Theirra shrank back. "I am your queen—" She started again, a little more composed. "—and, as your queen, I order you to take these stolen people back to their world. If this is a task you are unable to complete, then I will find someone else to do it for you, and I will reassign you to a less strenuous work load, as your current one has proven to be too much for you to handle."

Theirra flinched and Aura felt a deep throb in her chest. The two had been such close friends for so long, relied on one another so much—had Aura abused that comradery? Maybe she'd put too much pressure on Theirra to return to whatever normal they had before the Great Battle. Maybe that version of Theirra was lost forever.

The last thing Aura wanted to do was hurt her, but was it worth it if hurting her kept Theirra out of harm's way?

"I understand," Theirra said without emotion. "I will take them back immediately."

Aura nodded, crestfallen. She sensed something fragile had broken between the two of them just then, and she wanted to be able to take it all back, to put back all the pieces. She didn't want to have to keep Theirra in check. Aura didn't even think she would be in a position to rule if her friend had not been by her side all these years, but Theirra had become foolish and reckless since she'd lost Kolas. Aura was at a loss with what to do for her to snap her out of whatever trance she'd fallen in. She felt terrible having to yell at her, demean her like she did, but she thought it was the only way to jolt Theirra back into reality.

As Aura watched Theirra turn and walk out of the room, she caught a flash of movement out of the corner of her eye. A figure rode out of the tree line to the south of the castle walls. It picked up speed as it covered the gap toward the castle. A flashback of panic arose in Aura. For a moment, it was as if no time had passed and she was back in the Great Battle yet again, poised to defend herself and her homeland.

The rider disappeared around the side of the building.

Aura was about to say something, to call out to the others, when the door burst open. Afternoon light poured in from the hallway and momentarily blinded her. All she could see was a figure blacked out against the light in the entryway. The woman closed the door behind her and moved to the table in three large, rushed steps. It was clear from the yells in the hall several guards had unsuccessfully tried to prevent her entry to the room.

Amaline bowed as she tried to catch her ragged breath. "My queen."

Theirra had heard the commotion, had returned, and stood behind the newest arrival.

"Amaline?" Aura was confused, but the expression on Theirra's face was of pure delight as the two woman came into the room.

Theirra marched up to Amaline and grabbed her shoulders. "You found her, did you not?" she asked.

"Yes, along the northern borders in the woods," Amaline answered.

"Found who?" Aura asked.

"Lady Grustmiener, my queen."

Silence filled the room. Aura stood frozen, a half formed word poised on the end of her tongue, but unable to fall into speech. Theirra's pleased look was replaced by resignation, as if she was glad to hear her quest had validity, yet at the same time she wished it were not actually true.

Aura shook her head. "That is impossible. Levi killed her."

"No one saw her dead body," Theirra interjected. "It was never found. *We* never found it, and the explanation for that was never satisfactory to me. I know you wanted her to be dead. I know you wanted it to be over, and so did—" She caught herself. "—so *do* I, but it's not. We have to finish it. We have to finish her, or she is just going to come back." She turned to address Amaline. "Does she have an army?"

"Yes," Amaline said. "I do not know how many, but from what little I saw and heard, it sounds like hundreds, maybe thousands."

"So you did not actually *see* her?" Aura asked.

"My queen?" Amaline looked confused.

"Did you actually see Lady Grustmiener, or just hear people talking about her?"

Amaline looked at Theirra, as if for clarification. Theirra's eyebrows pulled painfully close together, her mouth in an almost grimace.

Amaline looked apologetically over at Theirra. "Well, no, not exactly," she answered.

"Then maybe she is not alive after all."

"Aura," Theirra started, and then remembering herself, corrected, "my queen—"

"Theirra, listen to me." Aura tried to make her voice soft but firm. "Maybe she is not really alive. That does not mean, however, that there may not be people fighting in her name. There may even be people who believe she is alive and getting others to fight with that belief. Maybe there is someone else trying to get to power, and they are using the threat of her return to gain followers. I am not saying that they are not dangerous, that it is not a force that needs to be stopped, but maybe it is not as bad as you think it is."

Theirra got up and walked away from her. It was clear she was not happy with how the conversation had gone.

"Amaline," Aura continued, "I want you to do something for me. I want you to tell my guards where exactly you found these people. As best you can, I need you to tell them where they can go. Then I want you to return to your home and tell Omire what you discovered. Go, now."

Amaline was out in a flash. Aura stood and paced the room. She put each foot so deliberately it was as if she expected the ground to fall away from her at any moment.

Chapter 13

Confrontation

A figure rushed toward Levi. His blood turned to ice in his veins, and it took him a moment to realize why.

His thoughts were still foggy from that time, but he remembered her face. Along with an older man, they'd taken Levi away soon after he'd reached this land.

She passed by him as he instinctively reached out and grabbed her arm. Amaline turned to face him, her eyes growing wide with the recognition of who he was.

"W—what?" she stuttered.

Levi's grip tightened and she let out a soft cry.

He looked around him. "I need a guard. Guard!" he yelled.

"Levi, please," Amaline said.

His gaze flew to her. "How dare you? How dare you ask me for mercy after what you did to me?" His voice trembled with anger. "What you made me do. What I almost did."

He thought back to meeting Emily in the woods. Her words reached down inside him and pulled him back. The knife clutched in his hand, the blood on her, the regret and confusion. His eyes met Amaline's, and she shrank back.

"I know what we did was terrible," she whimpered. "But we did not know at the time. I swear, we did not know." The words rushed out of her. "As soon as Omire and I realized what Abaddon and Lady Grustmiener were doing, we ran here and told Queen Aura. We tried to make it right."

He let go of her, and she staggered back as she rubbed her arm. "By leaving me there?" he bellowed.

They must have made a tremendous amount of noise, because out of the castle appeared several guards followed by Aura and Theirra.

Aura pushed through and stood between Levi and Amaline. "What is going on?"

Levi pointed toward Amaline. "You need to arrest her. She needs to be punished. Guard," he said as he looked around. "Arrest her!"

The guards looked from Levi to Aura, but made no movements forward.

"I told you," Amaline said.

"I don't care what *you* say. Arrest her."

Aura reached forward to grab his arm, but he shook her hand off.

"Levi, come inside please. You have been through an ordeal these last few hours, I am sure."

"Levi," Theirra's voice was firm. "Come inside."

For some reason, her words reached him and he followed her into the castle, Aura and Amaline following close behind.

The castle was as he remembered it, which comforted and disoriented him in equal parts. The door to Aura's office wasn't even fully closed before he unleashed on them.

"What's she doing here? What were you thinking, allowing her into these parts? Don't you know who she is? Who she works for?"

"Yes," Aura said calmly. "This is Amaline, and she works for me."

"Ha," Levi barked.

"Levi—" Amaline began.

"No." He cut her off. "No, you don't get to talk."

"Levi," Aura said, her voice sharper.

Levi pointed at Amaline. "Tell them, tell them who you are."

"I—I—" Amaline stuttered.

"Tell them or I will."

"What is he talking about?" Theirra asked.

"Tell them how it was you who ambushed us," Levi snarled. "That it was you who kidnapped me when I first came here all those years ago. *You.* You who started this whole war in the first place." The anger rose in him so quickly, he heard glass in the chandeliers over-head tinkling.

"Levi, you do not know what you are saying—" Aura started again.

"Tell them," he said.

"I—I did not mean for any of it to happen. I—I was simply following orders," Amaline stammered. "I did not know."

Aura turned to her with her brows raised in a question. "Amaline?"

"I did not know!" Amaline repeated.

Theirra moved closer to her, which caused Amaline to step back and crash into a chair. She inched toward the door, but something in Theirra's look froze her.

"I did not know. I swear. I swear as soon I knew, I came here right away." Amaline turned back to Aura. "I came here right away and told you everything. I tried to fix it, I tried."

"And Omire?" Theirra said.

Amaline closed her eyes and nodded.

Aura put her hand to her mouth for several moments before she was able to compose herself. "I need you to leave."

"My queen. Aura. Please," Amaline said, but Aura raised her hand to silence her.

"Please Amaline. You have a task. I need you to complete that."

"B—but—"

"I am going to need time to process this, yes, but you have done great things for me and my kingdom. That will not be ignored, but for now, I think it is best if you go. Allow us to talk to Levi."

Amaline nodded, tears in her eyes, and left.

"What is there to talk about?" Levi said. "You heard her, you heard what she admitted. Aura, she's the one who took me, who allowed that terrible person Abaddon to do those things to me. She…" His voice trailed off.

"I understand."

"Do you? How could you possibly know?"

"We did not know the extent of her involvement, but she did come to us and tell us what they were doing with you—" Aura said.

"She came here with information for us," Theirra broke in.

"Oh, so she can seem like she is saving the day when she is the one who wrecked it in the first place?" he asked.

"Levi." Aura addressed him kindly for the first time. "I am sure you heard about your cousin."

He shot a glance at Theirra who stared right back at him. "Yes, that's why I came."

"If the information Amaline has brought us is true, then it is possible that whoever is behind this uprising also has her. It may have been a way for them to lure you back here, to eliminate you and your powers."

"My powers?" he couldn't help but ask, his anger momentarily forgotten by his curiosity.

"While you have not been involved in our world for many years, your presence is still felt here. The possibility that you are out there, that you can still affect what happens here is known by few, but those few may stop at nothing to use that power for themselves."

"I thought we already went through this," he said, exasperated. "I already did the whole kidnap thing, unless Amaline is back to take me again."

"Levi, please," Theirra said. She made no attempt to hide the frustration from her voice. "It may be more complicated than that this time. They may be looking to do more than just take you..." She tried to choose her words carefully. "They may be trying to kill you."

"Kill me?" Okay, it was time to get out of this place.

Aura looked sickened by this new information. After a minute, she nodded. "There are protections in your world for people like you, people who exist in both worlds. They cannot enter your world and hurt you, which is why Winester had to bring you back here all that time ago. Your powers are fully formed here, but your protections are only truly formed there. They needed to lure you here to have any hope in defeating you. Unfortunately, I think Theirra bringing you here, whether she knew it or not, was part of their plan." She looked pointedly over at her, but Theirra remained fixed on something outside.

"It is not even something I fully understand," Aura continued. "Resbuca explained some of it to me, but your powers are so ancient and singular because of their source, it is hard for us to understand the full breadth of them."

Anger boiled in Levi. He felt like he'd just gotten his

life together. He had direction, a career, a reason, and just when it all started to go right, the rug got pulled out from under him. If he thought it would do him any good, he would have walked over to Theirra and shaken her, hard, but even through the back of her head he could feel her remorse, hot and palpable.

She turned to look at them. Tears cut caverns in her cheeks. "Aura—"

"Theirra, I know your intentions were pure. I know you thought what you were doing was for the best. It is unfortunate that sometimes, even on the most noble of quests, there are unintended consequences."

"But who could possibly want me now? Who is even left, other than you two, who knows my secret?" he asked.

"Lady Grustmiener," Aura said. "Or at least her sympathizers. Amaline told us there is an army building. She came here to warn us, to help us."

He had killed Lady Grustmiener. He knew he had killed her. He felt the power build in his body and release toward her, a feeling he'd never experienced before. There was no way she, or anyone, could have lived through that. He was certain of it.

"No," he said, "that's impossible. I killed her. She is dead. I saw her dead body."

It couldn't be true, he told himself. It was a huge mistake. Theirra thought she heard something, Amaline thought she heard something, and at any moment Emily would walk through the door. A misunderstanding, that's all this was. Emily got lost. No one took her. Lady Grustmiener was dead, everyone was safe, and he could go back home.

"We are still confirming this fact," Aura said, "but it may be true. We need to prepare ourselves for the possibility that she may be back, and she may have Emily."

Aura's voice sounded a thousand miles away. Levi sat. The weight of the last several years crashed down upon him. He looked out the windows of her office, but where there was once sunlight, now only darkness poured in.

Chapter 14

Information

Emily's lips cracked and bled with the slightest of movements. She tried to stay as still as possible when she breathed, but pain still radiated through her. She had lost all concept of time. Had she been here hours? Weeks? Her throat ached. Her screams and lack of water had made it raw and tender. She was desperate for something to drink, even just a drop. Her saliva had long since dried up, and it was difficult to swallow.

The door flew open and Emily had to turn her head against the bright light. The movement which sent shooting pain through her again. She squinted and tried to force them into adjustment so she could see who had entered, but it was no use. Her eyes were just too sensitive.

"Relax."

The voice shocked Emily with its delicateness. She kept her eyes pressed shut and jolted back against her restraints when she felt something cold touch her lips.

"Drink," the voice said.

The coldness returned to her lips, and she let the relief of it devour her. She gagged on the water, but still guzzled it. Just as quickly as it had arrived, the glass was removed. Emily tried to croak out a protest, but her voice was too weak to project above a whisper.

"Not too much." The woman had a soft, slight accent Emily couldn't place. It almost sounded Italian. "You have had nothing for a long time. I will come back."

The door opened and closed again. Emily wanted to cry, but was too exhausted for even that simple act. Instead, she slumped in her chair and tried to regroup her thoughts. Somehow, she was going to have to get out of here. Maybe this strange woman could be turned into an ally. She didn't sound like she was from these parts, so possibly she was a captive as well. Emily was determined to speak to her the next time she came, but the woman never did return.

Emily drifted in and out of consciousness, but was snapped awake by a large amount of water thrown in her face. Instinctively, she tried to lick at it, but the small amount of liquid she was able to get simply made her more thirsty.

"No more water until you have listened to my demands."

The voice was female, but not the same woman as before. Emily tried to place it. It sounded vaguely familiar, but she was unable to recall it. She pried her eyes open and forced them to adjust to the light. She blinked in time with her heartbeats as they burned in protest. It took several minutes, but she was finally able to open them fully again and let the views around her pour into her sluggish brain.

It couldn't be right. There had to be something wrong with her. Maybe she knocked her head hard against something and had scrambled some internal process? She pressed her eyes tight together and shook her head. That was a mistake. Pain shot throughout her body to the extent that she was unable to even pinpoint its origin. She

took a breath and opened her eyes again. She hoped
something different would meet them, but no luck.

"How?" she pushed out gruffly.

Lady Grustmiener laughed. "How what? How am I
here? Did you think that silly boy could have defeated
me?" She laughed again and her two guards, whom Emily had just noticed, joined in as well.

Emily had never seen her in person before, but after
the fall of Grustmiener, she'd ventured to their city center
with Milskar. There were paintings of all the former rulers of the land and he pointed out the one of this woman.
She looked evil, even in art. The image was burned into
Emily's memory, brought to life before her eyes.

"What do you want from me?" Emily asked, though
not really sure she wanted to know the answer. Nikolas's
face flashed into her mind and made the pit in her stomach turn into a frozen ball.

"I have gotten what I want out of you."

"Then let me go," Emily said. She tried to keep the
plea out of her voice, but some of it seeped through.

"Oh, heavens no." Lady Grustmiener laughed again. "I
have gotten what I want, though I still need you. The plan
will only work if you stay here. Do not worry, you will
soon understand. You will understand why you are here,"
she called over her shoulder as she exited the room. "And
what you can do to help."

"Help?" Emily was in full panic mode now, and she
didn't care how shrill her voice sounded. She pulled and
bucked against her restraints. She didn't care about the
intense pain it caused. She had to get out of here. She had
to get out *now* or she had a feeling she would spend the
rest of her days in this window-less room.

A man walked into the room. He was impossibly old,
yet still moved with a fluid purpose that it seemed he
should be incapable of. There were two large guards be-

hind him. They all had a sinister look on their faces. Emily fought harder, but the ropes did not slacken at all.

"Relax." His voice was thicker than she expected it to be. "We are going to take you out of here. I want you to not fight us. We are not going to hurt you."

"Who—who are you?"

"A friend of your cousin Levi's, actually. My name is Abaddon."

They released the restraints on her, and she slumped forward. Her muscles had gotten so weak, she'd been relying on the ropes to keep her upright. She felt like all the strength in her middle and legs had vanished in the time she had been kept here. They had to drag her to her feet and out of the room. She tried to protest, to fight against them, but the last five minutes of effort had taken every ounce of energy out of her. She was helpless and feared they knew it.

She tried to memorize the way they were going, the hallways, the number of doors, just in case she was able to escape and had to re-trace her steps, but it seemed like they went around in circles. Each turn faced them with corridors that looked identical. Emily wondered if they maybe had even gotten lost a few times and backtracked. Turning one corner, they stopped at a very solid looking door. It was made out of a different material than the other ones they had passed. Emily knew if she went in there, she would never get out.

She tried to fight again, but the two men were just too strong. In the center stood a chair with what she thought were screens around it. It looked like some kind of torture chamber. They pinned her down in the chair and put newer, stronger restraints on her.

"Just try to relax," Abaddon said. "We are still working out the kinks. Moving an entire operation such as this takes time, so you will have to bear with us, but I think it will work." This last bit he said more to himself than to anyone else in the room.

Emily looked wildly around the room as the three left. In a burst of sound and color, the screens came on, filled with images and music. The last thing she remembered was the loud thump as the door shut her in.

Chapter 15

Introductions

The hybrid children sat in the courtyard where the others had left them. They sat in silence, enthralled with their surroundings, even as darkness moved in around them. While it had been days since they'd left their world, it felt like lifetimes ago.

When they'd first arrived, they were immediately met by dragons. They had all screamed, except for Kiya who seemed to sense what they were before they even came to the clearing. She was twelve years old with skin a shade darker than Theirra's and was four-foot-nothing, yet she was the only one to take a step forward when the rest took a step back.

"They're intelligent," Kiya had said to Theirra in her sing-song voice.

"Yes, they are," Theirra said, pleased with the girl.

After a few moments, Theirra brought them to another clearing surrounded protectively by tall trees and left them there with tents and previsions.

"I will be back as soon as I can, hopefully not more than two days. I need you to stay right here and wait for me."

They nodded, but were not sure why they went along with this woman who had, for all intense and purpose, kidnapped them one by one. Not that they weren't willing to go. Each of them jumped at the chance to get out of their current situation, but as they looked back on the matter, some wondered if it was, in fact, a good idea.

Adam had just turned sixteen and wondered what would come next in his unfulfilled life when he saw this strangely dressed woman approach him outside a twenty-four-seven convenience store. She blabbed something about Adam being special and needed in some magical other world. Having no better prospects for his future, he agreed and followed the woman who had two other school-age boys with her. Their introductions were brief before they were transported to a sprawling estate. A young girl, Adam later found out her name was Kiya, sat on a patch of grass so green it hurt your eyes, a wild rabbit in her lap. Kiya took one look back at the house, put the rabbit down, and followed them into the unknown.

While they traveled, they added to their numbers every few days. They kept whatever powers they had relatively secret from one another. The girl named Galina was forced to show hers when a sudden rainstorm moved in while they set up camp one night. She took several deep breaths; moved her hands in concentric, methodical circles; and the rain abruptly stopped. The other kids looked over at her, but no words were spoken. There would be time, and it didn't seem like out in the open was it.

With a loud creaking noise, three figures exited the castle toward them. The group stood and flicked glances at one another. They had barely spoken, yet somehow they felt a connection to each other. Maybe that whole-shared-experience-brings-people-together thing that hostages got. Either way, they instinctively moved closer together. Theirra asked the group to accompany them inside the castle and they moved together to the disserted great hall. She waited until they were inside before she began to speak.

"Everyone," Theirra started, "this is Queen Aura. You have already met Levi, of course."

Levi raised his hand to wave but dropped it halfway through the motion. Aura wondered how much he had talked with the new arrivals during his and Theirra's journey here.

"And this—" Theirra spread her arms and gestured around them. "—is the castle at Esotera."

Confusion rippled across their faces. Tab, the oldest of the group at nineteen, stepped forward, his eyebrows pinched together. "Esotera?" he asked.

"Yes." Aura came forward. "My name is Aura—" she repeated and was about to continue when she was interrupted.

"The queen," one of the girls repeated in a whisper.

The visitors at each other in disbelief. Now it was Aura and Theirra's turn to shoot confused glances at each other.

"Wait a minute," Galina said. "You're Levi? As in Levi Roberts?"

"What is going on here?" Aura asked Levi.

Levi ignored Aura's question. "Yes, I'm Levi Roberts."

"So it's true then?" Tab asked.

"Yes," Levi said again.

"Levi," Aura said. She was frustrated that she was unable to follow their conversation.

"I wrote a book." The words came out in a rush. One of the girls gasped, but Aura didn't know why. "A book about Esotera," he continued. "I just—I just never thought I would come back here again. I thought that part of my life was over, and I could write about it. Keep it safe by telling such a fantastic story that no one would believe it was true."

"You have read this piece of work?" Aura asked the group.

Most of them nodded. Aura turned to see a light pink coloring spread over Levi's cheeks and neck.

"How much do they know?" Aura asked him.

"Pretty much everything. I had to make up some of the back story—you'll have to forgive me—and fill in some of the parts for when I was gone, but everything is basically in there. Aura, I'm sorry—" he began, but she put up a hand to stop him.

A few of the kids still looked around, a bit confused. Galina summed up the story quickly to catch any of those up to speed who didn't know.

"I never made the connection," one of the boys said. His fair skin and red hair matched Aura's.

"I suppose that will make this a bit easier then. Again, my name is Aura, Queen of Esotera, and I am sure you have all become well acquainted with Theirra in your—" She paused. "—travels. Theirra will be taking you back to your homes."

"Leave?" Kiya asked as she stepped forward.

"You do not belong here," Aura said. "There may be danger coming to this place. It is not your battle, not your war."

"I want to help," Tab said. "And I think I am old enough to make my own decision on the matter."

"Yeah," several members of the group said.

"I am not sure what Theirra said to each of you, but this is not a matter that needs your attention. We have guards in this land and in Grustmiener. If there is a threat against us, that is not something you need to trouble yourselves with. Theirra—" Aura turned to her. "—please take them to their rooms. You may stay here for the night. A group will bring you home at first light."

She noticed how tired Theirra looked. Aura wasn't sure if it was the stress of the last few hours, the possible dissolution of their friendship, the potential danger to the kingdom, or something much deeper.

"I have nowhere to go," the smallest girl in the group said. She had dark tan skin and black hair. She sighed. "At least, no where I want to go."

The group around her nodded.

Levi moved forward to stand next to Aura. She felt his breath tickle the side of her neck as he leaned in to whisper. "Maybe they can help. Theirra said they are hybrids. Well, if they're anything like me, maybe they have some talents you can put to use."

"And put them in danger?" She kept her voice low to match his.

"Maybe you really do need their help. Maybe you can use a bit of magic on your side. You have no idea how strong Lady Grustmiener's supporters may be getting."

"Lady Grustmiener? She is real? She isn't dead?" one of the boys asked.

Aura was certain she and Levi had whispered their conversation. It took a moment for her to register a strange, cool tingle in her head. She had seen enough magic in her life to realize that the two things must be connected.

"It seems that she may be," Aura said loud enough so the whole group could hear.

"They can help," Theirra said, desperation bordering on the edges of her voice. "I know they can. That is why I brought them here."

"They have homes," Aura responded.

What was going on here? In the last few days there had been a seismic shift in her entire world. Emily was missing. Aura feared that Theirra had slipped farther and farther down a road that Aura was unable to pull her from. Levi was back. And now all these kids—stolen from a foreign land—had pledged allegiance to her to fight again a woman Aura would have sworn a week ago was dead. It was all too much.

"Actually, we don't," one of the boys said, toeing the floor in front of him with his shoe.

Aura looked around the group. They looked so little, eleven or twelve up to maybe eighteen. It pained her heart to see these lost children, these kids without a place, but it was not her job to give them one. She was a queen in another world from their own. They had a place they belonged to, even if they didn't know it. "They are too young," she said to Theirra.

"You were sixteen," was all she said.

Aura closed her eyes, the memories of seven years ago flooded back to her—the sadness of her father's death and the terror of being thrust into a position of immense power, only to have that power challenged. It was true, she had been sixteen, but it was also true that she was too young. She did what she did because she had to.

Just at that moment, a middle-aged man ran into the room at full speed. His heavy footfalls echoed loudly. Aura saw Levi take a step back, but she remained relaxed and so he relaxed too, though he still stood a little behind her.

"My queen." The man looked terrified. "They are closed, the portals, they are all closed."

Closed? Aura's head swam.

Levi looked at her with a panicked expression. How would she get these foreigners out? Did Levi maybe have the power to open them back up again? She saw the man clutch at his stomach and take short, shallow breaths.

"Slow down," Aura said as the man gasped for air. "What do you mean the portals are closed?"

"Word had come from Vertronum that their portals are no longer working. I went to the one closest to here and found it solid. It should be open, but when I walked toward the tree it is next to, there was no glowing, and when I pressed my hand upon the area, I was met with a solid force. I have sent several men out to check on the other portals. They should be back in a day or two."

Aura looked over at Theirra, who seemed a little too pleased at the situation. Could she be behind this? Aura knew she didn't have the kind of power to do such a thing, but could she have learned in the time she'd been gone?

"Thank you. Let me know the reports of the others when they return," Aura said. She tried to keep her voice calmer than she felt. "I believe that makes the decision for us, at least for now. Since they are going to be here for at least a few days until we can get this situation resolved, tell me about these children."

Theirra beamed. The group moved and stood in a row, as if this introduction had been planned—and maybe it had been.

"This is Julia." Theirra started with the smallest girl. "Fourteen, can levitate objects."

Levi cracked a smile for a moment, before he realized it wasn't a joke. Aura tried to keep her face blank and smooth as the introductions continued. Theirra listed their names, ages, and powers in a very no-frills manner, as if magical children walked into their courtyard every day. The group also seemed interested while Theirra rattled off their information.

"Riagan, thirteen, can see through objects. Kiya, twelve, can talk to animals. Jada, fifteen, reads thoughts."

Ah, thought Aura, this confirmed her suspicions as he was the one who questioned her hushed conversation with Levi.

"Not exactly," Jada interrupted. "I see pictures, images in people's heads. When someone talks, I can sometimes tell it's not the truth by what they're seeing in their head. Ah…I know, but not really mind reading."

"Kalan," Theirra continued without any further prompt. "Sixteen, can become transparent. Adam, sixteen, impressive healing skills. Galina, seventeen, can control weather patterns." The kids looked at one another as if this explained something. "And lastly, Tab, the oldest of the group at nineteen, has immense strength compared to his size." She gestured at the group. "I think they will become useful."

Aura nodded at the group as she tugged on Theirra's arm. "They are not pack animals," Aura said to her friend.

"I did not say that they were."

"Theirra, I understand that you are trying to be helpful."

"I am being helpful," she said. "But you have to let me."

"Not at the expense of these kids. They may think they know why they are here, they may think they are ready for what lies ahead, but do they realize what can happen to them? Theirra, they could die."

"They can help in ways that will not put them in danger. We can figure it out. We need help, Aura."

Theirra's eyes were pools of hope. Aura could see to the recesses of her friend's soul that she thought this was the only way. It pained Aura to do so, but she had to disagree. She couldn't put any more lives in danger than absolutely necessary. She simply couldn't do it. She lowered her eyes and shook her head, unable to witness the expression that act created on Theirra's face.

Aura addressed the group of kids. "We will get you back to your homes at the first opportunity, for now, please enjoy your time here. Theirra will help show you around. I would ask that you stay within the castle walls as the forest is unfamiliar to you and contains a number of creatures and people who may try to take advantage of your naiveté. We will find space for you to sleep, meals are here in our great room. Help yourself to whatever you may need. Levi, if you wish, I can show you to where you will be staying." She also wanted to speak with him in private about what had transpired with Amaline.

She left the room of slack-jawed kids, who talked in hushed voices to one another about the strange turn their lives had just taken.

Chapter 16

Others

Far from the land of Esotera, the boy and girl stayed together, as they had since arriving. Luther was tall and muscular. It was clear that he had worked outside most of his seventeen years. His hair, once medium brown, had turned almost blond in the months that he'd worked in the field by his parent's house. He hated it there. Hated that he was expected to help all the time when he would rather be out in the woods hunting animals or building something.

Unna too had spent some time outdoors, but not nearly as much as Luther, and for different reasons. She was born on a reservation and was able to stay in their foster system until she turned eighteen. In the two years since, she'd drifted from place to place and often slept under the stars while she contemplated what was next. There was never anything next. Then one day she was approached by a man and now, here she was. She knew that sounded insane and dangerous. Basically the beginning of every poor run-away-murder story, but really, what else did she have going for her? So she went.

"How long are we supposed to hang around here?"

Unna asked in a lazy voice. Her head rested on her arms as she lay on the forest floor.

"Dunno," Luther replied. "That lady said it might be a little while."

"That lady," Unna said and turned over to face him, "is the ruler of this land."

"So she says."

"So all these people say as well," she said as she sat up.

"Don't know who you've been talking to. I spoke to some of them and they said she *used* to be the leader but was defeated in some battle or something." He got up and paced the area around her in slow loops.

"Well, it's not like you or I had better options back home."

"True." He laughed. "True."

She got up as well and started to move away from him.

Luther followed after her. "Unna, stop," He grabbed her arm, rougher than he meant to.

She took a sharp breath and he let her go. "What?" she snapped.

"What *is* this place? What are we doing here? And why do you seem so calm about it all?"

"Oh, Luther." She sighed with a tone as if she spoke to a five-year-old. "I know you came from the hicks and all, but do you have to be told everything. We are special. You are special. You can't say you don't know that."

"Well."

He shrugged and turned away from her. Now she grabbed his arm. The warmth spread through his body, and he felt a sudden urge to kiss her. He inched forward, but stopped himself. He figured he would get a swift kick in the face, or elsewhere, in return if he followed through.

"Ugg." She threw her hands in the air and walked away from him.

He jogged to catch up to her. "Unna, wait."

She turned around and he was shocked to see not her, but the high school love of his life, Sandy, in front of him.

"Luther." Her honey smooth voice dripped his name.

"S—Sandy," he stuttered.

She moved toward him. Her hot breath warmed his face as she got close to him. Her body, firm and real—*this was real*—was pressing into his. A moment before their lips met, his eyes half closed in anticipation. She laughed and pulled away. When he looked at her again, Unna was back. Luther was flabbergasted.

"You should see your face!" She giggled. "Oh, did I hurt your feelings?"

Luther turned away. He didn't want her to see his red cheeks or hear how hard his heart thumped. His brain replayed the scenario, and of course, he knew it couldn't be real. He was hundreds, maybe even thousands of miles away. A whole other world away. What would make him think that Sandy would appear in from of him, much less want to kiss him—an act she never wanted to do in his real life? But if felt so real! He was sure it had happened, as if the logic switch had turned off in his brain, and just because his eyes saw something, he believed it. This place had started to mess with him.

She looked at him under half-closed eyes. "So, I showed you mine," she said seductively, "now show me yours."

"I don't know what you just did, but it's not something I can do."

"No, of course not. Why would they want two of us? But there *is* something you can do. Come on, spill it."

She stood in front of him and blocked his path. For a

moment he wished she would switch back, or whatever it was she did, so he could finally get that kiss.

Luther sat in a heap next to a tree, his back rested against the firm trunk. It felt good to have something solid all around him, to remind him that he was real, and, as unreal as this all felt, it was actually happening. He lowered his head into his hands. He didn't want to look her in the eye.

"I can control—things," he mumbled into his palms.

She sat down next to him. "What?"

He looked up and sighed. "I've never told anyone this. I don't even know how they know."

She inched forward. "Spit it out," she said.

He hesitated. "If something dies, I can control it."

"Can control it how, exactly?" she asked, impatience giving an edge to her voice.

"It's almost like a trance, I guess. That's the best way I can explain it, but I can sort of go inside their head and work their brain. It's a lot harder the bigger the thing. Like small animals like squirrels and rats are pretty easy, dogs a bit harder, but people—" He thought it over for a minute. "People are really hard. I tried it once, but the feeling was a bit too creepy for my liking. Everything moved so sluggish, it was like I had a suit one size too big on and was trying to run through water. I don't know why I can do it or how exactly, it usually just sorta happens when my mind wanders. Scared the crap out of me the first time it happened."

"Why haven't you told anyone?" She looked at him with wonder in her eyes. He liked the expression on her face.

"I don't know. Well, that's a lie. I know perfectly well. I had a great aunt who swore she was a psychic, could talk to the dead, or something like that. Whether she was or not, I'm beginning to lean toward the former after seeing all this stuff," he said as he gestured to their surroundings. "She was inundated with requests. Bereaved widows, depressed parents who lost a child, even the stray pet owner heartbroken over the inevitability of the short lives of furry creatures. If people thought I could bring their loved ones back to them, they would never leave me alone. Plus, I can't do it all the time. It makes me tired. Not like take a nap and feel better tired, like deep down in your bones tired."

"Crazy," she said and sat back on the trunk next to him.

"Me, crazy? What's up with that stuff you do?" he asked, unable to hide the hostility in his voice.

"At least I can explain what I can do," she said. "Well, parts of it at least. I can change, obviously, you saw that. I just hone in on your thoughts, that's the part I'm not all the way clear on—it just happens—and I can picture faces, people. It doesn't always work the same way with everyone. Sometimes it's a person they're afraid of, sometimes it is someone they love, or even just miss. I'm guessing, from your reaction, it was love." He nodded, embarrassed. "But it's only looks. I still sorta sound like me. I try to change my voice a bit, but it still doesn't work that well when I become a guy."

She laughed again, that throaty laugh that used her whole body. The memory of Sandy slipped away.

"So what do you think we are doing here?" Luther asked. "This place is strange to say the least, but what is it they want from us?"

"She is ready for you now," a voice said from behind them before Unna was able to answer.

They both turned, startled.

A small man stood before them, though he was stocky and looked strong. He gave Unna just enough time to turn around before he moved off through the woods. She and

Luther had to jog to keep up with the stranger's long stride.

They were taken to a door that almost blended in with its surroundings. The man found a handle and pushed it open. He curled his fingers and beckoned Luther and Unna to follow him inside. They were plunged into light so dim, it took them several moments for their eyes to adjust. They moved through a corridor that appeared to go down and in circles as they went along. They passed a number of doors with muffled voices behind them before they stopped in front of one of the last ones. When the man knocked on it, an old man answered.

"I am finishing up now," the old man said. "I need someone to come and take her."

As the words left his mouth, two men appeared behind Luther, startling him again. They moved past, almost as if they didn't notice his and Unna's presence, and pushed into the room. Moments later, they dragged a semi-conscious woman out. From the quick glimpse he got, Luther thought the woman to be in her late twenties. It was hard to tell behind the bruises and caked blood, but he thought she might be pretty. Her brown hair hung around her shoulders as she was moved.

They were ushered into the room. Luther felt a web of dread weave through his chest and fought the urge to run. To turn and go back the way he had come, all the way back to Prairie Farm—literally, that was the name of his town—and his mind-numbing, boring life. Boring, but without danger. Yet something made him follow Unna into that room. Unna, this girl he met just three days before, but he felt an instant connection with her. She was unlike anyone he'd ever come across. It almost felt as if there was a thin string which tied him to her. It tugged when she went inside, and he obediently followed.

The room was spacious with a single chair in the middle. Luther noticed some blood on it, but quickly tried to put it out of his mind. There were various screens around the room, like TV screens but something was off about them. They all showed a blue screen, but the color undulated in such a way that wasn't like the set in his living room.

The door shut with a loud bang behind them, and Luther turned to Unna, but she appeared unfazed. Honestly, she appeared unfazed by everything they had been through. She seemed to accept what happened much easier than he did, almost as if she'd expected something like this to happen in her life. Not him. He only followed because she was good looking, and really, what else was he doing with his life? She was twenty, three years older than he was, but was still several inches shorter than him. He wondered briefly if he had a chance with her.

Then Lady Grustmiener walked into the room. It was only the second time he'd seen the woman. She looked just as powerful and fierce as he remembered.

"Unna, Luther," she said to them. "I require your help."

The way she spoke took Luther aback. It was as if she told them to do something and yet asked at the same time.

"You have special powers that I need, in order to keep, not simply my world safe, but yours as well. We will show you how to harness those powers, how to become masters of your craft, and when the time is right, you will unleash those powers on our enemy. I will be grateful to you both for your help, and you will justly compensated for your troubles."

What the heck is this lady talking about? Luther wondered. Master of your craft? Enemy? Compensated for your troubles? He was in a strange land with an even stranger girl next to him while this lady tried to tell them to go to battle for her.

After a long pause, Luther said, "Umm, I think I'm confused."

The look that flashed on the woman's face sent such a jolt of fear through him, he took a visible step back. Just as quickly, though, her face softened. "Luther, we know what you can do. There are people in this world who are threatening not only my existence and that of my people, but also your world. If they are successful in their quest, they will infiltrate your borders, destroy your people and everything you know. Your whole way of life will be a thing of the past. It is imperative that you help us defeat them. Nothing will be the same if you do not."

Luther looked over at Unna, but she stared straight at the woman, and he was unable to read the expression on her face.

"I know life must not be easy for you on the other side," the woman continued again in that soft voice. "If you choose to, you could stay here the rest of your life and never have to be worried about being called a negative name ever again. Here, you would be a hero."

This last part, as he was sure that was why she had said it, seemed to speak directly to him. How many times had he been made fun of? Been ostracized in school? How many times had he been made an outcast because he was weird, strange, a freak? To have an opportunity to change that—

He took a moment to mull the thought over.

She introduced them to Abaddon who would help train them. He seemed to almost salivate when he discussed how he was going to aid them. They spoke for a short while more before Lady Grustmiener dismissed them and the guard wove them back out of the underground.

As soon as they were deposited back outside, the two ran back to where they came from. It felt good to Luther to have fresh air push through his lungs as his heart raced to keep up. Unna grabbed his hand once again and pulled him forward before she stopped. She wheezed as they reached "their" tree and placed her hands on her legs.

"Well, they obviously want to use us for something big," she said. She still hadn't caught her breath and spoke in halted words. "Did you see that girl they brought out of the room before us?" Unna looked over her shoulder and, while there was no one around the, she whispered all the same.

"Yeah, I may have watched one too many movies, but seemed to me she was being tortured or something. Do you think they will do that to us if we don't help them?" The two looked gravely at each other. What was this mess they had gotten themselves into?

Luther longed again for his simple, boring life. *We're not in Wisconsin anymore*, he thought.

Chapter 17

Resbuca

Levi found Theirra as she sat in front of the stables, the group of stolen children scattered around her. They seemed to be in conversations with one another while Theirra gazed off into space at some far off place. From that distance, Levi was able to get a good look at what the last few years had done to her.

Time in Esotera moved more quickly than it did in his world, and while he knew it was seven years that had elapsed for them, it looked as if twenty years had been added to her features. Even from across the yard, he could see the sharp edges of her, like her whole body was made up of pointed angles, not the soft features he remembered about her. Even the kids seemed to sense there was something destroyed in her, and they kept a fair distance, worried about being sucked into whatever trap she had entangled herself in.

"I heard you spoke with Aura more about Amaline. Do you feel better about her being here?" she asked, though she kept her gaze on the sky.

"I guess. Enough," he said.

The stress of the day and Amaline's appearance had

caught up with him when he and Aura walked through the castle. She tried to reason with him, let him know all the wonderful contributions Amaline had made to help in the aftermath of the battle, but he found it difficult to allow her words to penetrate. She gave up and left him alone in the same spacious room he'd occupied the last time he was here. His sleep was fitful, but he did feel a bit better the next morning.

Levi came and sat next to Theirra. Her eyes gave the faintest flick in his direction before she resumed her vigil. He turned to see what it was she was looking at. There was a small black speck against the blue sky. A creature of some sort, and, while it was very far away, he could tell it was headed their way.

"What is it?" Levi asked.

"I am not sure," Theirra said.

"It's a bird," Kiya confirmed.

They both looked at her.

"A bird?" Theirra asked with the amused expressed she seemed to take when she conversed with one of the kids.

"Yes, and there's something special about him, but I can't quite figure it out. He knows this place, though. He's intent on coming here. He has been traveling for some time and he's tired." Kiya turned in the same direction as the other two, vigilant alongside them.

Levi still struggled to get used to being in this place again and being surrounded by a gaggle of X-Men wanna-be kids did not help the transition any. He had to get out of here. Find Emily and return back home as quickly as possible. If it was even possible. Earlier that day, a woman had arrived to confirm the portals along the borders of Esotera were also sealed. The memory of the encounter caused Levi's guts to tighten.

The three kept their gaze on the bird, but it made slow

progress against the great expanse that separated them. It wasn't until almost dusk that the bird's whole form was fully visible. Bright green, red, and blue feathers popped against the darkening sky as the creature dropped in height, preparing for its landing.

"Oh my," Theirra exclaimed and they all stared. She turned to one of the stable boys and asked him to fetch Aura right away.

"What is it?" Levi asked a second before it dawned on him. He recognized this bird.

Aura came moments later, out of breath with her hair half out of its long braid. It was clear she'd been getting ready for dinner when she was interrupted. "Theirra?" she asked as she ran up.

Theirra pointed wordlessly to the sky. Aura took in an audible breath.

"So, it's a bird. I don't get it?" Kalan asked.

"They know this bird," Jada said. "They are worried this means someone's dead."

The group fell silent.

The bird called as it floated down toward them. Levi wondered if it had been doing that the entire time, but they could only hear it now that it was close. It was eerie to see Busu again. The last time Levi had laid eyes on him, he'd been perched on the sorceress Resbuca's shoulder. The bird carried so much emotion and memories on its thin, feathered wings. Aura put her arm out and the bird landed upon it with relief.

"He is very hungry and tired," Kiya said.

Levi felt the statement was obvious, magic bird talking powers or not.

"Theirra?" Aura asked, worry crinkling her forehead.

Theirra rushed into the barn as Aura walked toward the castle. Levi was not sure if he was supposed to follow. Who did he belong with? The gang of misfits from his world or the two women he knew from this one with the creepy witch bird? He chose the bird and took the bag of seed from Theirra's arms as she returned and passed him.

"I wonder if something happened to her," Aura said when they were all in her chambers. Busu drank deeply and ate large mouthfuls of seeds. He dropped half of each bite in small puddles like rain on the polished floor.

"I am sure she has passed," Theirra said softly.

Aura sat heavily on a chaise and watched the bird intently. Once he had gotten his fill, he hopped to an opposing chair and curled up, his beak under his wing, and fell asleep.

"Should I ask Kiya to come in here?" Theirra asked.

"No, let Busu rest. He seems to have had a long journey."

The three sat in silence for some time before Levi spoke.

"Are there many witches in this area?"

"Not that I know of, not in our kingdom, that is," Aura said. "Resbuca was the only one I knew personally. And Winester."

Levi remembered the two ancient sorcerers, the latter was the bird's first owner. He wondered how old the creature was and about its life expectancy, which then made him wonder the same about witches and wizards.

"They can die? Like naturally?" he asked. He remembered that Winester had been killed by Resbuca, otherwise would the man have lived forever?

"They live much longer than you and I, but they are not immortal," Aura said. "Over hundreds of years, though, as their kind died out, they began having children with non-magical people. 'Hybrids' is what we call them. Those kids out there, they are products of magical lines. True blood witches and wizards, though, are rare, and thus any true blood offspring are unlikely. I knew there were some clans in the North, that is actually where Resbuca was from originally, but I do not know how many of those are actually left."

Levi saw Theirra shift, but she didn't speak.

"I am sorry about your friend," was all he could think of to say.

Aura nodded somberly. "Is this war really going to happen?" she asked Theirra.

"I am afraid so, my queen."

Aura wiped a tear from her cheek. "Theirra, I am so sorry."

"You were trying to do what you thought was best."

"I have acted like a fool."

The women walked forward and embraced each other. Levi wondered if he should give them space, but just as he took a step back, they let go.

Aura cleared her throat. "What are we going to do?" she asked, her voice still thick with emotion.

"We will figure it out together," Theirra said.

Aura sighed. "We will need to prepare. I know Milskar has both a heavy heart and mind, but we will need him to help gather an army."

Levi felt like she wanted to say something else, but she stopped herself. They probably thought the same thing—that this time they would be without Kolas. Levi wondered what, if any, disadvantage this would put them in.

"Theirra," Aura said. "Would you please tell Milskar I would like to speak with him before dinner?"

Theirra nodded and left the room. Levi got up to go also, but Aura stopped him. He turned and looked at her properly for the first time. There were worry lines which had started to run around her eyes and mouth, but she was even more beautiful than he remembered. When she didn't keep it up in her typical bun, her red hair reached all the way down her back. She looked every bit a queen. Any insecurity she had about ruling when he'd seen her last had vanished. Even with the vulnerable moment he'd witnessed between her and Theirra, he could tell Aura was a powerful woman, and it suited her well.

"Levi, you have done much for my kingdom, and while you are under no obligation to stay and help with whatever this may turn into, I would hope that you would lend us any assistance you can." Aura relocated to a small desk and flicked a sporadic glance at the bird as it slept. "I know seeing Amaline yesterday was a shock. I know this will be difficult for you on many levels, but we—" She paused and corrected herself. "—I could really use your help."

"I have a life now," he said.

The words sounded cheap as they came out of his mouth, a lame excuse, but it was true. His career had started to take off, and what would happen if the hot new writer of the hot new best seller just disappeared? He could hear his agent in his head now. 'What do you mean you want to take some time off?' Kailly would say. "Time off is for those who have given up, now get your butt out there!"

Aura nodded. "I understand. Once we have determined that the portals are working properly again, I suppose…" She let the silence apply the pressure for her.

He sighed. "I will help in any way I can to find Emily, but I don't think I can fight in another war. Aura, I'm sorry, but once we find her, once I know she's safe, I really must go. Well, if the portals are open, I guess," he mused. "I don't know what help I can give you here. I haven't the faintest clue where Emily is or how to get her back…"

His voice trailed off as his brain clicked through the

reasons Aura would want to keep him here. "You want to use me as bait," he said slowly.

"That is a little dramatic for my tastes," Aura said. "But, yes, I do think your being here will come to the attention of Lady Grustmiener. It is probably why she took Emily, to get you here. Once she knows you are in the kingdom, I am sure some kind of contact will be made and we will know where she is and what, if any, plans she has with those she is gathering. When that happens and we know where she is, we will be able to recover her. Then we can sneak you out so no one will know. As far as all parties are concerned, they will think you are safely in the castle here and, hopefully, that will drive them out of whatever hole they are in so we can finish this once and for all."

"So I just have to flush them out, like they're a burrow of groundhogs?" He didn't feel particularly reassured by the supposed simplicity of the plan, but he didn't allow his mind to wander to the simple fact that there might be no way to leave.

"I am not sure what groundhogs are, but I believe, yes, something like that," Aura said.

She looked back over at the bird who snored louder than a creature his size should have been able to.

Chapter 18

Broken Things

Milskar entered the room moments later, a hollow shell in human clothes. Levi excused himself, even though he could see in Aura's eyes she wanted him to stay. He didn't want to be privy to the conversation, especially while he was still trying to figure out his own emotions.

He hadn't had much contact with Emily since he'd left, and it was strange to think of this whole life she had. Like when you passed strangers in cars and you had to remind yourself there were millions of other people out there in the world that you would never meet, each with their own lives and stories. It could blow your mind if you thought about it too much.

Now Levi, who had been so involved in his own life for so many years, was thrust back into a place that had moved along perfectly without him. Well, almost perfectly.

It scared him seeing Milskar. He remembered him as such a strong and formidable person that, to see him so broken now unnerved him.

Levi needed time to get his thoughts together and in

the presence of his cousin's husband was not the place for it. He took one look back and exited her office.

こうこう

Aura felt some of her resolve walk out the door with Levi when he left. She didn't know why his presence gave her a sense of strength. The pull she felt toward him was strange and confusing. She'd thought little about him in the years since he'd left. She'd been so busy rebuilding not only her lands, but also the Grustmiener kingdom, that she had little time to think of anything else. Levi unexpectedly coming back into her life, flagged by Theirra and all those children, threw Aura for an emotional loop.

It was not the time for quiet reflection, though, no matter how much she wanted it.

Now her attention needed to be focused on the job at hand, and she tried not to feel crestfallen at the sight before her. It had been only two days since she'd last seen Milskar, but the bags under his eyes had turned a dark, bruised purple, and his skin appeared pale and clammy. Maybe a task to focus on would be exactly what he needed, Aura hoped.

"Milskar—" She stopped herself and didn't ask how he was doing. There was no point in the formality. "I have some new information and am in need of your help."

"You found her." It was a statement, his voice cracking under the hope of it.

Aura paid no attention to the tight feeling in her chest. "Not exactly." He sagged, hope dripping into puddles on the floor. She placed her hand on his arm. "But we think we know who took her and why. Lady Grustmiener—"

"Impossible." He cut her off and quickly paced one length of the room, clearly agitated. "Are you listening to

Theirra's ramblings again? You know she is not well."

Aura ignored the fact that this statement came from someone who appeared not to have bathed in days. "Lady Grustmiener, or her sympathizers, have assembled an army. This information has been confirmed by Amaline, but I am still waiting for information on who's leading them. An army is being assembled. I believe Emily was taken as a message and warning, and—" She took a deep breath. "—as a way to bring Levi back here."

Confusion momentarily replaced all other emotions on Milskar's face. "Levi?"

"Yes," Aura said hesitantly, "you passed him on your way in." No recollection passed over him. "Theirra brought him here along with several other hybrids from his world," she continued. "Milskar, it sounds like this may be a larger war than the last time. I know you have a lot going on, especially with being alone with Nikolas, but Esotera needs your help. I need your help."

"What do you need from me?"

Aura was happy that her assumption proved correct. Maybe putting his mind elsewhere would help Milskar, at least in the short term. She didn't want to think of the possible repercussions if the outcome turned out not to be a favorable one.

"I need someone to lead my army." Her pause lasted long enough for them both to think of the past and Kolas. "There will be many from the last battle who will be called on to remember their training, but there will also be enough new members that I need a strong leader to show them the way. Can I count on you?"

"Always," Milskar replied firmly. "When shall I begin?"

"Immediately. I will dedicate one of my aides, Cassney, solely to the task of looking after Nikolas. He will be in exceptional hands."

"You sound as if you will not be here to oversee preparations."

"No." Aura smiled weakly. "I will be first traveling to Grustmiener to meet with Omire, then to Vertronum to meet with King Piester."

"You are involving the other kingdoms?" Milskar asked incredulously. "Do you feel that is necessary, especially at this point?"

"From Amaline's information, there is a building army in the northern regions of Lady Grustmiener's former realm. I can only assume they will eventually try to recruit King Omaner, if they have not already done so." Milskar nodded solemnly. Aura sighed heavily. "If we can get the backing of Vertronum, especially before they can, I think we stand a better chance. I will be taking Heza and the rest of the fleet. We must focus on speed."

"I think they will notice a flock of dragons," Milskar interjected.

"We have to operate under the assumption that these fighters are aware of our knowledge regarding their attempts. Speed is our lone hope to gain any sort of advantage. I will travel lightly, bringing only a few guards with me so as not to interfere with your work."

"I would feel much better accompanying you myself," Milskar said.

"I know, but I need you here. I need my best in charge of training, but also in the event of any surprise attacks." She said a silent prayer that it would not be the case. "I plan on limiting my time away, but I cannot have my kingdom at risk while I am gone. I trust you Milskar. I know you will protect this land better than anyone else."

"Then allow me to pick the ones who will travel with you." Some glimmers of life seemed to return as Milskar's thoughts were refocused on how to help her.

"I would greatly appreciate that," she said and placed

a small hand on his broad shoulders, which now carried
the weight of so much upon them.

Chapter 19

Choices

Julia looked around her and at the other misfits scattered around this strange place. She felt…not homesick, that wasn't the right word for it…maybe just an ache for something normal. She laughed inwardly at herself. Normal. What did that even mean? She was certainly not normal. She used her mind to twirl a piece of grass in front of her. It spun in lazy circles against the light breeze.

Riagan sat next to her. The girl seemed nice enough, kept quiet, and mostly to herself, but there was something about her that unnerved Julia. Like she could see not just through objects, but through people as well, right down to their souls. Julia shuddered at the thought.

It was strange being around these other kids with somewhat similar abilities. While all slightly different, they shared an innate ability that somehow brought them together, and they seemed to know it. Separately, none of these kids would have talked to her, nor would she have talked to them, but now thrown into this mix together, they'd become quite friendly with one another. Kiya and Jada were deep in a conversation with a horse as they tried to figure out if Jada's gifts translated to beings other than just humans. Kiya laughed as Jada tried to relate what the animal pictured with its actual thoughts. They were too far away for Julia to hear the conversation, but Kiya's shrill laughter sometimes cut through the distance.

Kalan seemed to disappear for hours at a time. Julia was never sure if it was because he'd actually made himself invisible and snuck around them, or if he just liked to wander the grounds. Either way she made a point to never speak about him, just in case.

Tab had gone with a large man who introduced himself as Milskar. He seemed menacing, with a darkness about him that frightened Julia, and she told herself to stay away from him if she could. After the two had left, Jada explained that there was something terribly painful that all parts of his mind were centered on, though he tried desperately to not focus on it. Something about a woman who was taken and a battle. They speculated for almost an hour on what it could all mean but, without any additional information, had to abandon their discussions.

While Jada's powers were useful, he had to be within close proximity of the person to actually be able to use them. With Milskar gone, any attempt to uncover more information went along with him. The pair had been gone for hours and Julia worried about what the strange man wanted with Tab.

Adam and Galina, two who seemed to take immediately to one another, were a little way off from the rest of the group. They talked with their backs against a tree. They were the best looking of the group. Adam was dark skinned and impossibly handsome, muscles visible even under his shirt.

Galina was tall and slender. Her blonde hair skimmed off her shoulders in a fashionable cut. They did not look like they belonged on the island of misfit toys like the rest of them, and the way they sequestered themselves from the rest of the group seemed to show they knew it was well.

Julia noticed Queen Aura moving briskly around the castle grounds all morning as several men followed her. They didn't look like traditional guards. It was hard to tell, honestly—what, with the kind of clothes they wore—but Julia assumed, by the way they walked around her, they were there to protect her. They were carrying packs and soon after lunch, Julia noticed a group of dragons had arrived near the stables. She held back a shriek, still not used to the large and dangerous-looking beasts.

Aura had walked up to one, a smaller—if that word could even be properly used in relation to dragons—and petted its head lovingly. Soon after the group climbed up and, with an earth-shaking rumble, took to the skies. Julia watched until they had become specks in the distance.

"What do you think that is about?" Riagan had asked her.

"I don't know. Do you think it might have something to do with Tab leaving? That war stuff Jada was talking about?" Julia asked, her eyes still on the spot that had occupied the dragons and their riders.

"What was I talking about?"

Julia jumped as Jada spoke behind her.

"The queen," Riagan said, "just flew off on a dragon with a bunch of other people. On their own dragons." She said these words so normally that Julia almost felt like she was the strange one for not acclimating to this place fast enough.

"They're traveling to some kingdom," Kiya said as she joined the conversation. "I can't understand their word for it, but there was some kind of war. They are proud of how they helped in it, and now think they will be needed to help again. Dragons seem to be extremely simple minded though," she added, frustrated. "It is hard to get any real information out of them. And they are narcissistic. It's quite humorous actually, how highly they think of themselves."

Kalan laughed. "Maybe it's the whole breathing fire thing, gives them an ego," he said.

Where'd he come from? Julia asked herself.

The group stood there for some time and looked up at the sky before they gave up and resigned themselves to sit back down and wait for whatever it was they were here for.

As the day passed, hordes of villagers moved through the courtyard. Some embraced one another quickly, shook hands, patted backs, as if it had been some time since they had seen each other. Others, usually those who traveled alone and appeared quite young, seemed scared and out of place in the mix. They all went the same way through the grounds toward the woods, a steady stream that did not let up until close to sunset.

Out of the mix walked a face Julia recognized. Levi moved toward them with slow yet purposeful steps. The others looked up at his approach and got up to stand by Julia, Adam and Galina included.

Levi waved half-heartedly and shrugged his shoulders. "Hi," he said.

Julia wondered why he seemed so shy around them.

"War?" Jada asked and the others looked from him to Levi again.

"I think so," Levi answered matter-of-factly.

"Why are we really here?" Julia asked. She tried to sound more authoritative than she felt.

"I think for the same reason I'm here," Levi said. "They think your special talents can help in this battle."

"Battle?" Riagan asked with a hint of fear in her voice.

"You're different than them, and us," Jada stated.

"Yes. I'm from the same world as you, but I'm a descendant of this one."

"But so are we," Tab said.

"Yes," Levi said, "but my ancestry goes back a little farther than yours, I suppose."

"Is everything in the book true? You are the Missing Link, or whatever you called it?" Galina asked.

Levi hesitated for a moment before explaining in detail the events that brought him to Esotera all those years before. He hadn't included all the details in *Saving Esotera,* especially the part of his torture. Some of it was too painful to recount, even if others thought it was fiction.

The group sat stunned, glancing at one another throughout the story. Some nodded, while others sat open-mouthed, unsure of whether to believe his tale or not. When he spoke about the details of what Abaddon had done, something he'd hadn't told anyone, they all dropped their eyes from him. They sat in silence for some time when he finished.

"So it's a true story then? Your book?" Galina asked.

"Pretty much. I was taken hostage. A great battle followed, and Esotera secured the land of Grustmiener after Queen Aura defeated their king, resulting in the surrender of his army. And I killed, or—" He paused. "—I thought I killed Lady Grustmiener."

"And now they think she's back?" Galina asked. "What happens next?"

"I don't know, exactly. An army has formed, in hopes of defeating Queen Aura, and we aren't sure who's at its helm. Theirra thinks it's Lady Grustmiener, but we can't be sure, not yet. I believe Theirra assembled you to help assist in this fight against them. Your powers may prove useful."

"Useful?" Julia asked. "You make it sound as if we are cattle raised for slaughter."

"I would not put it in those terms, exactly," Theirra said, surprising them with her sudden appearance.

"Oh, I—" Julia stammered, feeling every bit as young as she actually was.

"No matter." Theirra waved her off. "Yes, you were brought here in preparation for an impending battle. One that you may think you have no stake in, but you are all decedents of members of this world, and, as such, you owe a part of your life to it. I understand that you are young, some of you very young." She looked purposely at Kiya, who blushed and lowered her eyes. "The decision is up to you if you would like to fight and use your special talents in protecting these lands. You have some time before a decision has to be made. Meet the people here, talk to them, get a feel for this place, and then determine if you think it is worth fighting for. Whatever decision you make will be accepted. If you do not wish to fight, we will find a safe place for you until you can be returned home."

The last statement she made was casual, but Levi took it as conformation that they had not been able to open the portals yet. He tried to ignore his building alarm at the thought.

"Where's Tab?" Adam asked as Theirra turned to leave.

"He has already made his decision. He's with Milskar, head of our army. Tab has already begun his training."

And because there was nothing else to say, no more words to give them, Theirra left them to make their decisions.

Stunned, the group looked from one to the other. None had homes that they could speak of. None had a real life to get back to, but did that still make it worth the risk—o risk the possibility of a future for whatever this endeavor might become?

Julia prayed for bravery above all else. Bravery, and a way to see herself through whatever the future might hold.

Chapter 20

Omire

Aura walked cautiously through the castle grounds at Grustmiener. While she'd been coming here for years since the end of the war, she still felt slightly out of place in these grounds. Before the conflict, the kingdoms of the Four Corners did not interact with each other often. Esotera produced almost all of its own goods, so trade was not necessary in most factions of their lives. It was not out of the ordinary for people to move between kingdoms, but typically members stayed where they were born and got married. They had children and died not far from where they grew up. The war changed that.

The members of Grustmiener who had decided to return and stay in the areas which surrounded the castle began to travel in greater numbers back and forth between their homes and Esotera, and vice-versa for her people. She was happy to see this, happy to see that they could so easily forgive what had happened in the past. It was not their war, not really.

They went along with it willingly because their rulers bid them to, but when it came down to it, peace was everyone's preferred method of existence. It interested Aura, all the same, to see how different their castle center was from her own.

Esotera's grand building was like a beacon. It could be seen from miles around even in the lush, wooden lands of her kingdom. She felt it gave her people comfort to know exactly where she was, exactly where they could go for help.

In Grustmiener, small portions of the castle showed through the ground. If you did not know exactly what to look for, it could be disregarded as a cluster of simple houses or dirt mounds. It was beautiful too, though, in its own way. Dark-green moss-covered trees draped all over the area, their branches looked like they laid protective arms over the building. Being half buried to help keep it protected from the elements also helped hide the structures. It was quite unassuming, in stark contrast to the castle at Esotera.

She was lost deep in thought when an aide ran up to her and handed her a letter. The man hadn't traveled with her party and she was confused to see him until she unraveled the note and read Milskar's slanted writing. Her heart sank.

She spotted Omire as he stood by the main door to the entrance and spoke with several people. Aura brightened and quickened her pace to meet him. She trusted Omire greatly and was pleased with how he ran Grustmiener. What was more, she liked him as a person.

He was a fair ruler, widely regarded as just by the people here, and came off as a strong presence when needed, though open enough that people were not afraid to ask him for help. It was a wonderful combination to have in a ruler that Aura tried daily to emulate, and she was just slightly jealous of how easily it seemed to come to him.

But what was she to think now? Omire had held a terrible secret from her. It was true that he'd spent the last seven years paying back a debt to her kingdom. But the words Amaline had spoken still rang through her mind. Aura had placed him in a position of power, and he accepted it without any word of how he got there. Of how the war started or what his role was.

Did this truth change who he was? Or who he was to her?

"Aura," Omire said as she reached him. "To what do I owe this pleasure?" He kissed her lightly on the cheek. He looked at the direction from which she came and saw the dragons being held by two guards in the distance. "What is this about? Is everything all right?"

"I apologize for interrupting," she said to the group around him, leaned in, and lowered her voice. "Is there somewhere in private we can speak?" She looked around to check if Amaline was close by, but she didn't see her.

"Of course, of course," he said and gestured her inside. He waved several of his guard away which left him and Aura alone as they walked into the castle.

Everything about this place spoke of darkness and hiding, Aura thought. It was hard for her eyes to adjust as they walked through the corridors. Small shafts of light broke through in various parts of the wall. Dull bulbs in the ceilings cast only soft light and gave the place an eerie, abandoned feel.

It was strange that, with how light and warm Omire was, he did not try to redesign these aspects of his new home.

"It is so dark down here," Aura said.

"Yes, I know," Omire said. He looked around, as if he'd forgotten himself. "I thought about changing it, but the people here are so used to it, I did not want to change their perception of home too greatly. Though, I am sure you will be happy about the changes I made to my own chambers."

He smiled as he opened the door to a spacious and bright room. After being in the darkness for several minutes, Aura had to blink hard against the bright light. She'd almost forgotten that it was still daytime.

"So tell me what is this about?" The sound of Omire's voice broke Aura out of the daze she was in.

"Have you spoken to Amaline lately?" Aura asked.

Omire wrinkled his face. "I have been traveling. You are lucky, actually, I just returned home. I believe she has been in the outskirts scouting these last few weeks. Why, what is it? Is everything all right with her?"

"She came to see me," Aura said.

"Came to see you?" Omire looked confused and slightly annoyed by this confusion. "About what, exactly?"

Aura had to take a deep breath to calm herself before speaking again. It all still seemed so preposterous. "Lady Grustmiener is forming an army in the north along the Grustmiener-Omaner boarder."

"Impossible!" Omire slapped his desk and caused Aura to jump. "Amaline is a child. She has fantasies and great imagination."

"She is older than I am," Aura said defensively.

Omire flitted his hand as if he batted away a fly. "She does not know what she says."

"It has been confirmed." She recalled the image of Milskar's note. The terrible realization of the truth. "I received word moments ago by my scouts. I did not want to believe it, but she spoke the truth, and now I need your help."

With a sigh, Omire sat at a large mahogany desk on one side of the room, his head pressed firmly into his hands as he tried to get his thoughts together.

Aura stood erect. She didn't speak so as not to interrupt whatever thoughts was going through his mind. She needed him to come to terms with the news, and quickly. Though she did wonder why Amaline had come to her first. Was it simply because he'd been away? Surely, she could have sent a message for him to return.

Aura wondered if something had been going on between Amaline and Omire, so that she did not trust him to take her seriously with the information. Though if his current emotion were any indication, Amaline probably knew he would brush her off. Going to Aura first ensured that the information would come not only from someone whom he trusted, but who also, in a pinch, he would feel obligated to listen to.

Omire looked up at her slightly. "What has she seen?" he asked.

Aura explained how the frenzied woman burst into her chambers and re-told what Amaline had seen and heard. He listened intently to her words, though Aura could tell there was a slight anger that brimmed behind his rapt attention. When she told him that she had sent along her own people to see the truth firsthand, and that they confirmed her worst fears of a gathering army, he lowered his head again.

"I wish she would have waited for me to return," Omire said as he raised his head from his hands. Aura realized it was not anger on his features, but hurt. "What do you need from me?" he asked.

She brightened considerably, but it was short lived. What did she want? What exactly had she come here for? For the first time in many years, she felt incapable of the responsibility she had. She suddenly felt very young and embarrassed to discover herself on the verge of tears. Quickly, she banished such toxic thoughts from her head.

"I think I may need your input on that," she said and

looked directly at him. If the last several years had taught her anything, it was to not be afraid to rely on others. Especially when those others knew more than you did. "Do you think your people should be made aware of the situation?"

"Well, there is a risk of sympathizers. Those who are going along with the norm because there is nothing to put their back up to fight against. The prospect of getting their lands back under the control of who they feel is their rightful ruler may cause some to turn against us."

"That is what I am afraid of, but I am more afraid of them catching wind of it, and then turning against us just on principle," Aura countered.

It felt good to be having this discussion. She again felt gratitude toward the man she left in charge of this place.

Omire came to the other side of the desk and sat closer to her. "Interesting theory," he said.

"Plus." She hesitated. "I am afraid that we will need their help. That without them we will be outnumbered and not stand a chance. That is why—" Another hesitation. "—I am also going to Vertronum to ask King Piester for his assistance as well."

"Aura." Omire stood, shock in his voice.

"This is not up for discussion," she said as she got her footing back. "I cannot risk Lady Grustmiener getting an army larger and stronger than mine. I will not lose my kingdom. Not to that woman, not to anyone."

Omire looked at her with a level of respect she hadn't seen in him before. Technically, Aura was above him in rank, though Omire always seemed like more of an equal or "big brother" in his role in the kingdom. He appeared both annoyed and pleased with her as she took control of their conversation.

"What about the North?" he asked.

"I believe from Lady Grustmiener's location and what

I have heard from Amaline and my scouts, I think they are already trying to align with King Vertronum, though I do not know to what measure of success she has had."

"That is unfortunate," he said and paused. "So you will travel to the South?"

"My plan was to travel there after our meeting," she said.

"I will assist in any way I can," he said. "I think the people that we will lose by telling them this information will be greatly outnumbered by those who will be willing to help. I think the majority of people in this kingdom have led better lives since the war. I believe they will be willing to help maintain that. I also believe that King Piester will be willing to help as well. He is a meek man, but also does not want to lose what he has. He relies too heavily on trade with the other regions. I have not heard much confident talk about him as a leader, though I think he surrounds himself with powerful and skilled people. I trust he will choose to ally on the simple fact that he cannot afford not to."

Aura smiled and thanked Omire. They spoke quickly about logistics, and it was decided that anyone willing to stand with Esotera should go to the castle there to train and fight. Aura hoped that a number of his people would choose to help, but any who didn't, or decided to join the opposition, should be found out now. Plus, she hoped once Lady Grustmiener came through this land and found it deserted, she would assume that Esotera had acquired most, if not all those missing.

She told Omire to encourage those who decided to stay behind, those unable or unwilling to fight, to find a place to hide, deep in the woods where they would not be discovered. Aura already feared the casualties of this war to be greater than the last, and wanted to limit that amount as much as possible.

Omire offered to accompany her to Vertronum, but she graciously declined. She needed him to help with the organization here and assured him that she would be back to her castle as quickly as she could. In all honesty, she hoped it would take only a few hours to convince King Piester to follow her, but since she'd only met the man once briefly at her father's funeral, she had no way of knowing how the ruler would respond to her request for help.

They embraced quickly and Aura was about to join her companions once again, when she could put it off no longer.

"Omire," she said, as if sounding out each letter of his name.

He narrowed his eyes at her, detecting the shift in her emotions. "Yes?"

"Did you and Amaline take Levi? Did you deliver him to Lady Grustmiener?"

His whole demeanor changed, and he seemed to disappear into himself. His shoulders rounded and he was unable to look her in the eye.

"Please tell me the truth," she said.

He looked up with a pained expression. "Yes," he said. "And I have regretted it every second since. I was mindlessly following commands. Once I knew, once we knew…" He trailed off.

"Amaline told me."

"I have been trying to atone to you and to your kingdom ever since," he said.

"And you did not think to tell me?"

"I was afraid that you could never forgive me. That I could never repay what I owe you," he said.

"You have repaid it ten-fold. You did not know what you were doing." She saw that truth clearly now. She took a deep breath. "Levi is here."

"In Grustmiener? How?"

"In Esotera," she said. "Theirra has—" She hesitated. "Theirra has brought him here with others to try to help. He saw Amaline, which is how I found out about what happened."

"I should have told you," Omire said. "But I did not want to burden you with my confessions when they could not change anything."

"I understand. I am telling you this because Levi was less than pleased to see her, to say the least. If his reunion with her is any indication, you may want to bring a guard with you when you travel to Esotera. I have spoken with him, and will continue to do so, but I feel the need to warn you."

"Thank you, my queen."

She touched his arm and turned to leave. As soon as Omire slipped back into the castle, her group mounted their dragons and took off. This place made the hairs on her arms stand up, and she was glad to see it growing into a smaller and smaller speck as Heza and the others rose higher in the sky.

Chapter 21

Ground Work

Memories floated around Emily's head, but she was unable to tell what was real anymore and what had been forced into her mind. She had a son, right? Yes. Nikolas. And Milskar. She could see the outline of his figure, but couldn't seem to focus on his face. He flashed so quickly in front of her eyes that she could never get a good look at him. There were other memories, ones she wasn't sure where they had come from. A house. Was it her parents? Her own? It seemed so familiar, yet she couldn't figure out where she knew it from. She heard voices and tried as best she could to tune them out, but at times it was as if they screamed at her to listen.

'*Get up. Get out. You have to get out of here,*' one would sometimes say.

'*They are the enemy. You must stay and fight against them. Everyone you know is a liar and must pay for those lies,*' another would whisper in her ear.

She would shake her head violently and, sometimes, that would help. Jostle the voices around in her head enough so they needed time to collect themselves again before they started back up with the chorus, but it always reappeared without fail as soon as she closed her eyes for sleep.

She had terrible nightmares. Terrible in their content and how real they felt. In one, she remembered being in a room. It was warm and felt safe, but then all she could hear was the cries of her son, his panicked screams for his mother, and she found that she no longer had legs to get up and go to him nor lungs to yell back to him.

Emily would wake with a scream trapped in her throat, covered in a thin film of sweat, despite the bitter cold temperature her room was kept at. Though, as terrible as the dreams were, waking was even worse. At least in the dreams she was somewhere else, there was the possibility of hope. Even without her legs, maybe she could use her arms to drag herself to the screams, but in real life? There was no chance of escape. She couldn't even cry any more. They gave her such little liquid, she did not want to risk the loss of any of it through such a trivial thing as tears.

She wasn't sure how long they planned to keep her there, or what their intentions were. Yes, they beat and tortured her, but never to the point that she could actually die. They kept her just on the brink. Just close enough to wish for it, but then slowly dragged it out of reach, right before she could embrace it with relief.

She also didn't know what they wanted from her. She had no useful information. The last seven years had been peaceful in the kingdom, so there was no real army training. Aura had kept a larger group of aides and guards than before, but they were nowhere near battle ready. From the questions her captors asked—asked putting it nicely—Emily surmised that Lady Grustmiener had formed an army, in hopes of getting not only her own land back, but Esotera as well. Any information Emily was able to provide them seemed minimal. Unless they'd used her for bait, but for whom? Even if she hadn't been kidnapped, Milskar would have fought against them. When they took her, all it did was let everyone know that something was about to happen.

Emily wasn't sure if Aura knew what was going on, but she hoped that the queen and the people of Esotera were preparing. From the sounds of people who moved in and out of the corridors all day, it sounded like the army was a large one, but how large, she couldn't know. These thoughts, though, were limited, as her mind was unable to stay lucid for very long. Soon she drifted back into sleep, pulled into the hope of dreams unattainable.

❧❧❧

Above ground, it was a different world entirely. The clang of forged metal reverberated off the trees for miles. Birds and small animals fled the noise in droves and filled the skies with their laments. The bigger animals had largely left the area as well, save for a few that had been captured and slaughtered by the training, and hungry, growing army. There was movement everywhere, and it made Lady Grustmiener entertain a rare smile on her normally stony face.

They'd set up in an abandoned annex of old training barracks on the eastern edge of Grustmiener. Left vacant for decades, the half-buried buildings remained surprisingly well preserved. There was even old weaponry—machines that Lady Grustmiener put to immediate use.

She could feel it, feel that it was different this time. She would get her revenge on what Aura and her people had done. Lady Grustmiener's army was stronger, better trained, equipped, and prepared than before. This war was on her terms. She no longer had her husband, weak and concerned with waiting for the other side to make a move. She was free to press forward and attack.

The people of Omaner had arrived in a steady stream for days now. King Theaus was true to his word. He gave not only his subjects, but also some of the exotic animals from his land. He sent word that the half lion-half bird griffins would arrive in a few days. She looked forward to their arrival. They were majestic and frightening beasts and would be a great asset to her fighters.

The only thing left was to convince the pair from the other world to join her in this battle. It had been Abaddon's idea to find them and bring them here. He thought if they had some ties to the other world, it would help them against Levi and Queen Aura. While they would not have the power the boy possessed, Abaddon was hopeful that some of their magic would be able to counter Levi in a way that she alone might not be able to.

She had largely left the two alone since they had arrived, although she ensured that her assistants stayed on top of their every need and wish. It was important for them to want for nothing so that, when the time came, their loyalty would have been bought many times over. The plan had gone smoothly, and both the boy and girl appeared to settle in well, though they largely relied on the company of each other. In a pinch, she could use this as well to get them each involved, whether they wanted to or not.

She saw the boy as he stood off by himself for once. He stared at the metal forgers as they molded red-hot pieces of iron into swords of various lengths and thickness. This was it. Now was the time.

She moved in steadily for the kill, just as she had done these last miserable years. Her time soon approached. She would not be at the bottom of the food chain for much longer.

‿✷‿

"She is very beautiful," Lady Grustmiener softly drawled.

Luther startled slightly. He hadn't seen or heard her as she walked toward him.

"You like her," she continued.

"W—what? U—Unna?" he stuttered.

The statement and, frankly, simply the fact that the lady had even addressed him had thrown Luther off.

She laughed quietly, which jarred him again. He would never consider himself a ladies' man, by any means, but he thought he possessed at least some limited skills. Since he'd arrived at this place, though, he began to wonder if he'd ever known anything about the opposite sex.

"So?"

"So what? Yeah, I guess she's pretty. I guess I like her," he mumbled. "But so what? Not like I have a chance."

"No?" she said in almost a hum.

"No," he confirmed. "Not only am I younger than she is, I mean look at her. She's gorgeous. She wouldn't give me the time of day out in the real world. Here, any conversation is based purely on necessity." It hurt to say it, but he knew it was true.

"Woman love power and the men who know how to wield it," Lady Grustmiener purred into his ear. Her breath on his neck made him shiver involuntarily. "She will see. Follow me, and she will not be able to resist you."

Luther turned his head to face her but she was gone, her words still hanging in the air around him.

Chapter 22

Meeting

Aura's fingers and legs cramped from holding on to Heza for the six-hour trip from the castle at Vertronum. She was afraid several times that she might fall off the dragon and tumble miles back to the Earth. She went back and forth about caring if this bothered her. She was just so tired, mentally and physically, and was tempted to just let it all go and rest. Many times she would find herself slipping, but then her brain would wake in a jolt and catch her before she could fall. She could also feel Heza shift under her. The dragon was tired as well, but she made sure her master was safe.

When Aura saw the spires at the top of the castle that was her home, she lay closer to Heza's neck and willed the great beast to give it one final push home. When they finally did touch down, Aura needed help from one of her aides to dismount. Gustado, her head groom and animal caretaker, was already headed toward the group.

"Make sure Heza and the others get cool water, lots to eat, and soft straw to sleep on," she told Gustado. "They have worked hard and deserve uninterrupted rest."

"Yes, my queen."

"How is Netty?" she quickly added.

She couldn't remember the last time she had seen her beloved mare. It pained her to think of how she must be feeling neglected.

"Serenity is fine, though I think she is feeling a little cooped up," he admitted.

"I shall take her out tomorrow. I just need to rest for a little while."

He bowed and led Heza and the other dragons to the barn, their steps as slow and labored as Aura's. She was pleased that she'd promoted him to Theirra's previous position. He cared deeply for the animals and their mutual affection toward him solidified his place in Aura's heart.

Her walk toward the castle, her home—an act that she'd looked forward to for days—did little to lessen the heavy burden which pressed against her chest. The task ahead of her seemed daunting. Even if she had a hundred years to prepare—oh, what she wouldn't give for that!—she would still feel like it wasn't enough time. Yet, she didn't have one hundred years, or even a single one.

While she'd been gone, word came to her that large fires burned in the far east of Grustmiener, a signal for the location of the growing army. It felt as if a swarm of creatures descended upon her to destroy everything in its wake and swallow whatever remained into its ranks.

She'd heard a story of a small farming village on the outskirts of the Grustmiener border that raised livestock for food and clothing. It had been attacked late at night. Three members of an already limited community were killed before the rest agreed to join up for the march west. It chilled Aura's soul. This horrid woman was coming for her with a band of captured slaves, members forced to serve out of fear of the alternative.

Aura was not sure if any army would be able to fight

against caged animals, more dangerous than any armed man.

It was all she could do to stand brave and tall to those around her and assure them that she was ready to fight. That her people would be ready to fight. The meeting with King Piester was tense, though she hoped that he would join them. He welcomed her—maybe not warmly, but with respect—and took her on a short tour of his palace grounds.

The buildings were massive and seemed constructed for the sole purpose of always allowing the inhabitants to view the water that surrounded them. It held windows that were probably close to forty-feet high. While they appeared wide open, with all the crystal blue around her, Aura felt strangely claustrophobic. At one point a gigantic sea creature reared up through the water and seemed to skim it for several minutes before diving back under the water. Its snakelike body coiled over the lake's surface and its towering fins that covered portions of its body were at full mast.

"You are lucky," King Piester said. "The lochni do not often surface, especially this time of year. It is a good omen."

Aura smiled at him and hoped he was right.

When they entered his office and began to talk about the reason for Aura's visit, any warmth left his expression. He was terribly angry that he'd been kept in the dark about the Great Battle. It was all she could do to have him listen to her and not throw her out. She reminded him that the Four Corners did not often engage in the affairs of one another, though remembered to thank him for his attendance at her father's funeral, and reminded him in a round-about way of how she attended the funeral of his wife three years prior.

It was a terrible and sad occasion. Aura was mortified

to have found herself crying openly at the service, the funeral reminded her of her father's, which she hadn't, and probably never would recover from. The king appeared weak at that time, but she'd assumed it was due to his wife's death and not a general characteristic of him. She was incorrect.

The man seemed to twitch at any loud noise and avoided any direct eye contact. It made Aura uneasy, but she disregarded this. Maybe the shock of her arrival and the news of the past events had thrown him off. She gave him the benefit of the doubt. He was not so kind to her.

King Piester doubted her greatly. He questioned if she could amass an army of any large number and if she could also train it and will it to do her bidding. She had doubts herself, but naturally she could voice those to no one. How she longed to see Theirra and speak with her over what troubled her mind. Her dear friend would know what to do, or at least know the correct words to say. Aura felt another ache, less severe but constant at the slow loss of her closest confidant. She hoped that she could fix what had transpired between them. When the current threat was vanquished and peace returned to her lands, she would put forth all her energy to help Theirra return to some type of normalcy. Though she wondered if she had better odds of gathering the great army she needed than fixing her friend.

Aura left the meeting in Vertronum apprehensive but hopeful. King Piester assured her he would send some help, but would make his final decision on how much future aid he would give her after he spoke with his counsel. She wished they had been there for the meeting. She felt that their conversation would have gone smoother and possibly in her favor, but he insisted that they meet behind closed doors.

Maybe the rumors she heard were true, that he relied

heavily on their input. Maybe he did not want that fact verified or to potentially look weak in front of another leader, especially when the talk of war loomed. Either way, she would know shortly how he would stand, either with or against her. She tried not to let the anticipation churn her stomach.

She entered the hall and almost ran straight into Milskar. His deep pain cut through anything she wrestled with and brought the strength of friendship to her tired body.

"Milskar," Aura said, half startled at their near collision.

"My queen," Milskar said with a slight bow to his head. "I am glad to see that you have returned safely from what I hope was a successful trip."

"As successful as I imaged it could have been," Aura said. She tried to sound more excited at her future prospects than she actually was. "King Piester agreed to send some people our way, mainly members from his guard and some servants he could spare."

"That he could spare?" Milskar looked incredulous. "Does he not understand the importance of this matter? Does he not understand that the events about to occur here will impact our entire world, *his* entire kingdom?"

Aura touched his arm. "If I had just brought you with me," she said. "He understands only that he was informed late of this, and thus assumes that it cannot be that important to him. I am hopeful that once he speaks to his counsel and hears the reports coming from the east, he will wisely offer up more help and support, and be looking for the same protection in return."

"And if he does not?"

"We have a strong army led by a strong man. I am confident that we will be successful, no matter the numbers either side may have."

She smiled again, but Milskar just shook his head. "That is a lot of hope placed on the heads of so few, and so few who actually understand," he retorted.

"Oh, they will understand soon enough I am afraid. Soon enough…" Her voice trailed off. "Milskar, I am terribly sorry to cut our conversation short, I would like to speak with you later regarding how the training is going, but I feel that if I do not get at least a half hour of rest, it may be my people who need the saving from me."

He nodded to her and walked away.

Chapter 23

The Take-Over

Lady Grustmiener looked arrogant atop of her horse as she gazed down at the fields below her. Men, woman, and horses screamed in pain and fear as fires burned all around them. There were bodies from both sides lying still across the land in front of her, but she cared not for their sacrifices. Their lost numbers no longer meant anything to her. Her army was so great, so vast, she could lose half of it and still be a force no one could defeat.

The newly captured prisoners of this small outskirt town sat dejected and blood covered in a makeshift pen, shared with what was left of their livestock. None, animals or people, were putting up a fight anymore. Some sat shell-shocked at the destruction and death around them while others wept loudly at their sudden losses. A mother wailed for her son who had been killed. The woman had begun annoy Lady Grustmiener. She turned her horse and went to address the group. She ordered the guards to remove the group and stand them in front of her.

"I understand what it is like to fight bravely for your

lands," she began. "I understand what it is like to lose them, but now is not the time for grief on such matters. Now is the time to join an army so strong that soon you will have more land than you could ever imagine. I offered your people a peaceful cooperation. I am saddened that violence had to be suffered by you and your people, in order for that cooperation to be taken seriously. You will all join my army and fight for me, and, in return, your rewards will be great. We will march west and take my lands back, and for your help, you will be given a parcel of rich, fertile land on which you may remain in peace for the rest of your and your children's days."

A man stood and spat in her direction. A guard promptly hit him hard in the head with the hilt of his sword, immediately dropping the man in a pool of blood. The others in the group averted their eyes.

"You do have options," Lady Grustmiener stated. "I am not an unjust ruler. You do not have to fight for me if the cause is not something you will give all of yourself to. I only want those who are willing to fight for me to pick up a sword. I will not have the liability of an unwilling fighter on my side. Treason on the battlefield is not acceptable and will not be tolerated, so if fighting is not something you are willing to do, speak now, for this will be your one chance to do so."

She looked around at the group who snuck furtive glances her way, but made no efforts toward movement. Her impatience grew thinner still.

"Those who do not wish to fight, come forward," she ordered.

Three women and five men took small steps while the rest of the group looked at them with a mixture of terror and hope.

Another woman started to move as well, but froze in place when ten guards started toward them. They ushered the eight people over and stood them in front of the queen.

"Are you all stating that you would prefer not to fight for me and for my army?" Lady Grustmiener asked them.

"Yes," one of the women stated, quickly echoed by the rest of the group.

The "s" was still on her lips when a sword promptly appeared through her chest. She looked down at it, confused, and was about to reach a hand up to touch the blade, when it was withdrawn and the woman fell to her knees, dead before she came to rest on the ground.

The man who'd stood next to the fallen woman yelled in shock, moments before a blade cut the sound short in his throat. He too fell in a slump next to the first woman. Now the screams were all around them. Yells came from those who tried to back up and hide in the pen and from the surviving six men and women as the guards surrounded them. Lady Grustmiener held up a hand and the world seemed to freeze by her gesture.

"Would any of you like to reconsider my offer?"

"I thought you said," one man stammered, "that we did not have to fight for you?"

"Oh, that is what I said," Lady Grustmiener said with a sly smile on her face, "but that does not mean the same thing as you being allowed to live."

The group looked at one another and weighed their options before they backed up toward the pen. They never took their eyes off the queen on the coal-colored horse. They knew that she wasn't a fair and just ruler. She would never give them their promised land. She might not even keep her promise to let them live, but in that moment, the notion of picking up a sword and joining her side seemed the logical thing to do.

They walked with heads down back into the pen, unable to meet the glances of their enslaved counterparts,

ashamed at their inability to stand up for what they believed in. Ashamed that their fear of death overrode any
other instinct they had ever felt in their lives. They were
now part of the army of thousands. They would march in
the morning toward the next village, looking to add to the
ever-expanding force they were now a part of.

The next several days followed in the same fashion.
The queen's army would come across a small town or
village, make an offer of peace, and barely wait for a hint
of resistance before a small battle would break out. These
people they fought against were no match for her army of
trained and armed soldiers. Those they came upon were
farmers, merchants, animal handlers, who maybe had one
awl or ax between a hundred of them. Her army grew as
quickly as the death and destruction in her wake did. For
every ten people they captured to join, another twenty or
so lost their lives in the fight against her. It was no matter
to her. Anyone who stood in her way didn't deserve to
live anyway. They would be of no use to her and, thus,
were eliminated.

Soon word of her conquests spread across the kingdom and the death rates became less and less with each
village they came to. The ground would shake for miles
when her army moved. People and animals rocked the
Earth under their great numbers. By the time they would
get to a crop of houses, the residents had either already
fled, taking their chances in the woods and mountains, or
they laid down whatever arms they had and surrendered
immediately to her. This pleased her, though when they
came upon a deserted town, she would send a dozen of
her outriders into the surrounding area to find those who
tried to escape and kill them. She had no use for dodgers.

Word of that began to spread as well and people
stopped trying to flee their homes, resigned to whatever
fate might lie ahead for them. Yet for a largely unwilling

army, they were surprisingly ruthless in their fighting as time went on.

Soon it was difficult to distinguish the original fighting force from those who'd been captured and made to do Lady Grustmiener's bidding.

It would not be much longer before they reached Eso-tera, though their method of travel did slow them down considerably. Her scouts estimated three or four more weeks, her army likely to double in size by then. Nothing would be able to stop her.

Around this time, she'd begun to keep more of a close eye on Unna and Luther. They were typically kept with the trailing caravan, made up of elders, advisers, Abad-don, and Emily. They were far away from any danger and fighting, but now it seemed time to include them in the mission.

Originally, she wanted people from the other world to try to give herself an advantage and insight into what Le-vi might think and do. She viewed him as some kind of alien creature. While he'd been in her midst for months several years prior, she always kept a bit of a distance from him, unsure of what to make of him and his powers. From intelligence she'd been given, it was not normal for people of his world to have powers similar to his, so it came as a great surprise to find that there were more like him. She immediately wanted to get her hands on such individuals, and now that she had these two, she contin-ued to think about how she could use them for her own benefit.

They looked similar to herself and her people, but they acted very strange, very emotional, almost like animals that ran on instinct alone without logic. They constantly seemed to be upset at one another or those around them, snapping for no reason and slipping into silences that could stretch an entire day. She'd watched them for some time and decided she'd had enough. It was time to put them to work.

After her initial talk with Luther days prior, she felt like he would be more malleable than the girl, who seemed to be unsure of this place. Lady Grustmiener was not sure how to align her to the cause. Outside pressures may be her only way.

After they made camp that night, Lady Grustmiener called for Abaddon to meet her at her tent. The old man seemed more frail than normal, and she wondered when the last time she had actually seen him was. He must have been a hundred years old, but only recently had he started to look his age. Yet she wondered if he were even capable of dying. He seemed a force impossibly strong even if his body wasn't.

"My lady," he said as he entered the tent.

"Abaddon. Tell me about Unna and Luther."

He seemed to brighten considerably at her question and began pacing the tent. He murmured to himself before looking up at her.

"They are amazing creatures," he stated. "But I wish we could be back at my lab, and I could fully test their capabilities."

"Capabilities?" she asked him.

"Oh yes, they have very strong powers, but I think with a little manipulation…" He trailed off and paced the tent again.

"Abaddon." The frustration was clear in her voice.

He turned back to her. "Oh, oh, yes. It is the most amazing thing. I have only seem her do it a handful of times. It is typically directly at the boy and only when she thinks no one is viewing them."

"What is it?" she asked as she leaned toward him in anticipation.

He beamed. "Shape shifting."

"Shape shifting?"

"Oh, yes, the girl, she is able to transform herself to look like other people. Well, I assume anyone, but I have only ever seen her become this one person, this other woman. It upsets the boy greatly. I am not sure how she does it or what triggers the reaction, but it is quite complete and remarkable. Nothing of her seems to remain."

"Shape shifting," Lady Grustmiener repeated to herself. "How can we use this?"

"The possibilities are endless!" he exclaimed, his excitement palpable.

"Example?"

"Well, if we can figure out the person a foe cares most about, we can send her in looking like that person. It would completely disarm that individual and then we would be able to quickly defeat that person. It would be as if the king—" He stopped short and flashed his eyes in her direction. She either had not heard him or chose to ignore his line of thought.

"Where did you find her?" she asked.

"A scout actually," Abaddon said. "Though he was not sure what she was at first, but she used her power on him. After a short...err...physical altercation, she agreed to come here."

Lady Grustmiener raised her eye brows. "Altercation?"

"Oh, yes, she certainly is not afraid to use her powers. Though she seemed eager to leave whatever was behind her."

"And the boy? What are his abilities?"

"That one is trickier. I am not sure how far it reaches, but several days ago one of our soldiers lost his horse in the fighting of a small outlying village, a beautiful white stallion. I am sure that I saw the horse fall and die, but Luther walked up to the animal. There was so much going on I do not think anyone else saw, but I was watching him. He placed his hands upon the fallen creature and soon it sprung to its feet."

"You think he can raise the dead?" Her shock and excitement now matched Abaddon's.

"I think it is possible. The horse was dead. I am sure of it, however—" For the first time he seemed to hesitate.

"What is it?"

"There was something different about the animal after. It did not seem the same."

"Same how?" she asked.

"The eyes. There was something lost in its eyes. And it did not seem to breathe or move like a typical horse." Abaddon went quiet, lost in thought.

"What happened to the animal?" she asked.

"The solider walked up to it cut its head clean off." He got up to leave.

"Killed it?"

"If you can call it that. I am not sure what it even was. I am certain that it was dead. The boy looked startled though, as if something that man did to the horse had done something to him as well."

"Why did the soldier kill his own horse?" Lady Grustmiener asked.

"Like I said, there was something not quite right about it when it came back. It did not seem quite alive, but also not dead."

Lady Grustmiener's mind swam with ideas. These two might prove be more useful that she'd originally thought.

"Send them to my tent immediately. There are some matters I need to discuss with these foreigners."

They smiled knowingly at each other before Abaddon quickly turned to leave and collect the unsuspecting objects of her new-found affection.

Chapter 24

Memories

"They are coming closer. Maybe four weeks away. They are increasing in size with each step they take."

Aura rubbed her temple with her fingertips.

"They are coming closer," the aide repeated

"Yes, yes, I heard you," she snapped. The man's eyes widened in shock and hurt at her outburst. She sighed. "I am sorry. Thank you for your information. Please make sure it finds its way to Milskar and Omire as well."

The latter was still in Grustmiener sorting through who was going to fight and who was going into hiding. The last she heard, the numbers didn't appear to be in her favor.

"Yes, my queen," the aide said. He bowed, but it was clear from his tone that he wasn't convinced that her apology was sincere.

Each time Aura felt like she'd reached the brink of her exhaustion, it found another gear to grip her with. Her eyes now stayed open under sheer will. At times, she felt like she was too tired to sleep and walked around the castle in a daze. She heard parts of conversations spoken directly to her and trusted that if the information was truly important Theirra or Milskar would repeat it to her again later.

Her kingdom had felt so small and manageable mere months ago. She felt like she'd really figured out how to rule over this land and the people that it contained, but suddenly, it seemed to have quadrupled in size. People flooded the outskirts of the castle and she found it difficult to house and feed them all. She was grateful, so incredibly grateful, to be blessed with such strong and brave people, but it overwhelmed her, all the same. Even worse was the knowledge that this sea of people would be but a drop of water in the ocean Lady Grustmiener had assembled to bring to her gates.

Aura felt like she was running out of time more quickly than she'd ever had in her life. She walked the castle grounds, and people turned to her expectantly, as if they were waiting for her to say or do something to give this meaning. She thought back to all those years ago, to the original battle and the words she'd spoken to her people.

"I am more proud today to be your ruler than anyone has even been of their people," she had said to her tired, bloody, yet joyous people.

It was true. She felt those words in her heart and carried them with her. The truth weighed heavy upon her. These people had given her so much, and she felt like she hadn't kept up her part of the bargain. She hadn't kept them safe, as they had done for her. In some small way, she had failed them and brought this battle back to their gates. This time, she had no words.

A soft knock at the door interrupted her mind as it wandered.

"Aura," a hesitant voice said as Levi slowly entered the room.

"Levi," she said with a tired smile.

"How are you holding up?"

"I have no idea." She laughed. "Would you like to take a walk with me?"

"Sure."

They both exited her office, but she surprised him by turning left, away from the entrance, and to a set of stairs toward her chambers. She'd considered moving into the larger of the bedrooms, the one reserved specifically for the ruler of this land, but it felt too much like trespassing on the memories held within those four walls. Seven years later and she could still not bring herself to enter her father's room.

"Did anyone ever tell you where the name Esotera came from?" she asked.

"No," Levi answered.

He could tell wherever they were headed was painful and yet filled her thoughts. He wanted to leave it up to her what she told him. He didn't want to push the issue and end whatever could happen between them. Any questions she asked he made sure to keep his answers short and limited to what was completely necessary.

They walked up two levels of staircases before they turned toward a single mahogany door. Levi looked around to see if anyone would notice the two of them. He wasn't sure what the protocol was when someone accompanied a queen to her bedroom, but he was certain this would be frowned upon. Luckily, the corridor seemed deserted.

She entered and he followed, yet left the door open behind him just in case. Aura continued through the room and exited through a pair of glass doors. Levi fought the temptation to look all around his surroundings, but he thought the better of it and joined her outside.

Her balcony overlooked the rear of the castle grounds and the forest below. Levi noticed how high up they were. He hadn't realized how much they had climbed. He felt like he could see for miles through the lush vegetation.

"There." She pointed. He followed her gaze and noticed a giant waterfall in the distance. "This land was named after those mighty falls. She leaned in conspiratorially. "When our world was divided up, this was considered the jewel of the Four Corners. I think it still is."

"Wow," was the only lame word he could manage. But really, that summed it up.

"My great-great-great-great grandfather decided to call it that once Lord Vertrous bestowed this land to him. While the Four Corners go out in all directions, that waterfall is actually at the center of it all. He built this castle so that the upper rooms would always have a view of it."

The falls must have been massive because they even seemed impressive from here and he could tell they were far away. He could hear occasional noises from the mass of people below, but it was largely quiet.

"It's beautiful up here," he managed to say.

"It is my favorite view of my entire kingdom. It is even better than the views from the air I think. Just refrain from telling Heza that please," she said with a wink.

"It's incredible. So—" He hesitated, but decided to continue. "—was this your parent's room before yours?" He knew as soon as he asked the question it was the exact wrong thing to say.

"No," she replied curtly and turned away from him.

"I'm sorry. Aura, I'm sorry. I shouldn't have said that." He stepped forward and touched her hand. He cursed his stupidity. Even from her side profile, he could see that her eyes brimmed with tears.

"I miss them every second," she said. "Even my mother whom I never met."

"I can't imagine," Levi said.

The thought of losing his parents, while inevitable, was unimaginable to him. While he knew his birth parents were long dead, they held no place in his heart. His adoptive parents resided stronger in him than blood ever could. He hoped he would get to see them again. He felt like a terrible son and made a promise to himself to rectify that upon his return back home.

"I'm sorry," he said again.

"Thank you. I know it does no good to dwell on the past, but I feel the sadness of losing them like a snake in tall grass. Like it waits for me to stumble upon it so it can squeeze every last ounce of life out of me."

They stood there in silence, Levi's hand still upon hers, as the sun gracefully vacated the sky, and the waterfall could be seen in only the faintest of reflections of the moonlight.

Chapter 25

Griffins

The fires burned hot and bright around her. Lady Grustmiener walked through the forest, dark outlines of soldiers at various angles of sleep against trees, rocks, and other bodies. The light danced on their faces and made them look fierce, demonized. She wondered if there was a way to capture this look, to place it permanently against their skin. She would have to speak with Abaddon about that.

"Lady Grustmiener," a servant boy whispered to her through the darkness. "They are here. I was told you wanted to be informed as soon as they arrived."

"Yes," she answered tartly. "Show me the way."

She felt the vibrations on the ground long before she actually saw them. It was as if the Earth trembled at the inhabitants on top of Her. The though made the queen smile. The ground would tremble in fear for years to come.

They stood in a massive clearing, yet it was still barely able to contain all the beasts. Fire blazed around them and threw even fiercer shadows on them than it had on the people she'd passed.

Yes! she thought. This was the final piece she needed. Now she was ready.

"I am not sure what exactly you are planning to do with these majestic creatures," a woman said as she approached her. There was no formality or respect in her voice.

Lady Grustmiener's eyes narrowed. "I will plan whatever I would like."

"I am not sure you will," the woman continued. "You see, they are protected beasts. Beasts that I specifically am tasked look after. I am in charge of implementation of the Winged Beast Protection Act, which I am sure you are aware of, but I would be more than willing to outline for you if you need me to."

The woman barely let out a gasp when the knife slashed the front of her body. She looked down and registered a hint of pain before she fell to the ground, dead. The griffins behind her pranced in place, clearly upset with what had happened.

"Does anyone else have issues they would like to discuss?" Lady Grustmiener asked the group loudly.

They all looked away from her. She stepped over the woman's body and walked up to one of the beasts. She reached a hand out to touch its gold, shimmering wings. It flinched slightly under her fingers, making his handler strike the beast quickly and severely. This also pleased her, to know that while these creatures were innately powerful, they could also be controlled with something as simple as a firm hand.

"I am sorry, my queen." The handler bowed. "This one has been more trouble than the others. He does not seem to have the same willingness in him."

"I think we will be able to change that," she said, staring straight into the griffin's eyes. "What is his name?"

"I have been told his name is Gilbert, my queen."

Lady Grustmiener nodded and continued down the line. The rest of the animals were equally as impressive in size and stature, but there was something about that golden griffin that kept pulling her attention back to him. There was a darkness that loomed over its eyes, a certain level of intelligence that she didn't see in the other beasts. It made her want to break him. Break the independent spirit from its feathers and hair, mold the creature to do her bidding, and her bidding only. Maybe he would be her next project while the army prepared for the march to Esotera. She could picture it now, her atop the griffin that looked like molten gold, charging to take back what was rightfully hers.

She pointed back at the creature called Gilbert. "I would like that griffin prepared to be my mount," she told the handler.

The man bowed low. "My queen, he appears to be a very temperamental beast. I can suggest one better suited for your needs." He gestured to a pair of griffins that stood to the right of her chosen one.

"No," she barked. "That is the one I want."

Gilbert eyed the queen warily, and she stared right back at him. A small shiver ran through her. It seemed the beast was sizing her up as she did the same to him. They would be glorious together, she knew.

"I will view your training of him tomorrow at day break."

The man bowed, refusing to make eye-contact with her. "Yes, my queen."

After she made one final pass, she left the clearing and moved toward her sleeping quarters. Her tent was not as grand as it was during the last battle, but King Theaus had provided more than adequate housing for her. She was exhausted most nights when she returned here and had been used to sleeping on the ground for so many years, she immediately fell asleep when she lay down on the feathery mattress...

cɔeɔ

Her dream started in such a burst, it almost woke her. A griffin walked toward her, fire instead of feathers on its body. Its eyes were like dark pools of midnight oil, liquid and never-ending. Its mouth opened wide enough to swallow all the heavens. Flames poured out and encircled the two of them. She was transfixed as she waited for what would happen next. She could feel the hairs on her arms start to rise as the beast walked closer to her. It closed its mouth after showing her its great rows of teeth.

Its mouth opened and closed, and she could tell it was trying to talk to her but no words came out.

"Speak you inferior creature!" she yelled.

"Inferior!" it boomed back. Its voice echoed through her bones and veins. Then its mouth opened wide again, and she was plunged into darkness.

There was a small light far away and she walked toward it. Though no matter how many steps she took, she didn't seem to get any closer.

"Stop moving!" she called into the darkness.

"Why, so you can kill me again?" The king stood in front of her, his face illuminated by some unknown source.

She moved a slight half step back away from him. He didn't look the way she remembered him, strong and proud. He was merely skin draped over bones. His face looked vaguely familiar and he wore his crown, but were it not for his voice, she never would have realized it was him.

"I—I did not kill you," she stammered, fear creeping through her for the first time.

The grotesque version of her deceased husband began to laugh, laughing so hard that it shook the earth around her. His laughter filled her ears and reverberated through her entire body.

"It was you who wanted me dead!" the vision yelled. "It was you who coveted my kingdom, and look! Look around you at what you have to rule over now!"

"No." She turned from him, but it was as if she was running in place. Her feet moved, but the scenery around her stayed the same.

Another figured appeared in front of her. She gasped and held her hands over her mouth. What had happened to this man? This man she loved and lost on many occasions.

Winester stood and pointed a finger at her. "You," he boomed.

"No," she repeated. The terror made her gag.

"You."

"I never wanted anything to happen to you. I did love you. I did."

The world came back into sharp focus. Smoldering trees lay upon the ground. As they came into greater focus, she realized they were not trees at all, but bodies. Thousands of dead and burned bodies, stacked in piles around her. Winester began to laugh and shook the world under her feet again.

Lady Grustmiener's eyes snapped open. The ground indeed shook, but a quick search of her surroundings informed her that she was in her tent. It was all just a dream. She had tried not to think about Winester since hearing the painful news of his demise.

At first, her love for him was a game, a way to get him to do what she wanted. But slowly, she developed real feelings for him. When the king discovered what was going on between the two of them, Winester fled the kingdom. It was many years until she saw him again. While their reunion was brief, it rekindled her feelings for him. His death hit her almost as hard as the loss of her kingdom.

She brought her head out into the early morning mist and saw the griffins moving in various formations in the distance. Their great breadth vibrated the earth beneath their feet.

"Just a dream," she repeated out loud to herself. "Just a dream."

She quickly changed and proceeded to the clearing. A group of soldiers had formed around the area as well, close enough to see what was going on, but far enough away to indicate a level of fear and uncertainty at what they were witnessing.

The golden griffin, so similar to the one from her dream, danced wildly, yards away from her. His handler tried desperately to mount the creature, but it was clear that the beast had the upper hand. Each time the man grabbed a handful of feathers and tried to pull himself up, the griffin spun artfully, sending his handler spiraling to the ground.

She walked up to the head keeper to ask why someone else didn't try to break the animal.

"Oh, Molluk has had the best luck of anyone trying to tame that one," the woman said. "He can at least put a hand on him."

Lady Grustmiener had had enough. She walked purposefully toward the man named Molluk, unceremoniously pushed him aside, and promptly mounted Gilbert. Whether it was being taken by surprise so quickly or that he truly didn't mind, the head keeper did not know, but the animal planted all four feet firmly on the ground and did not move a muscle.

"Now, beast, move forward," the queen said in a terse voice.

Amazingly enough, he obeyed. The other handlers paused in whatever they were doing to watch the untamable beast being directed by their queen. Once, when the griffin hesitated slightly in its movements, the lash from her was so fast and determined, he quickly fell into step without protest. Soon after, she dismounted and handed Gilbert back to Molluk.

"There will be no coddling this one," she stated. "At the moment of disobedience, this animal must be swiftly punished. It is the only way he will learn that we are to be obeyed."

"Yes, my queen," Molluk said.

Gilbert watched her with those clear, black eyes, the same ones that had haunted her in her dreams, as she walked away. His gaze followed her until she was swallowed up by the morning mist as it curled around the forest trees.

Chapter 26

Decisions

Levi found Julia sitting under a huge tree that skirted the castle grounds. Initially, he thought it was an oak, but the closer he got, he saw how the leaves shimmered slightly, even though there was little sunlight for them to reflect. The day was fading and, like the ones that proceeded it, had ended in anxious dread for him. Levi felt like he should do something, contribute in some way, but found that most days he just wondered around and tried to stay out of everyone's way.

He knew he should train to strengthen his body and skills, which frankly he hadn't used much lately. He'd gotten comfortable at home and was often so exhausted from writing or book signings that he rarely had the energy to even notice that his powers had faded. Being back in Esotera seemed to strengthen them. That, or the simple fact that he finally got more than four hours of sleep a night but, whatever the case, he felt restless. There was a crawling feeling over his whole body. It was like when you swear a bug just landed on you, but when you go to brush it off, you find nothing there. He wished he could just explode, send out shock waves like he used to, and diffuse the feeling, but he found that he couldn't. Was it because he was older? Or maybe more controlled that didn't allow the outbursts of his past? He wished the sorceress was still with them. He hadn't known her very well, but he still felt that Resbuca would have been able to fix him.

So his temporary solution was to find the kids. He liked to check on them from time to time, felt somewhat of a responsibility to them. He was probably the one person who could truly understand their overwhelmed feelings and give them advice, yet he'd barely said anything to them since they arrived. Levi had always felt awkward around people, and his book tour had induced a certain level of anxiety in him at all times. He was concerned that he wasn't saying the "right" or "cool" thing. That as soon as the person walked away, they would spend the rest of the afternoon laughing at him. Emily was the closest thing to a friend he'd had growing up. It took being back here to realize how much he truly missed her. He tried to push the sinking thought out of his already cluttered mind.

Now as the battle loomed ever closer, Levi felt a kind of pull to the kids. He mustered up all the courage he had for those sorts of things and decided to talk to them. He was slightly disappointed when Julia was the only one he could find. Better than nothing, he thought, and much less daunting to have a one-on-one talk.

"Julia?" Levi said as he got close to her.

She startled at his voice. "Levi, I'm sorry I didn't see you coming," she said as heat spread over her cheeks.

He noticed that she had been making a flower rise and fall from her hand. With her concentration broken and now focused on him, it fell from her palm and landed in the grass by her legs. She followed his gaze and they both stared at it for a few moments.

"I know, I'm weird," she said.

It wasn't a question, more of a statement of fact wrapped in an apology.

The flower flew into the air. Ten, maybe fifteen feet up. Then it exploded, raining petals down upon them. One landed on Julia's arm which she rubbed involuntarily, as if it hurt, though Levi knew it didn't.

She stared at him in amazement, her eyes squinted, as if he were made out of a bright light she had to shield herself from—and not just because of his pale skin.

"I'm pretty weird, too," he said. "Sorry, didn't mean to scare you. It's been a while since I controlled something. The movement isn't as smooth as I remembered it to be."

"I didn't know."

"It was a long time ago that I needed to use my powers here. Once I returned to our world, I sort of stopped doing it. I was able to control it a lot better and since it had always created problems for me over there, I guess I just blocked it out. Kinda feels good to use it, like my skin had been itching for years and I never realized it until now."

He smiled again and sat on the ground next to her. He was relieved that he hadn't completely lost his edge.

"Why are we here?" she asked him flatly. "I mean, I get that there is some battle or war about to happen, and I get that this place is strange, but I don't understand what we have to do with all of it."

He was just about to speak, when he heard a rustle behind him. Senses already on edge, he jumped to his feet and whipped around to see who was behind him.

There was a slight scream and, before Levi understood what had happened, Tab hung upside down in mid-air.

Just as suddenly, Levi felt himself blown back as both men crashed to the ground. The rest of the group was gathered around Tab. They looked both frightened and in awe of Levi.

"He has powers too," Julia said, stating the obvious to the group.

A hand reached out to help Levi up and, at that point he realized that Kalan was standing next to him, not with the group.

"What happened?" he asked the boy as he got to his feet.

"I thought you might be attacking Tab, I got a little carried away and rushed you. Sorry," he said, not making eye contact.

"Right, Kalan, invisible. Makes sense," Levi said.

"Makes sense. Makes sense?" Galina said, her voice as shrill as always. "Okay, for real. Answer her question, what are we doing here? This crazy woman convinces us to leave our homes—or where we live, or whatever—" She quickly corrected herself as she looked around the group. "We are in a strange magical land with other people who have these abilities we thought only we possessed, which now I see are a dime a dozen. Some sort of war is going to happen and this queen person seems to be upset that the chick brought us here. She asks us to participate, but then doesn't tell us anything more or offer to get us ready for whatever the heck we're supposed to get ready for. Seriously, what are we doing here?"

"Fair enough," Levi said and sat again. "Come on, sit down. Sorry, Tab, instinct. Still a bit rusty too."

Tab brushed off his apology.

"It has been a number of years since I've been here," Levi stated. "Honestly, I never thought I would see this place again." He sighed. "As you've been told, Lady Grustmiener is building an army and has gathered people from all over this world and perhaps even some people from our world." This intel had just been given to them the previous day. While it wasn't a complete shock—naturally Theirra wouldn't be the sole person to think of going that route—it was still a blow, all the same. "Her goal is to defeat Queen Aura and take over this whole world, and—" The idea just fell into Levi's mind as he spoke. He hadn't though it before, but it made so much sense.

"She wants to rule our world too," Jada said. He'd obviously seen the thought flash into Levi's mind.

"I think so," Levi said quietly. "We need all the help we can get in defeating her. We need to protect not only this place, but our homes, families, and world as well. She has to be defeated. We cannot allow her to succeed."

"And what if we decide we want to go to her side? Or go home? What if we don't want to fight for this land and this world?" Riagan asked.

Levi had been thrust into this position all those years ago, where the option not to fight, not to participate, wasn't available to him. He never once thought that these kids wouldn't just go along for the ride like he did. How did one convince another person to do something, especially something so dangerous, when they had nothing at stake in the situation? Or at least when they didn't know if they had something at stake?

"This isn't a war you can be forced to participate in. I can't force you to fight or stand up for a cause that you don't believe in. What I can tell you is that this woman is ruthless. She will not end with solely taking this land. She will want to take over its entire people and move on to our world. She will want to rule everything and force those she rules to do whatever she tells them. I was imprisoned by her and her husband for a short period of time, and they had turned me practically into a robot. I almost killed my cousin whom I love and would never hurt." This last part made him break off. Emily. She crept slowly back into his mind. He tried not to imagine the horrible things Lady Grustmiener had done to her. Nor to think about the pain on Milskar's face, or the lost look on their son's.

"She has my cousin. Lady Grustmiener has taken her to be used as bait to bring me back and finish the war she started. I have a vested interest in getting back at the woman, yes, but it's more than that. I cannot let her do the things she has done to my family and myself to anyone else. I cannot allow her to enter our world."

"I will fight," Kiya said boldly. "I will help. I may be young, but I will do anything and all that I can. I may not have a family that I know I am fighting for, but I know they are out there somewhere, and I don't want to lose my chance to find them."

"Sometimes it's the youngest or smallest person who can make the biggest difference of all," Julia said quickly. "I will do whatever I can too."

Levi's heart swelled and his throat tightened. He felt like a fool to be moved by such a simple thing, but it was amazing.

One by one, the group agreed to help, even reluctant Galina after a poignant look toward Adam. Levi left them to talk amongst themselves about the new information they had just been given and went to find Aura. He had to tell her about his new theory, which the more he mulled it over in his mind, the more he was sure of it. Lady Grustmiener was out for blood, and she wasn't going to stop with Esotera.

Chapter 27

The Arrivals

King Piester and his troops from Vertronum arrived in Esotera the next day. After his initial reservation, he finally agreed to help after his own group of scouts confirmed what Aura had told him. The numbers in the king's army were staggering. Just when Aura thought her grounds couldn't hold any additional people, more came.

Milskar beamed at her. "I think this will do," he said.

Aura tried to return the smile, but her thoughts flashed back to her dream from the night before. In it, she was in a completely white world, but as soon as she realized it was colorless, it burst into flames. The trees, grass, even clouds were made of plumes of smoke and fire. She tried to put out one of the fires that was by her feet and realized that they, too, were engulfed. Her entire body was on fire. Aura had panicked. It didn't hurt, but she knew, in the way truth comes to you in dreams, that she was about to die. It was so sad, she thought as she watched her arms turn to dust, how short life was and how abruptly it was all over. The finality of it angered her, and she tried to hold on to something, but she'd begun to disappear. She could no longer distinguish herself from the flames around her until, in one last gasping breath, she awoke.

She wished Resbuca were here. Aura felt somewhere deep inside her that if she had explained the dream to the woman, Resbuca would have been able to tell her what it meant. To let her know if this whole endeavor she was on was a mistake, if she should abandon it and go into hiding. It pained Aura to have these thoughts. She wanted to be strong for her people, for the people she had asked, once again, to risk their lives for the sake of the kingdom. Now she was asking even more people this time around to do to the same. What kinds of promises could she make these people to make it worth it? What could she give them in return that could possibly off-set the losses they were sure to endure?

"Queen Aura."

The voice shook her out of her daydream.

She nodded. "King Piester, I am honored and more thankful than you will ever know," she said, allowing the man to take and kiss her hand.

Aura introduced Milskar to the king, who, in turn, introduced them both to his army leader, a beautiful woman named Calanthe. She had olive skin; long, dark hair; and eyes so fierce they would probably make do if she found herself in battle without a sword. Aura was taken aback and intrigued by this woman, who bowed almost imperceptibly toward her.

"Shall we discuss training and plans of attack?" Calanthe asked. Her voice was harsher than Aura had expected it to be, as if she'd strained it the past few days by shouting.

"Of course," Milskar replied, "come. We can settle you into the castle and speak there more privately."

Aura and the king nodded at the pair as they left. The new army started to spread out as much as possible, though it soon became clear that the grounds in front of the castle would be too small to contain them.

"You possess a large army," Aura stated.

"They are the entirety of my kingdom."

Aura was shocked. *Everyone? He brought every person to fight this battle, my battle?* Then she remembered that this was not just her battle. How silly of her. How narcissistic of her to think that these people, that any people risked their lives just for her. This was their future too. They fought just as much, if not more, for themselves as for anyone else.

"My people and I are very appreciative for the generosity of the people of Vertronum."

"And my people," King Piester said, "will thank you to remember that generosity when the fighting is over and we have won."

Aura nodded without really being sure what she was agreeing to. Did they want part of her lands? Possibly part of the North and East? It was a subject that she had not thought of before—what would happen to Omaner and Grustmiener when all this fighting was over. Surely she could not think that Esotera would rule it all, could she?

"Your soldiers are welcome to camp in any lands in this area. The woods are secure, at least for now. Any space they can find they may use. The people in the village will try to feed and water them the best they can—" Aura started before the king cut her off.

"We have brought food and water, but could use housing for the creatures we have brought with us."

"Of course," Aura said. "My head stable hand, Gustado, would be more than happy to find a place for any and all you brought with you."

Aura caught Gustado's eye and signaled him toward a number of people who stood next to large, scaled beasts called mostlespries, which were actually native to Eso-tera. Aura wondered if the scaled clothing the people wore was from these creatures or the number of sea ani-mals that lived within their lakes and streams. She decid-ed not to ask. As she looked around, she also noticed that a number of the larger men and women held large birds, snow white in color, that looked like malformed vultures. Aura had seen them before on her travels to the east, but she didn't know what they were called.

"Jadwiga," Piester said as if he'd read her mind. "We have been able to train them to send communication be-tween parts of our land and thought they would be most useful in relaying information for us here. They are actu-ally native of Grustmiener. We have to import most of our land creatures, as the majority of our animals live in the sea. As you can see—" He gestured around. "—we have some animals from your lands as well. As for the ones native to my own kingdom, I did not think I could bring you any of those," he said with a chuckle.

"What you have brought will be perfect," Aura said.

With all who were involved, they needed any help they could manage in getting information disseminated.

"May I show you the castle and your room?" she asked.

"That would be most appreciated." He sounded very relieved to have a place away from the preparations.

The two strode into the castle as the swell of noise outside ebbed and flowed around them.

Chapter 28

Late Nights

As night fell upon the castle grounds, Levi once again wandered toward Aura's office. It had become an unofficial ritual at the end of each day that he, Aura, Milskar, and Calanthe would meet in the queen's quarters.

King Piester came once, but he was distant and contributed little to their conversation. After that, Calanthe was sent in his place. Amaline sometimes popped in, but she typically didn't stay long, still a little nervous to be in a room with Levi. Theirra was usually missing, though Levi learned to stop asking where she was, or if she was coming.

The group would start with a discussion of the day, and, when that got to be too monotonous, the conversation would weave around themselves. Sometimes they'd catch on stories, while other times it would turn into long, quiet stretches of silence. These meetings were some of the few times that Levi felt useful in this foreign place.

He'd trained, or tried to, with the help of Milskar. Levi had found it difficult to the point of impossibility to fight both with his hands and his mind. If he tried to do it simultaneously, he ended up not being able to do either one particularly well. With practice, he'd gotten a bit better, but more so in being able to switch between the two more quickly than actually doing them concurrently. The work exhausted him, and he was always ready to be done when they broke for the day.

It was also during these nights, bathed and smoothed in soft candlelight, that Levi began to notice Aura in a new way. The way the days draped on her like a cloth that slowly slipped off late into the evening. How sometimes she could look so young and at other times older than all her years.

Milskar too, Levi thought. When Nikolas was with him instead of his nanny, or if Milskar had just put him to bed, all his hard edges went momentarily soft. The effect didn't last long, though, and was soon replaced by pain so visible, it reached down into Levi's heart and gripped it tightly. Levi had been held prisoner by the same awful people who caused Milskar's pain.

He hoped that Lady Grustmiener's lack of a concrete home base could somehow spare Emily the terrors he'd gone through. He'd lost himself in the depths of Grustmiener, and it was Emily who'd brought him back. He trusted that he wasn't too late to return the favor.

The arrival of the army from Vertronum seemed to breathe new life into the fighters of Esotera, and also an amount of anxiety into Milskar and Aura.

"They are very well trained," Milskar said to her and Levi the next night when they were alone in her office.

"Is this a bad thing?" Aura asked.

"Not necessarily, but it does seem to be discouraging some of our people. There are mutterings as to what is the point of them fighting when one of the Vertronum soldiers seems to be able to do the work of two of ours."

"How do we quell such talk?"

"I do not know." Milskar sighed. "Calanthe and I are trying to integrate everyone as best we can, though it tends to result in a lot of our people standing around while theirs complete drills. It is a bit embarrassing, frankly. I think she is getting quite annoyed with it."

"To the point that we may lose them?" Aura asked, worried.

"I doubt that. They seemed very interested in the outcome of this war. I think they will fight, no matter what, but how loyal they will be to our cause remains to be seen."

"We should break into smaller groups then I think," Aura said. "You and Calanthe split the fighters up, have Amaline help you as well. That way they can learn a little more one-on-one and not get as distracted."

"Yes, my queen." Milskar shifted slightly and looked away from her. "We also need to discuss The Kids,"

"Discuss?"

Milskar began rubbing his temple. "What are your plans for them? What are they really here for? Were they just brought here to be killed, or are we going to be able to do anything specific with them? Do you think it was truly wise to bring The Kids here?"

"Theirra—" Aura started.

"Yes," Milskar said, uncharacteristically interrupting her, "she brought them here, but now they are here. One way or another, we will have to deal with them. I have worked with Tab, the oldest one. He is strong and a good fighter, but the others, I do not know what to do with such powers."

"Levi?"

It was the first time he'd been spoken to that night.

He nodded. "I can work with them, show them what I know and what Milskar has been teaching me. I can try to help them hone and improve their powers, but frankly,

I'm still trying to get mine back," he added as the feeling of uselessness entered his mind again.

While it had been a few weeks since his arrival, and the initial shock of being back here had worn off, he struggled to settle into a routine.

Aura opened her mouth to say something, and Levi hoped she'd come up with an answer, but when nothing came to her, she promptly shut it.

They stood there in silence for several minutes, each tried to figure out the next thing to say, or if there *was* a next thing to say. His mind wandered again to Emily.

"Hey, where did you go?" Aura quietly asked him.

He jumped and looked around the room, surprised to find himself still in it. "Where did Milskar go?" he asked, confused. He swore Milskar stood right by his side just a second ago.

Her fingertips brushed a piece of hair off his forehead as she smiled at him. "You really did go somewhere."

It how such a simple act could transform her whole face.

"He left about ten minutes ago to speak with Calanthe. He said his goodbyes. Are you all right?" She touched his hand softly and the warmth of her fingers radiated through him.

"Emily," was all he managed.

Aura faced him and grasped his hands firmly in hers. "We will find her," she said with authority. "I promise you, we will find her and bring her back."

A hot, burning feeling caught in his throat and, for a moment, he was terrified that he was about to cry in front of her. It was so hard to hold in his emotions, partly to not explode and hurt someone, and partly to not explode and hurt himself. The sheer effort exhausted him, and he wished he could simply go home, lie in bed, and forget any of this ever took place.

He looked up and her eyes locked on his. He wasn't even sure how it happened. One second they were apart and, the next moment, his lips had found hers. Their hands broke apart and Levi's fingers tangled in fistfuls of her flaming auburn hair. It felt like a lifetime had passed when they pulled back. Pink color flushed her cheeks and their chests rose and fell in quick succession. His hand was still covered by her hair, and he felt his smile crooked on his face as he pulled his hand back by his side.

"Levi—" Aura started, still somewhat breathless.

Levi cut her off. "I'm sorry." He backed up slightly, keeping his eyes anywhere but on hers.

How could he have been so stupid? How, with everything that was going on around them, could he think that she could have romantic feelings for him? And why the heck did he think that now was the time and place to act on his feelings toward her? He was still trying to figure out what those feelings were himself. He felt like such a fool. He turned to walk away. Maybe they could pretend that it had never happened. He had almost reached the door when he felt her hand on his wrist.

He turned back toward her and was about to apologize again when her lips stopped him. It was as if she was everywhere. Levi felt her pressed against him as their hands reached and grabbed and explored. There was an underlying desperation to their actions, as if they could stop some inevitable force by being together like this. Just when he thought he would be lost in this forever—oh and how he wished to be lost in it forever!—he pulled back. Their arms still around each other, they both smiled nervously at one another.

"Well then," Levi said, and Aura burst into laughter. It was the sweetest sound he'd heard in some time.

Chapter 28

Training

Julia was scared. The fear was deep in the pit of her stomach and, at times, seemed to bubble and rise up inside her. Though the edges of her panic held a sort of exhilarated anticipation. Or was it excitement? She had read somewhere once that thirst in the human body sometimes masked itself as hunger. Even with years of evolution, the body still couldn't distinguish between the two. Could fear and exhilaration work the same way? It brought a small amount of comfort to her to think that it could.

She looked to each side of her and tried to read the emotions on the other faces around her. Their entire group was on a knoll which overlooked the thousands of fighters below them who partook in various activities of training and preparation. Julia was unsure of what they should call themselves collectively for she felt they needed a name. The Outsiders seemed to fit, but also had the air of cynicism and she was trying hard to stay positive.

"The Kids" was the maddeningly inferior name everyone else seemed to refer to them as.

"What should we do with *The Kids*?"

"When should we start training *The Kids*?"

"Do you think it was truly wise to bring *The Kids* here?"

This last one was spoken by Milskar to Aura the evening before and overheard by Kalan who had begun to use his powers to spy around the camp and castle.

"It's not right to do that," Jada had protested when Kalan told them what was said.

"Oh, and reading their minds is perfectly fine?" he retorted, which turned Jada's face a bright shade of scarlet.

"Stop it you two," Galina said lazily. "They seem like they haven't the faintest idea about what they're doing about themselves, much less with us."

"You take that back," Julia said fiercely.

"Honestly, Julia," Galina continued, "I don't know what you see in this place."

"Then why are you here?" Julia asked.

"No place else to go," Galina answered matter-of-factly.

Now the group—maybe The Group would work?—stood around and waited for instructions. Tab, who normally wanted little to do with them all, was actually the one who suggested that they should take it upon themselves to train. He'd been participating in some of the training exercises with Milskar, while Kalan had observed some of what the new woman from the other army had been doing with her troops. They decided that it was doable for them to tackle some of the same training themselves.

Tab, being the oldest and most intimidating of the bunch—oh, The Bunch?—had become the natural, albeit reluctant, leader.

"All right," he said, walking slowly in front of them, "I think we need to first see where your powers are at, how you are able or not able to control them, and maybe areas where we can improve, and go from there."

"I thought we were going to be fighting, like, *really* fighting," Galina said.

"You can throw punches soon enough if you want," Tab said. "But first, I think we need to see where we all stand."

"Fair enough," she said in her usual uninterested tone. "And how are we supposed to go about this, dear leader?"

"Kiya," he said, ignoring Galina's tone, "can you find us an animal, maybe a rabbit or something?"

Kiya closed her eyes momentarily before quickly running off to the left and into the woods. A few seconds later she returned, a small creature cradled in her arms.

For an instant, Julia thought it was a rabbit and was about to wonder out loud how it could have crossed over here before she realized that it looked slightly off. Its fur shimmered and its ears, while larger than a squirrel's, were definitely smaller than a rabbit's.

"What's that?" she asked.

Kiya looked down at the fluff in her hands. "Umm...an adrasteia. Sort of a funny name, but that's what he says."

Tab put his hand out for the animal. "Good, thank you Kiya." She hesitated slightly. "I won't hurt it, I promise."

Kiya passed it over and Julia could see a flash of panic in the creature's eyes.

"Ask it to stay still please," Tab said to her. "We won't inflict pain."

"He can understand you."

"All right, let's begin then. Julia, can you pick up the andrea...what's it called again?"

"Adrasteia," Kiya answered.

"Right," Tab said and put it down. "Please stay still," he asked it.

"Julia, you're up. Let's see what you can do. Pick it up and try to put it down in the same place."

Julia concentrated on the creature with all her might. It quickly zoomed twenty feet into the air. The scream of the animal, mixed with Kiya's cry, broke Julia's concentration. The adrasteia began to fall and, before any of them registered what was happening, it crashed to the Earth with a sickening thud and made no attempt to get up.

Julia squeezed her eyes shut tight as she heard the others move around her. "Don't be dead. Don't be dead," she repeated over and over at a whisper.

The tone of the voices around her changed slightly, causing her to open one eye cautiously. The group stood in a circle with Adam kneeling down in the center of it. There was a shimmering in the grass at his feet and a flash ran toward the woods.

Adam rocked back and sat on the ground. He looked dazed, as if like he was about to get sick. Jada reached a hand out to him, but he shook his head before putting it between his legs.

"You okay?" Tab asked.

"He's just tired," Jada said. "It drains him." He stared at Adam with his head cocked to one side.

"You didn't kill it," Galina said to Julia with a breathless laugh. "Well, actually you *almost* killed it, but look on the bright side, Adam was able to practice his talent too."

Adam slowly regained his strength and stood. They lined back up, the bubbles of fear brewing in Julia's stomach again.

"Okay," Tab said, trying to get back some control. "Julia, how about we do something a bit simpler." He picked up a stick and handed it to her with a slightly uncomfortable smile before he moved back to the front.

Julia fought the building urge to run the same direction as the animal. She was mortified as she stared at the puny twig in her hand and debated whether she should walk back to the castle to ask to go home. Was there validity in what Milskar had asked? What *was* the purpose of them being there?

"All right," Tab began again, as if the previous moments events hadn't just happened. "I think maybe we need to take a more…err…intellectual approach to this."

"Intellectual?" Riagan asked skeptically.

"Maybe if we can first figure out *how* our individual powers can help, we can hone them for a specific purpose. Let's just go down the line. Julia?"

The sound of her name snapped her back to the present. She looked from face to face, as if an answer would appear by the simple act of staring at them.

"Well, it's obvious, isn't it?" Galina laughed. "She can just swing people up, drop them from great heights, and kill them. Just work on your aim, not sure how many times Adam will be able to save your butt."

"Enough, G," Adam said quietly. "She obviously feels bad about what happened."

Julia was grateful that he stood up for her, but she noticed an interesting look pass between him and Galina. And what was he calling her "G" for? Julia wondered if something was going on between them.

"Well, that could be helpful actually," Kiya said. They turned to look at her. "I—I mean," she stammered, "this is a war, isn't it? I'm sure the fighting we'll be doing will be to kill. Only makes sense to fight back to kill too." She shrugged. "Just sayin'."

They stood in silence and looked at one another. It was true, each of them knew it, but it hadn't seemed real. The gravity of what they were doing hadn't hit them until that moment when Kiya said it out loud.

"Do you think we'll really have to kill people?" Riagan squeaked nervously.

"Don't think like that," Jada said, "it wouldn't be like that." He obviously saw the terrible thoughts which flashed though their minds. "I'm sure we won't be doing a lot of fighting, and we can try to use our talents to prevent anyone from dying. Let's try to approach it that way," he said, smiling weakly at the rest of the group.

"Then I'd keep Julia away from battle," Galina said.

The cry of pain she gave as Adam stomped on her foot gave Julia only the slightest bit of comfort.

Chapter 30

Supreme Ruler

After two long turns around the clearing, Lady Grustmiener signaled it was time to make their decent. Obediently and without objection, Gilbert calmly lost altitude and brought them back to the earth. They had barely hit the ground before she was off of him, throwing a reproachful look at Molluk.

"See," she said and strode away.

Molluk grasped several feathers from around Gilbert's face and pulled him forward. The griffin's eyes flashed red and narrowed, but he did not fuss and did as he was told. If Molluk had only turned around, if he'd faced the beast and looked, really looked at it, he would have seen how hollow the creature had become.

Gilbert was deadened and empty inside as he turned all of his anger and resentment inward. Though, at the center of him still burned the image of Kolas. However small, he held it tight and would not let the picture go, for he feared that it would take the last bit of him with it as it fluttered away.

Lady Grustmiener walked through her camp, head high, filled with anticipation. Soon! So soon and she would be the queen and ruler of these lands, of every land. In her dreams last night, she climbed the mountain again and, though she worked very hard, she did not seem to make any progress.

Finally, she looked down and was surprised to see not earth beneath her hands and feet, but skeletons, thousands of them. Bleached white in the sun, they gleamed under her. They were no longer made of fire or ash. As soon as she'd made this realization, she had reached the summit. She looked down and saw a crown atop one of the skulls. She removed it and placed it upon her head in triumph. She would not fail, could not fail. The Four Corners would be hers. When she woke, she could still feel the crown's pressure as it encircled her head.

There were lines of soldiers around her now. Some marched in silent, perfect rows, while others were involved in hand-to-hand combat. She did not recognize most of the faces around her and soon they blended into one another. She saw King Theaus working with several of the heads of the various parts of the army. Lady Grustmiener scoffed inwardly. When a ruler was seen among their people, doing the same things they did, those people couldn't help but feel that they were on the same level of those who were over them. She kept an unapproachable-ness about her that instilled fear and respect.

She looked over at the group that surrounded the king. They acted as if he was one of them. It not only made him look weak, but also made the people of Omaner look weak as well. They would be just as easy to defeat as Esotera when the time came. She laughed to herself.

It was mapped out in her mind. She was anxious to implement her plan and revel in her victory. After her march on Esotera, she would slay Queen Aura and then King Theaus, as he would be no more use to her and needed to be killed before he suspected any further plans.

Before the blood of the battle had even been dried into the ground, her plans would be in full swing.

In their collective fear and love of her, what was left of the armies of Omaner, Grustmiener, and Esotera would march on Vertronum and capture that land for her. After the fall of King Piester, nothing would stand in the way of Lady Grustmiener. She would rule the entirety of, not merely their world, but would continue to the other world. She would rule over the greatest and largest kingdom ever known.

There was just one small roadblock. Somehow, Levi would have to be killed.

She didn't think that it would be that much trouble. It was luck that picked the boy over King Grustmiener and almost led to her destruction. She was so much stronger now than her husband had ever been. Now she had an army he would have been envious of. Distance and opportunity were the only things that stood in her way, but that would soon be over as well. Then, and the thought did nothing but create even more excitement and anticipation within her, she would move on and consume everything in her path.

It was Abaddon who had told her about a loophole, and the possibility of gaining supreme control.

"He is at the end of the blood line," Abaddon had said months before.

She had found him as he sat against a low wall that surrounded the abandoned barracks that became their command center for the rebuilding effort. He didn't seem surprised to see her. The only indication he'd even given of the events that had transpired was to simply state the following three facts: Queen Aura still ruled Esotera, Omire had been appointed ruler of her former lands, and they would be safe where they were for as long as Lady Grustmiener decided to stay.

Preparations happened almost immediately. As word spread of her whereabouts, others began to arrive. It wasn't until Lieal and Achan showed up that the army started to rebuild with any gusto. She was disappointed to learn that the former head of her husband's forces, Belial, had died, but these new successors proved just as competent. Achan, while older, had a hotheadedness that made him difficult to work with at times, but he appeared loyal. Lieal was the one who surprised her, though. She didn't remember him being much of anything the last time she saw him, but now there was a hatred which burned in Lieal that seemed to rival Lady Grustmiener's own. Her army was in the right hands.

It was during one of these early rebuilding meetings between her and Abaddon that he informed her of what he'd gleaned from the months he had traveled since the Great Battle.

"He is at the end of the blood line," he repeated.

"Yes, I know this. You have said it already," Lady Grustmiener said absentmindedly. She was still tired of all the inaction. While she knew she wasn't ready for battle yet, she was anxious to implement her plan to regain power.

"He has the power," he continued, not picking up on her tone.

"Yes, I *know* this," she said, looking up at him. "So?"

"If you kill him, you get the power. There is no one to take it after him, no one for him to pass it down to."

Lady Grustmiener froze. Her mind whirled. She hadn't thought of this, hadn't thought that there was a way were she could circumvent the bloodline requirement set up by the original creators Lord Vertrous and Lady Amadea.

"How do you know this? Why did you not tell me?" Her words were laced with anger.

"The witches and wizards of the North—" he started before she interrupted him.

"They still remain? Why do we not have them fighting for us?"

"There are few that remain, very few who are of full blood. I attempted to convince them of our cause…" He trailed off as he so often did.

"And…" she pressed him. She was in no mood for his idiosyncrasies.

"They were talking in theories about the Missing Link. I am not sure if they had any concrete information that he is real and that he once resided in these lands, but they were able to agree on that one thing, at least hypothetically if he did, in fact, exist."

They sat in silence for several minutes while she absorbed this information into her brain.

"Would I even need to kill the other rulers? Or would the killing of him make them bow to me?" Power flashed like fire in her mind.

"I do not think that is a requirement, though I think, for ease, they should be extinguished to eliminate any problems they may try to cause."

"Yes, yes of course," Lady Grustmiener said. She got up and began to walk back and forth. "Does anyone else know about this? Does anyone know killing him will exchange power?"

"I do not know. Like I said, it was spoken about in theory, but they have little interaction outside of their own, limited kind…" His voice trailed off again before he looked up at her. "I would think not, or he would already be dead. Though this will make you a marked woman, as his power would be transferred to you. I would not announce that these are your plans, which should keep you reasonably safe."

"Would I have powers and rights to the other world as well?" she asked excitedly.

"I believe, yes," Abaddon said, after contemplating the thought. "Yes, you would rule everything, if you wish," he added more firmly this time. "While there are others who have some powers as well, I think the blood is what makes all the difference for him. I do not think there is anything that can overcome that."

"Would I have to be the one to kill him?"

"Oh, yes, yes you must," he said.

Supreme power. She could almost taste it, as if it were edible, and she could not wait to consume every morsel of it.

Chapter 31

Joining Forces

Aura stood at the edge of her camp and looked at the bodies scattered below her. For a second, a thought flashed through her mind that they looked as if they were all dead. She shuddered and tried to push the picture away. She hoped that this image wouldn't be solidified in reality, that they would all be safe. It became difficult to breathe. *They're just sleeping,* she told herself. *Just sleeping.* As if to help her, many of the forms started to move and stir.

Her head spun. There were times where she felt sixteen again. Like her father had just died and she sat outside his room with the crushing realization of what she had to do and not the faintest idea of how to go about it.

The rustle behind her had barely registered before Theirra appeared next to her. Aura had not seen her friend, at least not up close, in days. Now that Theirra was near enough for Aura to give her a proper looking over, she saw how thin and frail Theirra had become. The circles under her eyes were so dark they looked permanent.

"Theirra." It was a relief to see her. "How did you

sleep?" Aura asked, trying to keep the concern out of her voice.

"Hmm?" Theirra asked distractedly. "I think we should start making final preparations," she continued.

"Is the army close?"

"Busu says the time is near. A fortnight," Theirra said. It wasn't until this moment that Aura registered the great bird as it clutched, painfully from the looks of it, to Theirra's shoulder.

"I think he has taken a liking to you," Aura said as she reached her hand out to pet the bird. He gave an indignant squawk and flew off and into a nearby tree.

"Frankly," Theirra said with the hint of a smile, "I think he is a bit of a jerk, but he will not leave me alone, so there you have it."

"Theirra."

"Aura."

They both said each other's names at the same moment. They smiled at one another. What had happened between them? Aura wondered.

"Aura, I—" Theirra started.

"Me too," Aura continued.

"I know I have not made it easy."

"I am the one who needs to atone, not you."

"When Kolas died—" Theirra said.

"You do not need to explain. There is so much more I could have done for you. I did not know how to help you, but I could have tried harder. Could have gotten someone to help you. I pushed you away when I should have brought you even closer."

Theirra smiled. "We each made our mistakes."

"You pulled away and I let you go. That is unacceptable. I should have made a point to find you. To bring you to the meetings."

"It felt like the world was moving on without me,"

Theirra said. Her voice was tiny. Aura felt a tear slide down her face. Theirra swallowed. "Being around you as you planned for the future. It became too hard. I lost my way, and it became too hard to try to get back."

"Theirra, I am so sorry."

At that moment a soft rustle alerted them to someone's approach and they broke off mid-conversation, still so much left unsaid between them. Milskar joined them and after a quick exchange, agreed that it was time to organize, and went off to speak with Calanthe.

The movement happening around her made Aura feel a bit better, though she wished she and Theirra would have had more time to talk. It was not simply that they needed to apologize and set whatever was wrong between them right again, but Aura needed to know, truly know, that everything would be okay. She had betrayed her friend, ignored her counsel, and refused to listen, and she needed to make it right with Theirra. Their conversation was a start, but Aura knew they had more work to do. If she could conjure a pause button, she'd use it to sit down with her oldest friend until they'd set everything right again, but such magic didn't exist.

Aura needed to shift her focus. She had always preferred action instead of waiting for something to happen. She found having a task to focus on made her less nervous about the bigger picture, and right now, she could use all the calm she could get.

Her dreams the night before were again filled with the fire, though this time it was a burning horse and the harder she tried to reach the animal, the farther away it seemed, and the larger the fire became. The horse looked vaguely familiar, but she didn't know why, and was unable to get closer and get a clear look. All the same, the dream frightened her and left her with searing doubts.

She turned to voice her concerns with Theirra, but she

was already gone. Aura's heart ached for her friend. They had known each other for so many years Aura couldn't pinpoint a memory that didn't in some way involve her. Though for the first time in their lives together, she felt like they were on completely different paths. So deep was Theirra's pain, Aura was frightened that not only would she not be able to recover from it, but she might drown and be lost forever beneath its grasp.

Before Aura could get lost any farther within her thoughts, she spotted Levi coming toward her. Her heart leapt slightly at the sight of him. The image of their kiss flashed across her memory, but she was unable to give counsel to such thoughts. They had not been alone together since that night, and part of her felt like Levi wished Milskar and Calanthe would leave them alone one night.

She was so grateful for the help the two gave her but, at the same time, she wished she could pause what was happening and get lost in time with Levi. There were even times where she was tempted to ask him to take her away from this place, from all this strife and fear, to take her back with him to his world. These thoughts left her feeling shameful and she regretted them as soon as the notion occurred to her.

Aura saw that he was with a boy, maybe fifteen or sixteen. She vaguely recalled his name being Jada, but she couldn't be sure. She chastised herself that she hadn't spent more time with the children Theirra had brought with her. Her initial anger over their arrival was so great, she had basically ignored the fact they resided in her home.

"Levi, and…" She hesitated. "Jada is it?" He nodded, much to her relief. "What may I be of service for? I hope you have been taken good care of. I apologize I have not been able to spend much time with each of you—" She broke off and gestured feebly around her, hoping this was a sufficient explanation for her neglect.

"It's, fine, fine," he said. "Everyone's been great."

"Tell her why we're here, Jada, tell her what you saw," Levi said.

"Well." The boy looked nervous and would not meet Aura's gaze. "I'm not sure what I've seen. With all these people here, things have been getting sort of jumbled and I'm still getting the hang of seeing visions from people who aren't near me." He half-smiled at her, embarrassed.

"What have you seen Jada?" Aura asked.

"These great winged beasts. I dunno what they are. They sort of have feathers I think and lion bodies?" he said in a questioning tone. "I can just picture them flying over an army—and—and, well, eating people." The boy looked almost horrified as he stared up at her, fear in his eyes. "I'm not sure what it means," he said in a rush. "Sometimes I see things as they are really happening and sometimes I see what someone *wants* to happen."

"That is very helpful, Jada, thank you," Aura said, trying to keep her voice calm and even.

"I thought that might be helpful information," Levi said as he looked at her knowingly. He and the boy turned to leave.

"Griffins," Aura said to their backs.

Jada turned around. "Sorry?"

"They are called griffins, the things you saw. It really is very helpful, you telling me that."

As they walked away her mind reeled. She fought the urge to cry out in panic and relief when she saw Milskar and Calanthe walking toward her.

"Griffins," she said shakily.

"Sorry?" Milskar asked, looking over at Calanthe.

"They are using griffins. It is confirmed. Lady Grustmiener has aligned with Omaner."

Her words hit Milskar and Calanthe, as if they were physical things.

Chapter 32

Comings and Goings

A ll right," Levi said, somewhat awkwardly to the children who were gathered around him. "So I guess first and foremost, you each need to work on controlling your skills. I know Jada's been improving his range, but we need to have you all doing it, too."

"We've been working on that," Galina said with an exasperated sigh.

"Right, then that will make this go quicker." He tried to say it with a laugh, but he suspected that it came off as self-conscious.

"Would you like us to go over what we have done so far?" Julia piped up.

"Yes, that would be helpful."

"We've each been practicing," Kalan started, "on our individual talents, and then as much as we can, we used them against each other, but just to disarm or stop the other person from being able to do their, um…" He paused, as if searching for the right word. "…magic?" he said with a questioning look at the others.

"You make us sound like wizards or something," Galina said. She picked at some dirt that had been trapped under her nail. It was evident that she found that task of greater interest than the present one.

"Don't they have witches and wizards here?" Julia asked.

"Yes…well, at least they did," Levi said. He wasn't sure how many there were or if, after the death of Resbuca and Winester, any more still existed.

"Do they use wands?" Adam asked.

Galina huffed under her breath.

"Let's stay focused," Tab said briskly to the others, and they seemed to take his order instantly.

Levi made a mental note that he was the clear leader. "Right," he said. "I want you to line up. I will try to block what you are doing, and you try to stop me."

They lined up obediently—Galina, Kiya, Jada, Julia, Kalan, Riagan, Tab, and Adam. Levi's heart raced. He'd been working very hard on getting his strength and skills back, and, while he felt stronger than he ever had, he wondered if he would be any match for those in front of him. As he stepped forward he hoped he didn't make a complete fool of himself.

He felt the air around him shift, and static tickled his skin. The sky above them became a dark gray color and rumbles could be heard in the distance. Before Galina was able to send down a bolt of lightning, though, Levi pushed the clouds away, forming an invisible bubble over the two of them. She hardened her face in concentration and pushed more forcefully against him. It was difficult, but he was able to resist her, though he could hear rain not far off from where they were.

"Good!" he said, as he felt the tension break and dissipate around them.

Galina, however, glared at him.

Next Kiya stepped up, and Levi was unable to stop her having a great black bird—he later heard someone calling it a hethronian—land on his head. The kids all laughed and he felt himself crack a smile, though he was frustrated that he wasn't able to figure out her skills well enough to prevent her from using them. He gingerly removed the bird and hefted it to the ground before it took off into the woods. It must have weighed thirty pounds and he rubbed his head where the bird's claws had grazed him.

He had better luck with both Jada and Julia. It was a strange feeling, having someone try to enter your thoughts. It felt slightly warm and fuzzy, and, with a bit of a shock, he realized he had felt this before, but it was so brief he didn't know what had caused it.

A picture of Aura and him kissing flashed into his mind before he felt a push like a strong hand thrust the image back, as if behind a door. The look he gave Jada was clear, if he ever repeated what he saw, he was a dead man. The boy averted his eyes and moved to the back of the line.

Julia was quickly thwarted as well. Her almond eyes were on him for just a second before he felt his feet shift up slightly from the earth, but he was easily able to drive them back down. The force of his block made her stumble back slightly, and she looked sheepish as she moved away. Levi could tell she was powerful, but her lack of confidence would be her undoing—and, thus, she reminded Levi a little of himself.

He was no match for Kalan, though. One second the boy was directly in front of him, and the next Kalan had him by the arm. Levi almost jumped out of his skin at the touch. Being invisible gave the boy an incredible tactical advantage, but Levi was determined to figure out how to outmaneuver him. He made the boy stand in front of him again. This time Levi closed his eyes and concentrated on the air, much like he had done with Galina. While he could feel a slight shift, he was unable to pinpoint it, and again Kalan was able to touch him without Levi having the slightest idea where he'd come from.

Levi was still a little shaken, his thoughts on how he could improve his own powers, when Riagan moved toward him. He wasn't sure how to block her powers of being able to see through him, mainly because he did not quite understand them and how they could be used against him. She seemed to have the same problem, and after staring at each other for several moments, she shrugged and moved to the back of the line.

"We'll work together one-on-one later," he called after her, trying to make her feel better.

He was however, no match for Tab's incredible strength. While Levi had gotten better at his multitasking, Tab was too quick and too strong for him. In what seemed like a second, a large body hovered over him as Levi struggled for breath. He couldn't even remember how he got on the ground, but every inhale burned and he felt like his ribs may have punctured a lung. Adam was promptly by his side and the pain subsided almost as quickly as it had arrived.

"I'm not sure if you want to block my power," Adam said with a smile.

"No, maybe not," Levi said forcefully. He stood, a little shaky, and they went through the rotation once more before breaking off into pairs and groups.

Levi encouraged Jada to work on trying to see images "live." That way, he could potentially see, through someone's eyes, what actually happened, instead of what might happen. Levi thought if they could pinpoint exactly where Lady Grustmiener was, they would have a huge advantage. The task seemed daunting, though. As soon as one of them hid behind a tree or got too far away, Jada had little success in accessing their mind. He promised to work on it.

They'd also figured out a more useful application for Riagan's talents. With complete silence and immense concentration, she was able to see through a group of trees and rocks and pinpoint several of their hiding places. It turned into a fun game—they hid and she tried to find them—though, it was clear after the fourth round, that Riagan was so exhausted it was difficult for her to see through anything.

Toward the end of their session, Milskar arrived. He gave out some pointers, sparred with Tab—he seemed to be the only one truly capable—then they broke for the day.

After two more days of training in this similar fashion, Levi and Milskar agreed that The Kids were ready to start training with Calanthe and the combined armies. Amaline had also been joining the preparations. She'd previously been helping the new recruits in her own army, so she became the perfect liaison to blend all the new fighters from the three kingdoms. The soldiers appeared to like and respect her and even some of The Kids gravitated toward her when their structured training was complete.

Several times Levi had caught Aura with a smile on her face as she watched the girl. It was clear she cared for Amaline very much. He tried to open himself up and forgive Amaline, to see her the way Aura did.

"I think we are ready," Amaline had announced to him after a particularly disastrous training exercise.

"Really?" Levi asked worriedly.

"You should have seen your face!" Amaline remarked with pure laughter. "Gosh no! They look terrible. But they *will* be ready, do not worry about that," she said, grasping his shoulder lightly.

She walked off, a chuckle still in her voice as she barked out orders.

Despite himself, he laughed. The anger Levi felt when

he first saw her had begun to melt away. He'd started to like her very much.

Now that Levi saw everyone in one space and the contained chaos of the scene, he realized how breathtaking it was. It was hard to imagine any army being able to defeat them, or even come close to their numbers, but the limited scout reports they had been receiving told them that it would still not be enough.

Lady Grustmiener's army was apparently so large in size, their numbers could not even be calculated. The Esotera scouts recounted an alarming picture. The glimpses of the army they saw contained fighters marching in lines so long, they went so far off in the horizon, their numbers seemed endless.

By the end of the third day the small group of kids were mingled in with the other soldiers, who seemed to get great entertainment at seeing their powers in action. In return, The Kids were extremely intrigued by the clothing and body armor of the Vertronum army. They marveled when they were told stories about the sea creatures that resided throughout their land. Levi stood back with Milskar and Calanthe, a slight smile plastered on his face.

"Gratifying, is it not?" Calanthe asked in her thick accent.

"It is."

"Let us hope they can remember this training and camaraderie when the fighting begins," Milskar said, somewhat solemnly. "I would hate for anything to happen to any of them."

Levi had been so busy preparing for battle, he almost forgot that they were actually preparing for a *battle*. He looked around at the group—little Julia picking up soldiers and putting them back down as the men and women laughed. Kalan disappeared and reappeared feet away, to

much applause. The pit in Levi's stomach began to grow
again. He no longer feared just for his life and Emily's
but for everyone in front of him. What would he do if
something happened to one of them? How would he be
able to live with that? And Aura. That was a line of
thought he couldn't even bear to go down.

"The training is going well," he said to Aura proudly
that night.

It was a rare evening in which the two of them found
themselves alone. Milskar and Calanthe had decided to
work late into the night with the troops. Theirra had come
into Aura's office for a few minutes before said she
wanted to investigate some thought she had and left the
two of them, her mind already far away in contemplation.
Finally alone, Levi told Aura about how worried he was
for the lives of the children.

"I know what you mean," she said seriously. "That is
how I feel about each and every one of my people."

"How do you stop? How do you turn off the panic?"

"I do not." She laughed without humor. "At least not
most of the time. I try to keep busy, but as soon as I let
my thoughts wander—" She paused. "It is best to try to
not let your thoughts wander, I believe."

He smiled at her. "They are so skilled. That gives me
some comfort. They are much stronger than I am."

Aura smiled at him. "I think you underestimate yourself. My kingdom and I owe you our livelihood."

"That seems like a lifetime ago," he responded quietly.

"We were so very young," she replied.

She was so close to him, he could feel the heat off her
body. He didn't look at her, but he could picture the way
she sat next to him in his head. Levi found it hard to concentrate. He couldn't quite remember what they were
talking about.

Why was it so warm in here? Was it always so warm

in the castle? Had she gotten closer to him? Why did it seem like she'd gotten closer to him?

Aura stood and faced him. "I mean it." She looked so serious and, for a second, he thought he was going to have to advert his eyes from hers. "I owe you everything." She cut him off just as he was about to protest. "I appreciate everything you are doing, especially helping with the preparations, but do not forget that you are an intricate part of this as well. You are powerful, and I—" She blushed at this last part before correcting herself. "—I mean, my kingdom needs you."

There was a piece of hair that had fallen just in front of her right eye. Levi found himself fixated with the strands. He felt a powerful urge to brush it back, but questioned his instincts. He couldn't take it anymore and moved his hand up. He lingered on her face and soon found himself kissing her again. Though just as their lips met, the door behind them crashed open. They both turned and saw Theirra, her hand still on the knob, face frozen in shock.

"Theirra," Aura said.

Levi noticed his hand rested on her neck and quickly pulled it back. He kept his eyes down and focused on a spot on the floor in front of him.

He heard movement around him and looked up to see a flash of red curl around the door and disappear. He heard footfalls running in the hall and whispered pleas. Levi shut his eyes in an attempt to block out what might be happening outside the room. He feared the glorious stolen moments they had shared would come to an abrupt and soul-crushing end.

Chapter 33

More Broken Things

Emily blinked hard against the light, but it did little to clear her vision. It felt like a film was over her eyes, giving which gave a soft blur to everything she looked at. The noise around her was deafening, probably even more so because of the relative isolation she'd been living in for what seemed like an eternity. She felt like a zombie as she moved through the small clearing and assumed she looked like one as well, due to the stares of those around her.

She was not sure how long she'd been kept underground, though it had been about a day and half since they hauled her back up into the light and made her walk on stiff legs behind a huge army. It felt as it if had been years since she had seen her home, her family. A sharp pang tore through her heart. She found it difficult to remember what Milskar and Nikolas looked like. They appeared in her memories just as fuzzy as her surroundings.

Anytime she thought something would come into focus and she stared straight at it, it seemed to shift and move away from her. Emily resolved herself to look straight down at her shackled feet as she shuffled along.

A burnt, acrid smell filled her nostrils. Fear prickled on her skin, as if it was a living thing that brushed up against her. She was roughly halted and noticed several sets of feet in front of her. She lifted her gaze, though it took a moment for her eyes to make sense of the sudden, even if minimal, movement.

Lady Grustmiener stood in front of her, with a wicked grin pulling at the corner of her lips. Several men and women in some type of thick body armor, one of whom Emily remembered from when she was first taken, flanked her. He was tall and appeared to be the same age as she. She wondered how they both could have gone on such different paths with the years they were each given. He whispered something that Emily didn't catch. It was difficult to get them into focus, but it helped to stare straight at Lady Grustmiener.

"Do you see the damage around you?" Lady Grustmiener opened her arms in a gesture at their surroundings.

Emily attempted to follow them, but became so dizzy she almost fell over.

"I see you are still not stable on your feet. No matter, I am sure you can *smell* what has happened. The stench of burning flesh, whether human or animal, is one like no other. Once you are able to recognize it, it lingers in your nostrils, able to be recalled with the slightest remembrance."

Emily's stomach turned. The smell of decay and burning filled her, and she knew Lady Grustmiener was right. It was a stench she would never forget as long as she lived. She tried to focus again and take short, shallow breaths through her mouth, as she fought the urge to vomit.

"This is what happens when someone resists me. Do you see that now? Do you see that it is a futile effort to fight against me? Your people, everyone you love, will die. I will spare no one."

The conviction in which she said these words turned Emily's stomach even more. She had to shut her eyes against everything around her, but as soon as she did images of Milskar, Nikolas, Aura, Theirra, and even Levi filled her mind.

The day prior she'd been informed that her cousin had returned to Esotera. The fear of one more person possibly in danger of being hurt by this woman sickened Emily even further. She could not bear such things happening to them. The thought of losing them would be more than her soul could handle. She would rather die that live a second without them.

"So you see," Lady Grustmiener continued, "why it is so important that you are able to tell your people what is happening. To convince them to surrender."

Emily snapped her head up. What was she talking about? How could Emily convince them? She was hundreds, possibly thousands of miles away.

"I—I do not understand," she stammered.

"Do you not?" Lady Grustmiener asked. "You are our pawn now, our Trojan horse. We are returning you home with a message."

Home. It was the only word Emily was able to hold on to, and she grasped it with hands so tight it was difficult to hear anything else.

She was going home. It was all going to be okay. She would go home and they would defeat this awful woman. Emily and her family could live the rest of their days in peace. Blessed, wonderful peace.

"Oh, Emily," Lady Grustmiener continued, as if she were able to read her thoughts. "Do not think that it will be as simple as us releasing you into their clutches. No, that is too much of a risk. Last, we thought we turned your cousin into such a thoughtless killing machine, we did not think that we had to watch him so closely. We were convinced that he would kill our enemies. We cannot take such chances with you."

"Then kill me," Emily said. "I will not aid you. I will not let you hurt them. I would rather die."

"Oh, so bold. So selfless and yet so foolish. You are worthless to me dead. It does nothing to help me. For you—" Lady Grustmiener stepped forward and placed a soft hand on Emily's cheek. "—that is not an option. Achan," she said and turned to the older man behind her, "apparently, she needs more convincing. A few fingers should start us in the right path."

Emily looked at her in horror and recoiled as the guards tightened their grips on her. She clenched her hands firmly to hide her fingers within her palms. Death, she thought, she could handle, but torture? She hoped that she had the strength to endure it.

"Oh, heavens, no!" Lady Grustmiener laughed. "Do not worry, my dear, we are not completely barbaric. We understand that we need you as whole as possible. If it comes to that, then yes, maybe we will need a flesh sacrifice from you, but for now, no. Not for now. Achan." She nodded again at the older man.

A depraved smile spread on his face now. Achan turned to the younger man who stood next to him and said something, but Emily wasn't able to catch it.

The younger man…Lieal?…moved away and came back several moments later, a large knife in one hand and a terrified-looking boy in the other. The child appeared to be maybe seven or eight. He kicked and scratched, trying to get away from his captor, but he was no match for the stronger man.

Emily was transfixed. She watched in horror, her vision momentarily, mercilessly clearing.

No, she prayed. No.

The screams of the boy, mingled with her own, would live inside her forever, just like the smells of death wafting around her, as the fingers on his right hand were skillfully removed.

Chapter 34

Conflict

Early the next morning, Levi found himself yet again in Aura's offices. After she chased Theirra, he stayed for several more minutes before he returned to his room. He found himself pulled in and out of a fitful sleep. Dreams of red flames and Aura's death wove through his mind and shocked him awake on several occasions. As soon as the sun crested over the trees outside his window, he abandoned any further attempts at slumber and decided it was time to find her, though he now regretted this decision. His stomach felt uneasy with nerves at seeing her again.

While he was worried all night about what she might say, he also feared the finality of what she might decide. Would she tell him that they could no longer see each other? That Theirra, wracked with sadness, convinced her to focus all her energy on the battle and forgo any thoughts of him? He could not blame Aura if she felt this way. Frankly, he even wondered these same things, but then the pull of her would wash all those qualms away and silence them to a soft murmur he was able to easily ignore.

He was just about to leave and pace the grounds when he heard the handle of the door turn. He braced himself, but was shocked to discover that is was not Aura that walked through the door, but Theirra.

"Oh," she said, equally startled.

"Theirra, I—" he stammered.

"I am looking for Queen Aura." The way she said it seemed so formal to Levi. What had happened between the two of them over the years since he'd be gone? He knew that discovering him and Aura together last night wouldn't be enough to strain their friendship like that. It had to be rooted deeper.

"I was just leaving," he said and made to move past her.

To his surprise Theirra shut the door and blocked his escape. "Actually, since I have you here, I need to speak with you," she said frankly.

"Theirra—" he started.

"No." She cut him off. "I need to speak. I understand that Aura cares for you, and I believe that you have similar feelings."

"I do."

"Be that as it may," she said, "there is a battle that needs to be fought. Lives are at risk and anything that may..." She hesitated. "...distract her at a time like this needs to be neutralized."

"You think I'm a distraction?" The accusation hurt him.

"I think she needs to focus on winning this war. This is not a game, Levi. We cannot go home after this is over. We *are* home."

"Is that what you think? You think I just abandoned you all here and left? Never thought of any of you again?" He found it increasingly difficult to keep his voice even.

"What else are we supposed to think? You left. You left and told our story, without informing any of us, and have carved out what I imagine to be a pretty lucrative life for yourself."

"You asked *me* here!" he bellowed. "You asked me! You said you needed my help and I came. Do you think I have spent one day since I have left this place where I have not thought about each of you? My cousin is here. It was all of *you* who could not protect *her*!"

"I asked you here," she responded calmly, "because you are the reason we are in this mess in the first place."

"Theirra." They both jumped at the sound of Aura's voice. Neither had heard her enter. "Theirra, please." Aura's eyes looked red and swollen.

"No, Aura, *my queen*." The words spat out of Theirra's mouth. "You are being reckless. Do you not remember what we lost last time? Are you willing to sacrifice it again so you can have some pleasures in your life?"

"I know what we lost."

"No, you do not, you have no idea. You did not lose anything," Theirra said.

"I did not lose anything? Theirra, these are my people! I lost my people. I was in charge of protecting them and I failed."

"And if you continue as you are doing, you risk failing them again."

This time Theirra didn't wait for a response. She brushed by Aura and out through the hall. Levi stood frozen. It was as if the air had left their surroundings. How could this happen? Why did it seem like everything around him was crumbling, and not a single arrow hadn't even been shot yet.

He met Aura's eyes and she collapsed, wracked with giant, gulping sobs. He reached her in one step, knelt on the floor, and held her tight in his arms.

"Where have I gone wrong with her? I have tried to help her, but she keeps pushing me away. It is like she wants me as miserable as she is so we can bear these crosses together. Does she not understand that I have my own miseries to shoulder? My own ghosts and demons that haunt me?" Aura turned her face up to Levi, a plea on her face.

"I don't know," he answered truthfully and at a complete loss at what to say or do.

The door burst open again and Levi saw Theirra there. For a moment, he expected her to either spit more insults or to apologize, but neither happened. She had a shocked expression on her face, yet it did not seem to be from the scene unfolding in front of her.

Aura stood just as Amaline arrived, the same shocked expression clouding her features.

"She is back," Theirra said in a confused whisper.

"Back, who is back?" Aura asked.

"Emily."

Levi's breath caught in the back of his throat as the words crashed into him.

Chapter 35

The First Move

Are you sure it was wise to release her, my lady?" Lieal asked.

"Yes. And I will hear no more questioning of my authority," she answered sternly.

"She is a weapon. A weapon they do not know the scope or breadth of," Abaddon piped in. "They do not know it, but she will be integral to our defeat of them."

In the days leading up to her release, they'd tortured Emily in ways only a parent can be broken. They marched her in front of buildings that held the rounded up children of villages and made her watch as the soldiers burned the structures to the ground. Before each assault, they asked her again if she would help them.

"No," she answered with tears in her voice.

It took five villages, but she finally agreed before they reached the next. Though they killed everyone in the town for good measure, just to be sure. Emily now held the knowledge of the terror they could inflict upon her, her fellow Esoterans, and worse, her son. They spoke of him by name. Abaddon described what they would do to the boy.

The soldiers of Grustmiener and Omaner seemed appalled by what the man said and by what they had done, but they had long ago learned to fear their ruler, and they obeyed without question.

As if Emily needed any more fuel to persuade her, Luther and Unna were brought in. They seemed apprehensive, yet they too had seen enough to know that not following orders was counterproductive and resulted in the end of life or limb.

Luther had been practicing with animals for days now, but this would be his first attempt at raising a human corpse. He looked over at Abaddon who nodded his head enthusiastically. Out of the burning embers, two figures of contrasting sizes began to move. It was difficult to make out their features, to determine if they were male or female, but due to their height they appeared to be an adult and a child. They walked as if their legs no longer had movement in their joints. The larger figure's foot caught on a branch and it appeared to be about to pitch forward when it righted itself, which caused those watching to shrink back in fear. Emily was transfixed with terror. She turned her head and, in the space Unna had occupied moments before, Milskar stood.

"Our son," Unna said in a deep voice.

Emily turned to the disguised Unna, unable to comprehend this new sight. She didn't even register that his voice wasn't quite as husky as it was in real life. He pointed a finger toward the charred bodies. "Do not let this happen to our son."

That sealed it, Lady Grustmiener knew. She was very pleased with the foreigners, glad that she agreed to bring them here. All of her moves and counter moves thus far had worked brilliantly in her favor. It was only a matter of time before everything did.

She ignored the pained and exhausted expressions on

both Unna and Luther as they were returned to their original selves. The burned bodies felled yards from them.
They no longer moved and were left to smolder in the
grass as Lady Grustmiener set her gaze on Emily.

"This will be your reality if you do not convince
Queen Aura to surrender."

"I understand," Emily answered feebly as tears fell
down her face.

"I hope that you do."

The following day, Lady Grustmiener had tasked
Achan to lead an out party to bring Emily back as close
as they could to the castle in Esotera. Lady Grustmiener
found that she had less and less use for Achan and his hot
temper. He'd been delegated to training the new members
of her army, and it appeared to be a role he was a little
too enthusiastic about. She was tired of the stories of how
he yelled and bullied everyone. She hoped these out-
missions would be a way to make him useful without
driving her crazy.

She sent them under the cover of night, right on the
cusp of the early morning. The battle did not need to start
quite yet. There was still more time, still more to prepare.
She instructed the group to ride near the edge of the opposing army and to send Emily forward without them.

Lady Grustmiener wasn't concerned with escorting
her the whole way to the castle. Emily knew the way.

Once freed she would be sure to run right back to
where she came from, the ticking time bomb that she now
was, poised right in the epicenter, ready to implode and
take Esotera down once and for all.

Chapter 36

The Message

Aura's group still stood around, dumbfounded, when Milskar barged into the room. No words were spoken. He went straight to Emily and swallowed her up in his arms. She almost seemed to disappear, she being so tiny and frail and he so big and strong. Soon a soft murmur emanated from their embrace, though it was difficult to determine what, if anything, they said to one another. It was a long time before they broke apart, and that only seemed to happen because Nikolas ran into the room as well. Cassney quickly followed and apologized in the boy's wake for the intrusion before she noticed Emily. She moved to the rear of the room and seemed to melt into the background, movement from her came in quick sweeps of her hands to remove the tears that spilled from her eyes.

"My loves, my sweet, sweet boys," Emily repeated over and over and clutched the two of them, as if she was afraid either one of them, or she herself, would float away. Bruises and cuts covered all visible parts of her, but she held them tight, all the same.

Aura glanced sideways at Levi and tried to catch his

eye, but he stared fixedly at his cousin. Aura felt the soft tender spot in her heart form even stronger as she looked at him.

For a moment, she wondered what the future would actually be like. When this war was over, what would happen to them? Surely, he would return home like before, surely, this would be the last time—hopefully, this would be the last time—they would need him. She longed for peace, could feel the weariness of it in her bones, but part of her also didn't want him to leave. Luckily, Emily started to speak and broke the momentary spell on Aura.

"I am sorry, what did you say?" Aura asked.

"We cannot go through with this war. We must surrender."

The terror in Emily's eyes bore into Aura. It made her blood feel cold and thick. "Emily, we are not going to surrender to that woman."

"She will kill us all," Emily insisted.

She released Nikolas and Milskar. He held on to her hand, kissing it, as he looked over her broken body.

"We have been preparing. We will be ready. Yes, we may lose some, but we are ready—"

"You do not understand!" Emily bellowed. "You will not win. You will not lose some, you will lose all. You must surrender!"

Her voice had become hysterical. Any attempt by Milskar to calm her down was pushed away. He looked at Aura with concern in his eyes. She shook her head infinitesimally. He hugged Nikolas and sent him away with the nanny. This was not something the boy needed to see.

"Emily," Milskar began

"No! No you do not understand, none of you understand!" She backed away from them as if she was a caged animal of some sort.

As if a switch had been flipped inside her brain, she

lunged at Aura and grabbed the front of her shirt. Levi was the first one to reach her. He'd already moved in her direction when he saw the shift in her pupils. He knew something had taken over inside her. Aura cried out in shock, but regained her composure almost immediately as Levi tried to pry Emily's fingers from her clothes.

"Em, Em, let go, it's me, it's Levi," he whispered in her ear.

If she heard him, she gave no indication. Levi noticed her eyes were almost completely black, the blue iris replaced by dark pupil.

"Emily," Aura said in a firm tone. "This is not going to accomplish anything. Let us continue to talk. We will figure this out."

"There is nothing to figure out," Emily said in a robotic tone.

"Help us understand, my darling, help us." Milkar's voice was soft and even as he moved toward her slowly.

"They will kill us all," she whispered. "I have seen what they do, what they are capable of doing. It is more terrible than anything you can imagine. We will not escape it, we will not be able to survive it, but she will offer us mercy! She will spare our lives and the lives of our children if we yield to her. We must yield!"

Aura, Levi, Theirra, and Milskar all looked at one another. Aura called in an aide and asked for them to fetch Calanthe and King Piester.

"Piester is here?" Emily asked.

For some reason this seemed to shock her enough that Aura was able to extricate herself from her grip. Emily made no acknowledgment about the events that had just occurred. Her pupils seemed to be close to their normal size now.

"Yes, his army is helping us. See? I told you, Emily, we are well prepared," Aura said.

"Good, that will be good." Emily acted as if she hadn't heard the last part. "That will make it much easier as you both can surrender. Then his people will not be in danger either. She will not have to march through these lands to get to his."

She paced back and forth while rubbing the hem of her shirt. She mumbled to herself as she took three steps in one direction, turned, and took three steps in the other. It was manic. They all looked at one another again. Milskar looked away.

Moments later, the king and Calanthe entered the room. Emily didn't even introduce herself, just went straight into her tirade. The pair looked taken aback. Calanthe even went so far as to place herself between Emily and her king.

Milskar was beside himself. "Emily," he said. "Emily, calm down. You have to stop this."

He walked up to her and placed his hands upon her shoulders. It was as if an electric shock went through the room.

Emily exploded. "Don't touch me!" she screamed and knelt on the ground. With her hand over her ears, she began rocking back and forth.

"Everyone out," Aura ordered.

They seemed relieved to have the option and also to be told what to do. Both Levi and Milskar hesitated, unsure if the two should be left together again, but Aura insisted that everyone leave. She thought that maybe this was all a little too overwhelming for Emily. Maybe if it was just the two of them, she would be able to get Emily to calm down and think rationally. Plus, Milskar would be just outside if she needed any additional help. For the millionth time she wished for Resbuca.

"Emily," she cooed softly.

Aura sat on the floor next to her, but did not lay a hand

upon her. Emily's only indication that she'd heard was to stop rocking. They stayed this way for several minutes before Aura repeated her name again.

"Emily, I know it may not feel like it, but you are safe here. Just tell us what we can do for you. Tell us what happened. I promise I will do everything in my power to help you."

"There is nothing you can do," Emily said. She raised her face and meet Aura's gaze. "There is nothing you can do but surrender."

"Emily, you know I cannot do that. This is my land, these are my people. I cannot, will not hand them over to that woman. She will destroy them."

"She will destroy them if you do not," Emily said.

"What did you see out there? I have heard stories—" Aura started, but she was cut off.

"The truth is worse than any story or rumor you could have heard."

"They killed those who would not side with them."

"They did not just kill them, they burned them. Tortured them. Killed their children in front of them, in front of—" Emily shuddered. "—me."

"That must have been a terrible thing you went through, but you escaped, you are home. You are safe."

Emily laughed, stood up and began pacing the office again. Aura stood as well. She took measured steps to her desk and leaned against it as she watched Emily move back and forth in front of her.

"I escaped?" Emily laughed again. "Do you think that's what happened?"

"Then what happened?" Aura asked evenly.

"They released me as a warning!" Her voice rose again. "Do you not understand that? They were able to get Levi to return. They took what little information I had and then they had no more direct need of me. She does nothing without planning. I would not have been able to escape. I would have died there if they did not free me."

"We would have saved you."

"Yeah, and how was that going?" Emily said bitterly.

They were quiet for several more minutes.

"Emily," Aura said.

"I know, I know. But Aura." Emily moved closer and grabbed the other woman's hands. Aura flinched, but tried to breathe normally. "This is real. She is going to kill everyone. She will burn this entire place to the ground. It means nothing to her. She only wants to defeat you."

"And what? Do you think she will let everyone else live? Do you think she will let Levi just walk out of here and go home? Emily, you know that is not true. You know we have to fight. If we surrender, there is no telling as to what she will do to all of us. Do you think she will just let us live and go on with our lives?"

"Of course not, I am not a fool." Emily stood again. "But she will let most of us live. She only wants you."

The determination in her voice scared Aura. Was she really suggesting that Aura march herself to Lady Grustmiener's army, surrender herself, so that everyone would get to walk away? If it were that simple, Aura would do it in a heartbeat. Of course, she would. She would gladly give her life if she knew it would secure the lives of her people, but she knew that wasn't the case. She knew the type of person Lady Grustmiener was, and time and isolation would have only strengthened those terrible qualities in her. She'd had a chance to start over, to hide away and try to make a life for herself, but she spent that time gaining an army. She spent that time poised for war, and Aura knew the only thing that would stop her would be success, or death.

"Emily." Aura walked up behind her, "I apprecia⁺

what you are saying, I hear it, but we are going to fight. We are going to do everything in our power to win."

"Then it is all on you," Emily said, turning to face her. "When this whole kingdom is burning, and everyone's charred remains surround you, you will have no one to blame but yourself. There will not be enough water in the world to wash away all the blood you will have on your hands."

With that, Emily left. Aura didn't even hear the door click shut she was so lost in her own thoughts.

Chapter 37

Continued Preparations

Julia's arms and legs felt heavy with exhaustion. They'd trained for hours and, while she wanted nothing more than a hot bath and a warm meal, the way Tab was barking orders at them, she knew neither was in her immediate future.

"Give it a rest, Tab," Galina said in a tired voice.

"Would you like to die then?" he responded.

"Don't be so dramatic." She ignored his protests and lay down.

"Galina's right," Adam said.

"Of course, you think so," Jada said under his breath.

Julia had to stifle a laugh.

"We need a bit of a break," Adam continued. "We've been at this all day."

"Yes, we have," Tab said. "And we still have more work to do. Kalan is finally able to make himself and one other person vanish, but that won't be enough."

Honestly, he was giving Kalan too much credit. While it was true they'd worked to make their powers stronger and to see if they could be transferred and used on others, Kalan was the only one having mild success. The best he was able to do was make himself and Riagan look fuzzy so they blended into the background, but if you looked down you were still able to make out her polka dot socks. After the third attempt Riagan put a stop to it.

"It's too creepy," she said, shivering. "And cold. It's like having ice water poured over your head. Let someone else have a turn."

For Julia's practice, she lifted and lowered a branch. She wasn't entirely sure how helpful this would be, but Tab insisted that she practice using larger and heavier pieces of wood. She soon left the group and ventured to the edge of the woods toward a downed tree. If she concentrated with all of her strength she was able to raise it several inches above the ground before it crashed back down.

"Nice work," a voice said beside her.

A gasp caught in Julia's throat as she turned to face Theirra. The strange bird was perched on her shoulder, staring at Julia with ink black eyes. Theirra smiled almost imperceptibly as if something funny had been said, but then the corners of her mouth returned to their neutral position.

"I—I didn't hear you coming," Julia stammered.

"I find that I sometimes move very quietly through these grounds," Theirra said dreamily. "I often find that people do not hear me coming."

"Right," Julia said. "Well, anyway, is there something I can help you with? Are you looking for Levi? I haven't seen him all morning."

She actually hadn't seen much of anyone all day. There was some buzz going on in the castle. They'd gathered that—well, really Kalan eavesdropped—the missing woman, Levi's cousin, had returned. Jada tried to figure out what was going on and where she'd been, but after a few seconds, he promptly said that he was unable to infiltrate her mind. Julia wondered if he'd told the truth as he'd been silent and appeared deep in thought ever since.

"I am not looking for him," Theirra answered a little sternly.

Julia was not sure what was going on between her, the queen, and Levi, but there was some palpable tension between them. She could feel it each time she was in their presence. She made a mental note to ask Jada about it.

"Then what are you looking for?"

"What makes you think I search for anything? I am making my way to the stables to visit the animals. They are very important in this battle and I want to make sure they are ready. I have asked Kiya to speak to them with me."

As she said this, Julia noticed Kiya extracting herself from the group, to the obvious protests of Tab. While Julia could not hear what was being said, their body language suggested that Tab felt her uses were better served right where she was. In what was probably the first show of defiance toward their self-appointed training, Kiya threw her arms in the air and marched toward Julia and Theirra with a look of frustration on her face.

"I swear, if this war doesn't do it, I may kill him," she said slightly louder than under her breath. If Theirra heard, she made no comment. "See ya, Julia," Kiya said before they walked down the worn path to the stables and left Julia to lift and lower the tree again and again.

After her tenth or so time, the tree suddenly felt like it was encased in cement and she dropped it. She'd being doing it so lackadaisically that it startled her when it was wrenched from her grasp. When she looked around, she saw Levi a few yards from her, jaw fixed in concentration.

Julia's blood boiled. She was tired of being messed

with. She averted her attention, found an even bigger log, threw it into the air, and began moving it to the fallen one. Soon it felt like it had hit a solid wall which quickly encased it. Next she picked up two logs. Logs, branches, rocks—each item she hurled got stuck in the same blockade.

At some point her anger gave way to enjoyment. She alternated between attempts to bring new objects in and adjust the old ones. Once the pile became as tall as her, she could feel the friction in the air melt away. Levi laughed and collapsed next to her.

"Sorry for interrupting your training," he said once he'd regained his composure, "but I needed to try that out on someone who is strong and could challenge me."

Julia was dumbfounded. Strong? No one had ever called her strong. Honestly, she couldn't even remember a time before being coming to this place that she was ever sought after for anything.

"No problem," she tried to say casually.

"Mind practicing with me again tomorrow?"

"Sure."

The words sounded far away as she spoke them, like the world was free and without limits.

Chapter 38

Insurance

L ady Grustmiener had the dream again. They were close. She was sure that, by this time tomorrow, she would be victorious.

The dream started just as it had before. There was the ring of fire, the horse, the king, but this time when she climbed the mountain of bones, they crumbled beneath her, burying her in their burning rubble. Lady Grustmiener awoke with a gasp. She felt the dusty taste of ash on the back of her throat.

A small thread of doubt and panic tried to worm its way into her mind. She needed another safeguard. Surely Emily would not fail. She saw the fear in the woman's eyes placed there by herself and Abaddon and nailed into place by Luther and Unna. She was sure that the woman would succeed, but just in case, she needed something else.

It was still the middle of the night when she exited her tent and made her way to the group of guards that stood not far from it. She spotted Lieal in the distance, as he talked with another group, and decided against placing her orders on him. He'd proved to be quite a useful tool and she did not want to risk him, at least not yet, at least not when they were this close. Instead, she turned to the stockiest man of the group and spoke to him. It was night time and she was not able to make out his face clearly, but his features appeared dark and hooded. She wondered if he was from Omaner or her former lands.

"I have orders for you," she said to the man.

The others melted into the darkness. Apparently, their loyalties were better served in combat and not favors, she thought.

He bowed deeply. "Anything, my lady. My name is Yontel."

"I need you to travel ahead and speak with Queen Aura."

"My lady?" he asked, obviously perplexed by this request.

"I need someone to move quickly. I need you there before day-break tomorrow. The army will take more than a day to move into position, but one person will be able to make it much faster."

"Of course, of course, my lady." While he appeared strong, Yontel quaked in fear. "Why? I mean—" he corrected himself. "—what do you need me to do for you?"

"I need you to bring them a message."

"A message?"

His constant questioning tone started to annoy her, but there was no one left around to ask, and she'd already wasted enough time. She disregarded his hesitation and pressed forward with what she needed. "I need you to speak with Queen Aura and tell her that if she and a man named Levi are to surrender, no battle will need to occur. She can save her people. She must lay down her arms and agree to step down as queen and Levi must surrender himself to me. If they do this, I will allow the people of Esotera to live the rest of their days in peace."

The man seemed stunned by this revelation. He looked at her skeptically.

Anger flared inside her. "It is important that you deliver this message and that she heed your warnings. Tell her of the carnage we have created. Tell her of our great power. Implore her to spare her people."

"And if she refuses?"

A wicked smile spread across Lady Grustmiener's face. "If she refuses, and I expect that she will, your next task is to let it be known that any member of her army who refuses to fight against us will be granted full amnesty and granted safe passage past the battle lines. Their lives will be spared. If they surrender to me, then once the battle is over and I have won, they will be allowed to return to their lands."

"I will tell them," Yontel said and turned to leave.

"And, Yontel."

"Yes, my lady?"

"Let them know that if they do not surrender, if they do indeed intend to fight, we will destroy every last one of them and burn everything they have ever known and loved to the ground. When we are through, there will not even be ashes left for anyone to mourn."

Yontel's face lost any color the moonlight gave him. He nodded curtly and had turned toward where the horses were kept when she stopped him and told him to take one of the griffins instead.

Time was of the essence. With a giant flap of the beast's wings, they were gone.

Lady Grustmiener turned to walk back to her tent but was stopped by a voice right behind her.

"Full amnesty?" Lieal purred.

She smiled and turned to him. "When they come to our side," she said and he snickered, "and they will come. They have heard stories of our conquests for weeks. Once they hear that we will protect them, save them, they will crawl over themselves for the chance."

"So how are we going to house all of these usurpers?"

"Who said anything about housing?"

"If we are giving them forgiveness," Lieal said.

"Who said anything about forgiveness? I do not want traitors in my midst. I do not want deserters. I am looking to rebuild my kingdom. Those who have not joined me yet are not going to be allowed in now with their tails in between their legs."

"So what shall we do with them?"

"We will capture every last one of them and hang their bodies from the trees. There will be no mercy given. Their army will be so terrified, they will prefer to die at their own hands then waiting for ours to do the deed."

"Hang them, my lady?" For the first time Lieal actually looked horrified at what she said.

"Preferably alive. I want their screams to reverberate throughout these woods until they die. I want every man, woman, and child of Esotera to know what their fate is."

She rotated on her heels and went back into her tent, the smile still tugging at her lips, as she lay back down and quickly fell into a dreamless slumber.

Chapter 39

The Visitor

It was so late in the evening, the morning sun had begun to erase the moon, yet the fire in Aura's office burned steadily. She had not slept in almost two days and the exhaustion of their preparations pricked around the rims of her eyes. Each time she blinked, a scratchy pain washed over them. She knew she needed rest, she knew the battle was mere hours away, but there was still so much left to do. She knew the others in the room teetered on the edge as well.

She was about to speak, to break the tension-filled silence, when her office door creaked open and Omire walked through. His clothes were slightly dirty, and he looked tired as well, but equally wonderful to Aura.

"I am sorry it took me so long to arrive, but I needed to ensure that all those who remained in Grustmiener would be hidden and safe. Several hundred did travel with me, I have left them with Amaline," he said in a breathless rush.

"Thank you for coming and securing your people," Aura said as she moved toward him.

Omire took her hands in his and dropped his voice low so only she could hear it. "How are you?"

"Tired," she replied honestly.

"You should be proud of what you have done here," he said, looking firmly into her eyes. Aura nodded and blinked hard against the tears. "We will defeat her," he continued. "We will be done with her once and for all."

An image of her father flooded into her memory. She was young, maybe six or seven, and there had been some conflict that she could no longer remember the details of. Her father had been away for days, dealing with it, and when he'd returned, he looked like ten years had passed. It was late at night and Aura had awoken to him sitting beside her in bed, holding her hands.

"Do you know what the most important job you have as a leader is?" he asked.

She shook her head, still too foggy with sleep to speak.

"You must be strong and trustworthy. People must know that when you make a decision, it is the right one. They must be able to put their faith in you. If you let them down, you will lose them forever."

The room around her came back into focus. She wasn't sure what had sparked such a vivid memory, maybe it was the conviction with which Omire spoke, but—and not for the first time—she was glad he agreed to rule the land of the east.

They turned away from each other and Aura sat at her desk. After he shook hands and was introduced to King Piester and Calanthe, Omire sat in the one empty chair in the room.

Levi was on the floor by the hearth when Omire entered. Aura saw him stiffen, but remain seated. She was relieved that there wasn't going to be another outburst, at least not yet. Calanthe, King Piester, Milskar, and an annoyed looking Theirra sat in chairs around Aura's desk. Attitude or not, Aura was pleased that she'd starting coming to their meetings with more frequency.

Emily resumed her pacing. "We *need* to surrender," she implored for the millionth time.

"Emily," Theirra said with a dagger edge to her voice.

Aura held up a steady hand. She looked over at Omire and said with her eyes that she would fill him in later.

"Emily," Aura said quietly. "I know your position, I know what you went through, but you have to understand that we are not going to surrender. You have to get that train of thought out of your head. If you do not think you can do that and help us with our preparations, I am going to have to ask you to leave."

Emily turned to her with a look of anguish on her face. She then looked over at Levi, begging him with her eyes.

"You're the only one who has seen them—" Levi started.

"I know! Which is why you need to listen me. Which is why we need to surrender."

Theirra stood. "Ugh, not this again."

Aura got up and asked her quietly to stay. She was relieved when Theirra sat back down.

"Emily, I know," Levi said in a measured voice. "But giving up isn't an option, at least not right now. So how about this? You tell us what you know, what their camp is like, who she is traveling with, and once we have all the information, we can decide what we want to do, up to and including surrendering."

Theirra started to protest as soon as Levi stopped speaking, but quieted after he locked eyes with her. Busu, who never seemed to leave her side anymore, also seemed to relax slightly. His feathers had been bristling all day.

"All right." This seemed to temporarily appease Emily. A palpable shift happened in the room as if each of them let out a breath they'd been holding.

"How many people do they have fighting for them?" Calanthe asked.

"I don't know exactly," Emily stated. "The army grew with each town we passed through and captured." She seemed on the verge of slipping back into her previous demands, but clearly thought the better of it, and censored herself. "I would say a couple thousand."

"A couple thousand?" King Piester echoed. "Queen Aura, I think maybe we do need to consider our options here."

"Your help has always been greatly appreciated by my people, but it has also been completely voluntary. You do not need to stay here and fight this war, but know that if you do not, if you go back to your home, she will come after you and your lands," Aura said.

"This is not my battle. This is your war," he protested.

"You are a fool if you actually believe that," Theirra said.

Calanthe shifted in her seat but the king put a hand on her.

"A fool? Do you know who you are talking to?" he asked.

"Theirra—" Aura started.

"No." Theirra cut her off. "It is true. Lady Grustmiener is not going to just stop with our lands. You are kidding yourself if you think that. She is not going to stop until she has our lands, her old lands, and I would not be surprised if her teaming up with King Theaus is a ploy to also gain his lands. It is only a matter of time before she comes after you. You have a better chance fighting against her with us. We are stronger if we are all together. She will come for you."

"Well, I—" he started.

"She isn't going to just stop there," Levi said quietly.

Aura hadn't even registered at first that he'd spoken.

"What do you mean?" Milskar asked.

"Look at what she's after. She wants lands, yes, but she also wants me."

"For revenge, for what you did to her in the past," Emily said.

"We will protect you, Levi, you need not worry," Aura said.

He smiled weakly at her. "I wish it were that simple, but I don't think that's the only reason why she's after me. Why would she stop with this land? Why would she stop with the Four Corners when she could have a chance to rule my world as well? I think she wants them both, I think she wants everything. I don't think she's going to stop until the entire planet is under her rule."

Levi's words hung in the air. Hearing them spoken out loud to this group seemed to give them more weight and meaning. Images flashed through Aura's mind of Lady Grustmiener as she walked through the streets of some city and destroyed everything in her path.

"Our world, too?" Emily asked, breaking the silence with her whispered question.

"I really think so, Em. I don't think it's as simple as us surrendering. I think that's just part of what she wants. I don't think it will stop her. I think it will only move this along faster. Anything we can do to delay it and possibly thwart her must be done. I wonder if what's left of her people and Omaner even know that this is her ultimate plan. I have a feeling she's going to cross them the second she can."

The room fell into silence yet again, then shouts and screams infiltrated the room from outside. Aura felt her blood turn to ice. Had they made it here already? She thought she still had at least a day. She looked over at

Levi and could see her own terror reflected in his eyes.

"I will see," Milskar said and instantly ran from the room. Emily reached for him, but grabbed empty air. Calanthe hurried out seconds later.

There were yells and a great rustling noise. It sounded vaguely familiar to Aura, but she couldn't quite place it. Levi got up and stood by her, clutching her shoulder in his hand. They both jumped when Milskar and Calanthe, along with a half dozen guards, burst through the door. They struggled to restrain a man. Levi began to put himself between Aura and the intruder, but she brushed him aside. Sometimes it was hard to remember that she was a queen and probably didn't need his protection—what little he was actually able to provide.

"What is your business here?" Calanthe demanded.

Strangely it seemed the closer she got to the man, the more King Piester seemed to shrink into the shadows away from her.

"Yontel," the man answered. He appeared to struggle more out of terror than an actual attempt to escape. "My name is Yontel."

"Where are you from, Yontel?" Aura asked.

"O—Omaner. Omaner, my lady—I mean, queen. I mean—" he stuttered.

"Omaner? Are you fighting with Lady Grustmiener then?"

"Yes, my l—lady," he stammered again. "I have a m—message from her."

Aura nodded to the group which held him back. The softened their grips and, all but Milskar, let go. The latter still kept a firm hand on the man's arm.

"What is this message?" she asked.

"Lady Grustmiener asks—I mean demands," the man replied, stumbling over his words again.

It was strange, Aura thought, to see this strong-looking

man reduced to a blubbering contradiction of his appearance.

"That you and a man named Levi surrender to her."

"We have heard these demands. We know what she asks. We decline."

"You do not know what she is capable of!" the man practically shouted.

"We do know, Yontel, but thank you for your concern. My lands and my friends are not a bargaining chip. She will receive neither, willingly or otherwise. We will allow you to return to her, as we have no grievances with you. Please let this be known through your army. We will accept anyone who wishes to surrender. You will be kept safe and allowed to return to your lands at the end of the battle."

"That is my second message. That is the offer she wishes to relay to you," Yontel said to the confusion of the room.

"Offer?" King Piester said as he peered from the shadows.

"Anyone who wishes to cross to her side will be given safe passage. They will be spared. Anyone else—" He hesitated for a moment and then a sudden a rush of confidence ran through him and gave strength to his words. "Anyone who does not wish to surrender will be slaughtered. No one will be spared. You have been warned. You have twenty-four hours. War is coming."

With this last word, he nodded, an indication that what he had come to say was said. He broke from Milskar's grip and the guards escorted him from the room. The loud noise happened again, and Aura looked out the window just in time to see a large, winged half bird-half lion take to the air. She knew the sound was familiar. Thoughts of Kolas came in with the morning light as the griffin departed.

It appeared Theirra thought the same thing because, all of a sudden, she went very still and shrank into herself. Aura swore Busu's feathers seemed to dull, even though the sun illuminated them.

Emily broke the silence. "Told you."

If it weren't for the fear in her voice, she would have almost sounded vindicated.

Chapter 40

Options

W e should at least give people the option," a resigned Aura said.
"You will allow traitors?" Calanthe asked incredulously.

"I will not make, nor do I want, anyone fighting and
possibly dying for me who does not wish to," Aura answered.

"Aura, do you really think that is wise?" Omire asked.

"I am not a leader who forces her people to do her
bidding. I did not think you were that kind of leader either," she said pointedly.

Omire nodded slowly and lowered his head.

King Piester cleared his throat. "I will let my people
know. I imagine a number of them will either want to
travel back to our lands or cross over to neutral territory."

"Yourself included?" Milskar asked.

"Well, I—" He hesitated. "I would like to stay with
my people, show them that everything will be all right.
Yes, I do think I will stay with them."

The breath seemed to deflate out of Calanthe. She'd
never appeared particularly fond of her king, but at this

moment, she looked to be beside herself that he was her ruler.

Aura sensed the shift in the room as well. "I would be most appreciative if you would allow Calanthe to stay with us, that is, if she wishes to." Aura looked over at her. "She has been an asset and I think it will help any of your people who remain to see her, as she has been instrumental in their training."

Calanthe visibly brightened. King Piester agreed before quickly leaving the room.

"Coward," Milskar said under his breath as the door shut.

"Tell me about it," Calanthe whispered back.

Emily stood and made her way to the door as well. She turned back expectantly toward Milskar. The outward marks from her ordeal had started to heal and fade, but it was clear her mental wounds were far from closed. Her outbursts occurred less frequently, but she fidgeted nearly all the time. Some internal battle raged in her as the external one formed around them.

"I will retrieve Nikolas, then are you ready to go?"

"To go?" he asked, confusion washing over his face.

"We are leaving." She didn't plea, she didn't even ask. She stated it as if it was an already decided fact.

"We are doing nothing of the sort," Milskar said as he stood abruptly.

"I have seen—" she started, but he cut her off.

"Yes, you have seen. You have seen what she will do. What? Do you think that she will give asylum to you, me, and our son? Do you think she will allow us to live, those who have twice fought against her? I am not going. *We* are not going." His tone was strong yet measured.

She instantly exploded in a tirade of obscenities. He moved toward her and whisked her from the room. Bits of their conversation traveled with them down the hall.

Aura, Levi, Calanthe, and Theirra all looked awkwardly at one another. None looked like they had slept in ages. Omire, lost in thought, stared out the window. It seemed as if he'd checked out of the conversation completely. He'd brushed off Emily's concerns when Aura had repeated them to him after his arrival. Any continued conversation about it caused him to get quiet and pull back into himself. Aura wasn't sure what his problem was, but it frustrated her that he wouldn't communicate about it.

"We need our rest," Aura said. "Please, at least lay down for a few hours, even if sleep will not come. It may be the last chance we get for a while."

They nodded and made their way to the door. Aura noticed that Levi walked slowly, maybe in the hopes that she would call him back, but she had other matters on her mind.

"Just a moment, Theirra, please," Aura said.

Theirra turned back. Levi locked eyes with Aura who nodded at him and smiled. He said his farewell and left.

She ached for her soft mattress and what little sleep she could gather, but it would have to wait.

"Theirra—" she started.

"I am sorry for the way I spoke to you before, when I saw you…" Theirra trailed off.

"You have nothing to be sorry about. For as long as I have known you, you have always had my best interests and the best interests of this kingdom in mind. And I know, in some matters, you may be smarter than me." The joke hung between them for a moment and Aura hoped that Theirra would receive it.

A smile cracked on Theirra's lips. "Definitely smarter," she agreed.

"I am not distracted," Aura added as she moved to stand in front of her oldest friend. "I know exactly what I am doing and what I am doing it for."

"I believe you," Theirra said as she looked straight into her eyes. "I just…" She trailed off again.

"You have been through some terrible things. I know you are just trying to protect me from going through them as well. But I know we will be successful. I know that we will make it and, when we do, Esotera will be better and stronger than ever. Once the threats against us are extinguished, we will thrive."

The two women smiled at each other and embraced. Aura felt her heart swell. She kissed Theirra lightly on the cheek before her friend left. Aura collapsed onto the sofa by the fire and closed her eyes for what felt like an instant before bright afternoon light pulled them back open.

Chapter 41

Retreat

She will not surrender," Yontel said.

"I did not expect her to."

"But I do believe they will have some that will," he hurried to say, trying to appease her.

She was unmoved. "I am not concerned with the peasant army they have assembled. They will be destroyed either way," Lady Grustmiener said.

"Either way?" he asked.

Lady Grustmiener turned to Lieal and the several men and woman who stood around him. "Anyone who comes, take them into the clearing behind the army. Hold them there. We will take them with us to display them where they can be seen. I want no doubts as to their whereabouts," she ordered.

The group nodded and walked away from her.

"Display them?" Yontel asked with fear in his voice.

"Do you question my authority and my decisions?"

"Never, my lady, never. I just thought you said…" He trailed off.

"Words do little to move me, Yontel. Armies, now armies can move people, but words—" She fluttered her hand. "—they are too light. They float away instantly in the wind. They do not win wars. They are merely instruments to be used, like a sword. Do you have a problem with this?" she asked as she stared daggers through him.

"No, no, my l—lady," he stammered and slowly backed away.

⌀⌀⌀

And come they did. By the hundreds. Men and woman walked through the woods as the sun was high in the sky. Some had carts of animals with them, others had no possessions, no weapons even! She laughed at their foolishness. At their trusting nature. They deserved to die for their stupidity.

In the middle of them—she almost couldn't believe it!—was King Piester, the biggest fool of them all. He wore a gilded crown on his head that looked one size too large—like a child pretending to be a leader.

"Lady Grustmiener," he said as he reached his hand out to her.

Lines of people walked by them headed toward the edge of the patch of forest they stood in. They had walked for hours, but appeared relieved that the end of their journey was in sight.

"King Piester," she said, allowing him to take her hand and kiss it lightly.

He disgusted her. Here he was, a leader, a king, and he was going to surrender. He'd run away from battle like a scared, pathetic creature and hoped that the gold hoop on his head would save him. He was sweaty from exerting himself for probably the first time in his life. It would please her to see him dead and take his lands from his open palms.

They stood there for some time until the last of the

surrendering people had passed them. It must have been close to a thousand she thought. It did not take long for their screams to start filling the air surrounding them.

King Piester looked at her questioningly. Several people began turning back and running toward them, but they were met with a wall of her fighters. Her people had moved into place quietly. She was quite impressed how so many could move so silently. Those who tried to flee back the way they came were cut down immediately. When several realized they were trapped, they knelt down with their hands in the air, the universal sign of surrender. They took little time to fall, as they were already so close to the ground.

"I—I do n—not understand," King Piester stammered as he backed away from her.

Lady Grustmiener advanced slowly on him. "You are all traitors and cowards. What part of this do you not understand?"

He raised his hands, palms toward her. "We were promised. We were told we could surrender."

"And you have, and I appreciate how easy you are making this on us. No unnecessary lives need be wasted."

"You cannot kill me," he said as panic rose in his throat.

"Oh, but I can. What use do I have for a former king?"

Terror washed over his face and he backed up at a quicker pace until he stumbled over a root and fell. His eyes were locked upon hers and his hands still in the air when she brought out her sword and slashed his throat.

The screams around her were quickly muffled. It was evident that her original plan to keep those captured alive was not going to happen. There were too many of them, and it would have been too much to corral them all. She informed several soldiers to tell the others that all those who surrendered should be slaughtered.

For a few minutes, a cry was heard through the trees, strong and pleading, but it soon too was silenced. The forest floor was stained red from their blood. The signs of her victory littered the ground.

"My lady," Lieal said.

She reached forward and wiped a splash of blood from his face. He caught her hand and moved in close to her. She felt the warmth of his breath upon her face. In that moment, she knew he would do anything for her. She leaned in and kissed him deeply.

"Slight change of plans," she whispered into his ear after she pulled away. "Instead of hanging them from the trees, gather the griffins and use them to drop the bodies from the skies. Let their loved ones rain from above. Let them know there is no hope for them."

Chapter 42

Veritas Lux Mea

Aura walked into the forest toward the main camp, flanked by Milskar, Calanthe, and Levi. She was pleased to see that, while she'd heard that soldiers had surrendered to Lady Grustmiener for her promised protection, the numbers who stayed behind were still formidable. Calanthe walked directly next to her, strong and erect. After some initial protests, she agreed to be interim ruler of Vertronum. Aura had a suspicion that the woman had acted in this capacity for some time. Aura had heard rumors throughout the years of the lack of true leadership in the southern kingdom and now felt that maybe Vertronum would have a chance to thrive under Calanthe's guidance.

Milskar, on the other hand, did not appear to have her confidence. Emily begged him not to join the battle. Aura was surprised at how desperate she'd become. While Emily did not have an official capacity in her kingdom, she did support Milskar and taught the local children about the other world. She was well liked and well regarded, but since her time in captivity, she had become crazed. Aura knew this stemmed from whatever Lady

Grustmiener and a man called Abaddon had done to her—based on Levi's reactions when she tried to bring it up to him, nothing good—but it was a distraction, all the same, at a time when they didn't need one.

Aura tried to sympathize with Emily, but found that she just wanted her to take her son and remove herself. Aura would deal with her and her road to recovery when this was over.

Theirra was with The Kids while Amaline and Omire were on the other side of the camp group where most of their people had gathered. Even though the various armies had trained together, they still gravitated toward their original alliances and broke up into small clusters as soon as they were able to.

Aura hoped it would be over soon. Noises from the woods had infiltrated a few hours after those who surrendered had left them. She assumed they were the roar from the other army as they celebrated their good fortune of having less people to fight, but there was a small voice in the back of her head that was worried. As the noises continued, the hairs on the back of her neck rose. She was unable to decipher anything sinister from the sounds to pinpoint why, but there was still something off about their cries. She said a quick prayer, in hopes that those who crossed over found solace and empathy on the other side.

As if some silent cue had gone through the crowds, the soldiers who comprised portions of three of the kingdoms assembled closer to her small entourage. She felt the ground start to tremble around her. The birds went quiet and large, winged beasts could be heard approaching.

"They are starting already? From the skies?" Aura swung her gaze to Milskar. He'd assured her that a foot battle would be the start of this war, based on how Lady Grustmiener had moved her army into position.

"Tell Gustado to ready the dragons now!" Milskar barked at a woman who stood next to him and whom Aura didn't recognize. The woman nodded, quickly mounted a horse, and began dodging people and trees to get to where the dragons were being kept.

"Please do not panic," Aura began, trying to be heard over the din of worried voices, but any further speech was cut off by a scream.

Then, all at once, it was as if the woods exploded. Sounds of crashes reverberated all around them, followed by cries. People began to panic, but unable to find the source of the terror, they stayed frozen in place, eyes wide with fear. Aura felt someone press against her and take her hand. She turned and saw Levi, a calm but urgent look on his face.

"Maybe we should go back toward the castle," he said.

"No, no if the battle is starting, I need to fight, I cannot leave my people," she said.

She opened her mouth to call again to those around her, but her words were stopped short when a crash sounded inches from her. She turned and saw something lying on the ground. It took her a moment for her brain to process what it was, especially since Levi had tugged her backward. She broke free of his grasp and walked toward it. Inches away, she turned back and locked eyes with Milskar.

"A person," she said in a whisper.

He moved up quickly beside her, reached a hand down to touch the body, and confirmed what she already knew—no one could live through this torture bestowed upon them. While the figure's eyes were wide open, the rest of it looked completely alien. Aura realized she kept calling it an "it" as…well, it was impossible to tell if a woman or man lay at her feet. The figure was covered in blood from several deep and terrible gashes. In some places bone was visible through the mutilated flesh. Then, as if it sensed her presence and wanted to assault her with one last horror, the smell reached her nostrils.

She jumped back and covered her mouth. She nearly lost her balance and fell. Another crash to her right presented another body. A few feet from that another. A splash of blood hit her in the forehead and ran down her face. Levi came toward her and wiped it off. Together, they looked skyward and saw a small body stuck in a tree. They moved back quickly. Aura hoped that its size was an indication of how far up it was and not that it was a child.

The thunder of loud wings continued, and Aura started to piece it all together. People rode the griffins and dropped their cargo. From the sounds around her, she suspected that hundreds of bodies were being scattered all over the woods.

"Emily was right," Aura said to Levi quietly.

"I know."

"What else is she right about?" As hard as she tried, it was impossible for her to keep the fear out of her voice.

At that moment another loud crash occurred right behind her. She whirled around and saw a body resting feet from her, its gold crown listing to one side on its bloodied head.

Chapter 43

Old Friends Return

L ady Grustmiener bobbed up and down slightly with each flap of Gilbert's giant golden wings. From her vantage point, she was able to see the figures in the distance and the specks they rained down to the ground. The muffled screams of the inhabitants below floated around her head like songbirds. She closed her eyes and let their cries fill her.

Slowly, she spiraled back down to the ground, pleased with what she saw. Her forces stood poised on the edge of the denser parts of the woods. They had traveled through parts of her old lands to get to this part of Esotera and she felt like it had invigorated her. She had spent so much time on the outskirts of her land or traveling back and forth between Omaner, it comforted her to be near something familiar again. She looked forward to the time when she could reside back in her old quarters in the partially submerged castle in Grustmiener. She knew she had other affairs to put in order before that could happen, but it was nice to have the picture of her home placed firmly in the back of her mind.

Moments later, she heard new screams mix with the

old ones. These appeared closer and she noticed those around her looking up toward the sky. Across the sky streaked a dozen griffins chased by large beasts. It took her several seconds to register that they were dragons. Their tendrils of fire licked the heels of the griffins as their riders cried out in fear. One became engulfed in flames. The man who rode it fell to his death covered in fire. The animal became frantic and flew in such sporadic patterns, he caught another griffin on fire in his terror. Lady Grustmiener heard the pair crash through the forest and finally go still about a mile away. The black smoke rose through the trees and mixed with the coming sunlight.

"March on to Esotera! Forward!" she bellowed at the soldiers behind her and snapped them out of their stupors. "Destroy everyone who fights against you!"

The dragons swooped and turned above them as they moved forward, scorching the tops of the trees, but they were too high up to reach any of those on the ground directly. The canopy also prevented them from getting closer, so while their cries and movement were incredibly loud, she assured those around her that they were safe and could move forward.

It was unfortunate to lose some of the griffins, though she imagined that most would find their way back. They had incredible homing devices. Once they partnered with a person, they had an innate ability to track and find that person again. While some of their handlers would surely be dead, hopefully they would travel back with their comrades and find them. She didn't want to risk taking to the skies again with them still so full of dragons. In the meantime, she still had Gilbert and they marched methodically close to the Esotera castle.

As they continued, a handful of the other griffins had finally returned, some with their handlers and others riderless. Those that could be calmed down joined with the group and began to march in line. Several were so crazed by their experience Lady Grustmiener had them immediately put down. She did not want to risk them falling into enemy hands.

The soldiers behind her did not speak while they marched, yet they made a terrific noise. Just like in her dreams and visions, the ground and trees around them quaked. She wished she could have seen Queen Aura's face as she heard this great swell of people coming toward her to defeat her. Though Lady Grustmiener would soon be satisfied.

She picked up her viewing glasses and combed the enemy line. Even without the magnification, Aura's bright red hair would have made it easy for Lady Grustmiener to pick her out of the crowd, though there was not much of a crowd to speak of, anyway. Lady Grustmiener laughed quietly to herself as she saw their paltry forces. This might be quicker than she could have ever hoped it would take.

She held the griffin back, allowing the troops to flow on either side of her. She was separate from them, and they needed to know this. They didn't need to see her as an ally. They needed to view her as their ruler. She would not fight alongside them—no, she would wage two battles and she would win them both.

∽✑∽

On the other side of the woods, Aura tried to regain her army. She called to those around her to quickly move the bodies. Groups soon assembled with make-shift stretchers, gingerly gathered what remained of those who'd surrendered, and took them away.

The scene was gruesome and she found that she had to

distance herself from it to keep from going crazy. It was all too much to process, but this was not the time. She began to feel the ground quake beneath her again as birds took to the skies, certainly startled out of their trees.

Aura heard the dragons in the distance, their bellows mixed with the noise that swelled around her. It was hard to raise her voice loud enough to be heard over the din. The other army was still a few miles away, though their footsteps were almost deafening. Soon there would be no good way to get orders through the crowds. Quickly she found Kiya in the mass of people and asked her to speak to the jadwiga.

"Please tell them to be available to relay messages. Once the battle begins, it will be difficult to communicate, and their help is critical."

"I will," the girl said and climbed a tree where several of the giant birds watched the commotion below them with almost amused expressions.

Aura turned to Levi. "Where will you be?"

"Right where you are," he said without hesitation.

She smiled at him. "Levi."

"I'm not leaving you."

She looked around nervously. "I need your help securing the castle, making sure no one can infiltrate the grounds. It is imperative to keep it safe. Can you guard it for me? With your powers, you will be able to do more than twenty soldiers, and I do not think I can spare a single one." She found that she had to raise her voice to be heard, even though he stood right beside her.

"What about you?" he asked, worried.

She reached up and kissed him lightly. "I will be fine. We have done this before, and we will be victorious again. I will meet you as soon as the battle is over, and if you need to get in touch with me, use the birds," she said and pointed up to the branches above them.

He kissed her once more, but this time it was not soft. He felt her press her body into his as he gripped her tightly. With the utmost restraint, they pulled apart. He moved away from her and motioned for Julia to follow him. Between both of their powers, Aura hoped the pair of them could do what she asked.

At that moment, the sound of branches and leaves breaking snapped her around. Her breath caught in her throat as she beheld the sight in front of her. Three dozen horses, all various colors and sizes stood with flared nostrils. Their necks glistened with sweat even in the cool morning air. They must have traveled a long distance to be here. Aura wasn't even sure from where exactly they'd come. Amongst the other horses, Serenity looked pleased with herself. Aura recognized several of them as mounts of fallen soldiers and former members of her and her father's counsel. As if reading her question, from the middle of them an old white mare made her way toward the queen. It had been many years since Aura had laid eyes on this horse, and the memories of that day flooded back to her. Of her and Theirra as they walked to the edge of the castle grounds and removed the mare's halter. Of thanking her for her service before they set her free.

Alcippe, as strong and mighty as she looked the last time Aura had seen her leading her father's funeral procession, marched right up to her. Aura reached out a hand to touch the soft gray velvet of her nose before burying her head in the horse's long mane.

"Thank you, sweet strong girl. Thank you for coming back. You did not have to. You have done your service to this kingdom." She pulled back and addressed the others. "Each of you have done your service to this kingdom and I thank you for returning. You have no idea what your presence means to me."

Kiya appeared next to Aura. "She says they traveled

for many days to get here and that your father tasked her with protecting you and this land. They are fulfilling promises from their people. They are a proud group," Ki-ya said, unable to hide a smile, despite the chaos.

"Do what you can, help where you think you are able," Aura said.

She gave Alcippe one last pat and the mare took off with a squeal in the direction of the oncoming army.

Aura said a silent prayer that the horses would be safe, but especially the one who held her father's heart for so many years.

Chapter 44

The Battle Begins Again

Aura had to push the memories out of her mind of the last time she was in this position. *It is going to be different this time*, she told herself. She knew her army was larger and better prepared than before but, still, she was shaken. The thought of those bodies that fell from the sky made goose pimples rise on her skin. What was Lady Grustmiener capable of? Aura thought she had known the answer to that, but now she questioned her prior assumptions.

As she turned to her left, she had to remind herself that she sent Levi away. While the guise may have been a real one—she did feel that he had the best chance to protect the castle with the least amount of reinforcements—she felt better knowing he was out of direct danger. While she wished he could be next to her to give her strength, it was easier for her to concentrate without him there.

The ground now trembled with greater force. She felt it like a secondary heartbeat in her chest. She saw Milskar standing a few yards from her, and they made eye contact before they focused their attention forward.

Aura wished for a happy outcome for him. The last

few weeks had been so hard on him, and instead of the relief the return of Emily should have brought, it seemed to bring a new kind of pain into his being.

The moments of doubt were behind her, but in her daydreams she would have been able to surrender and walk proudly and quietly to her death as she spared all those around her. Those gruesome bodies, some of which were impossible to clean up completely from the forest floor, reiterated that she'd made the right decision to fight on. Milskar was right. There was no way Lady Grustmiener would have upheld her promise and spared those Aura left behind.

In the distance, Aura could just make out specks as they emerged from the trees. Her heart raced and she gripped her sword tighter. This was it. Soon all this strife would be over and her and her people could live the rest of their days in peace. She prayed to the spirit of her father to look over them and end this war favorably and quickly.

She saw a huge golden griffin standing away from the other fighters as it was struck by its rider. Why was it separated from the rest? Suddenly, it morphed into a blur. It reared up and spun, throwing its rider. Aura watched the fallen figure grab some sort of weapon and throw it after the beast. She hoped the object missed.

Aura stood in shock as the giant winged lion charged right for her. Her terror quickly turned to joy, but then she heard the cries of those around her.

"No!" she yelled at the pair of archers pulling their bows back. "No, do not harm him! He is not an enemy!"

Her last word came out in a rush as Gilbert nearly ran her over. She stroked his neck and chest as the beast flapped its wings in a clear display of joy, dancing around her.

"Gilbert, Gilbert." She laughed. "Shh. Oh, I am so glad to see you!"

The forest seemed to go still. The griffin stood like a statue and stared slightly off in the distance. Aura looked behind her and followed his gaze. She saw Theirra, her expression frozen. In two giant steps, Gilbert repeated the same gestures to her, and Aura had to turn away, unable to stand the tears pouring down her friend's face.

It took her by surprise to see how close the Omaner and partial Grustmiener army was to her now. Aura had forgotten that time had not actually stopped while their little reunion had happened.

"The time has come!" She turned and addressed those who could hear her. "Defend your lands, defend your people, and defend your future!"

With Milskar in the lead, they began to march forward to meet whatever fate might have in store for them.

Chapter 45

The First of Many Days

J ulia thought the woods had been loud before, but now they simply exploded. It took all the willpower she had to not cover her ears.

Levi had brought the two of them closer to the castle grounds, but almost as soon as he gave her the rundown of what they were supposed to do, he disappeared. She was left alone with the sounds, a giant white bird, and what remained of a single body, overlooked by the initial clean-up crews. It was impossible not to stare at it, even though it turned her stomach. She was fascinated by the connective tissue and shocks of white bone, though she tried not to look at the eyes, still open as if caught in eternal surprise at what had happened.

A large explosion, followed by a scream, snapped her back to attention. She began moving some fallen trees to form a bit of a barrier through the most obvious paths. Julia thought it was curious that this castle did not seem very well fortressed, but from the indications she had gotten from the townspeople and whatever truth could be gleaned from Levi's book, being attacked was never a concern when the structure behind her was constructed.

After what seemed like an hour, she began to grow bored and moved deeper into the woods under the pretense that she was looking for more trees. The bird opened its wings, but she told it to stay. It must have understood her because it rested back down.

While the main fighting was clearly a few miles or more away from her, the noise of it still made her occasionally jump. She was torn, part of her wanted to be in the thick of battle, to play the hero and save the day, but another—probably larger—part of her was grateful she didn't actually have to risk her life. When it came down to it, she feared she didn't actually have any fight in her.

As if to call her bluff, a boy not much older than her appeared. They both froze, the boy held a simple rock and Julia had a tree trunk raised about a foot off the ground. They stared at one another, trying to figure out what each wanted to do.

"What side are you on?" the boy said. Once he spoke he seemed even younger.

"I—I don't know. I am with Queen Aura." Julia hoped this answer was the correct one.

She would never know for sure, but the boy nodded and seemed to vanish back from where he came. Did he spare her because they were on the same side, or because it was clear neither wanted to kill the other? Julia began to make her way back to the castle grounds where she was supposed to be. If nothing else, the encounter seemed to reiterate what she struggled with. There was no way she could kill a person.

ເ/ɔℰ/ɔ

Killing didn't seem to be an issue for those in the thick of the fighting. In only moments, sheer chaos rattled around the trees. Humans and animals alike fought, screamed, and, in some cases, died. At times, it was difficult to tell who was from which army. While Aura's forces appeared better dressed and fed than Lady Grustmiener's, Aura still feared that some of these casualties would be by their counterparts' hands. She started to weave her way back from the main fighting, trying to get a handle of what was happening around her.

The combat seemed to go for hours and, still, it did not look like the entirety of the opposing army had reached them. While both sides dispersed, as individuals were locked in battle, rows of new fighters seemed to constantly push in. Aura wondered, for the first time, how possible it was going to be to actually win this.

"There are so many of them," an out of breath Milskar said.

"We are strong," Aura responded, without looking in his direction.

"Thank goodness for that."

She turned toward him, but he was already gone. A sound reached her left ear and she whirled just in time to see a woman streaking toward her. In more of a reflex then with actual intention, Aura brought her sword around. She barely felt the resistance as it made contact, but the woman crumbled to the ground in front of her and moved no more.

The battle went into the early night before each side began to retreat. While the moon did give off its bright blue light, it was not enough to fight with any effectiveness. It was clear each side was breaking for the day.

This also gave the healing crews time to gather those injured, and also remove those who had died. Aura was not sure where they took all those bodies, probably to the same place as the ones who had dropped from the sky, but she was glad that it was not in sight of the living. Just like last time, there would be time to mourn and they would give appropriate thanks to those who made the ultimate sacrifice, but like so much else, this was not the time for such luxuries.

It wasn't until she had made it back to the castle grounds that Aura realized how the day had worn on her. Every inch of her body ached, and she realized that a deep cut ran the length of her left arm. She didn't even remember being hit, but it was clotted over, an indication it wasn't a particularly fresh wound.

She spotted Levi as he stood with the smallest of the hybrid children and was pleased to know he had listened to her wishes. Though the closer she got to him and was able to see stray cuts and a blackened eye, she wondered how accurately he'd followed her orders.

She was about to say something, but he rushed forward and enveloped her in a hug. It was slightly tighter than her aching body could handle, and while she made a slight noise of discomfort, he made no attempt to loosen his grip. When he seemed convinced that she was alive and standing before him, he let her go. He touched her injured arm, but she shook her head.

Aura began to walk around and speak with various people, including Milskar, Calanthe, Omire, Theirra, and Gustado. She was relieved to see they had made it safely through the first day of battle. It appeared that most of the animals had made it through all right as well. Tears sprang to her eye when she saw Netty and Alcippe grazing together, but she did not want to bother their peace with her emotions. As she made her way through the crowd, she encouraged those she saw to sleep or at least rest as much as they could.

A healer came over to her and, while she initially brushed the man away, he insisted.

"It scares them to see you injured," the man whispered.

Aura nodded, allowing him to clean and bandage her arm and wipe several spots off her face.

Long after the sun went down, Aura made it back to Levi and the two lay on the ground in the open air.

The next two days went in similar fashion, though their forces who regrouped each night seemed to get smaller and the healers worked harder to keep them in one piece. Aura was completely exhausted. She had not slept more than a few hours in days, but it was difficult for her to calm herself and let slumber take over.

"You need sleep," Levi said into her hair on the third night.

"I do not know if I can."

"You rest, I will stay up," he said. She protested but he quieted her. "I got some sleep last night. I'll let you get a few hours then wake you up so we can switch."

She relented and laid her head on his chest. She fell asleep to one of the greatest sounds known to humans, the beating heart of the person you love.

Chapter 46

Fight to the End

It was just before dawn when Aura awoke. Levi had slept little that night. He'd been so transfixed with how her mouth parted slightly as she breathed that she caught him by surprise when she stirred. He smiled at her and kissed her forehead.

"How long did I sleep?" she asked in a panic as she propped herself up on her elbow and looked around.

"You slept, don't worry. Nothing happened If something had, I would have woken you up." He kissed her again, but it was difficult as she moved to get up.

Those around them also started to awaken. Moans escaped tired lips, and everyone moved a little slower than they had in the days prior. Levi hoped the fighting would be done today. He was not sure how much more they could take. He tried to keep his participation to a minimum but, after five days of battle, found it increasingly harder to do.

When the blended army finally made their way into the woods, Levi kissed Aura one more time and made his empty promise to stay put. Moments later, he nodded to Julia and followed the stragglers.

If the days had weakened their side, it seemed to have rejuvenated the other. Levi could not understand how they seemed so fresh and so uninjured. Maybe they had so many soldiers they had substitutions when one got too tired or hurt. It was the only explanation as to why they were still able to fight at such a high level of intensity.

He'd tried to stay close to the castle, so he avoided the worst of the fighting, but there were still so many he'd battled. He knew if Aura discovered he'd disobeyed her, she'd be furious, but he couldn't just stand by and let her risk her life alone.

He'd gotten better with his sword and was able to kill a man a little larger than him before a man and woman descended upon him. Levi thrashed with his weapon, but it was clear he was badly out skilled as well as being out numbered. He was able to force his concentration and push them both away, momentarily, which gave him just enough time to sever a large tree branch above them and crush both fighters.

He'd never truly mastered fighting in both medians at the same time. He could do either a physical or magical move, but frustratingly never together. He was glad that he'd worked on his sword skills, though. It was too dangerous to drop trees and branches in close quarters. He risked killing himself along with his enemy.

Then just as quickly as that pair was neutralized, another man approached him. Their skills seemed to be more closely matched and their swords clanged in a hypnotic rhythm as others moved around him. He was so engrossed he did not even notice who those others were.

⌖

Lady Grustmiener saw him as he stood in the distance. It amazed her how the human eye worked. All the movement around her, but she was able to pick up on this one figure and hone in on him. It was as if the gods had willed their meeting to happen and a path opened up in front of her. It was as if she'd parted some invisible sea. People and animals brushed softly away from her. They didn't seem to notice her, yet some innate force compelled them to move out of her way. She had never felt more powerful, or more deadly, in her life.

Levi had not seen her. He fought some unnamed man from some unnamed kingdom. Lady Grustmiener did not recognize the fighter, but he could have easily been from her lands. She never felt it worth her time to get to learn their names or faces. These people around her were as replaceable as the animals she rounded up, and worth just as much to her. If one fell, her only sadness was from the realization that it meant one less body to fight on her behalf. Her rule over these lands would be absolute. It was almost time to claim her throne.

It had been a number of years since Lady Grustmiener had laid eyes on the boy, who now she had to admit, looked more like a man. Soon he would be nothing, though. Soon he would be a pile of blood, tissue, and bone ready to decay and be swallowed up by the earth. Her earth. Every bit of it hers. She wanted to run to him in her excitement and finish him, but she forced herself to walk forward calmly. There was no need to rush. He was not going anywhere, and she wanted to savor each moment leading up to his death.

The man Levi battled fell backward, though it did not look like he had been struck directly, and apparently hit his head on a rock before he went still. Levi panted from the effort, but seemed in control. He was looking around for his next foe when his eyes locked on to hers.

It was as if the world opened up and enclosed the two of them. Time and sound seemed to stop. The one thing that felt real to her was the rhythmic beat of her heart in her chest and her feet on the ground as they brought her closer to her destiny.

Her spear was clutched tight and steady in her hand. She was an exceptionally good fighter and walked forward with purpose, secure in that knowledge. A wisp of fear seemed to pass over Levi's eyes, and she had to fight the urge to smile at him. It felt delicious to her, like she could eat this moment and live off its energy for the rest of her days.

"You will not win this war," Levi said. His voice, while shaky, seemed to boom and reverberate all around her.

"I will win more than this war," she said, not able to keep the smile out of her voice. "I will win everything."

"You're wrong."

"Ha!" she barked and the sound was so strange and foreign in her throat it was almost painful.

A vine reached up from the earth and tried to entwine her foot. She expertly cut it away without having to change her stride in the slightest.

"Finally figured out how to use those powers?" she asked.

"I think your late husband can attest to that."

Anger flared in her. She wanted nothing more but to rip his throat out and hold it up as a trophy for those who defied her. How dare he speak of the late king in such terms? She slowed her breath and heartbeat. This was not the time to get emotional. She needed to stay focused. Again she felt the underbrush try to root her in place.

"Is this the one thing you know how to do?" she asked bored. A tree branch fell in front of her and she had to half dive to get out of its way.

"Better?" he asked.

She noticed he held a sword, but at such an awkward

angle, as if he feared it might turn into a serpent at any moment. He didn't seem comfortable with his movements. She knew she could defeat him.

She silently ran around the tree, twenty or so steps left of him. The advance took Levi by surprise and she was able to get in a blow to his arm before he was even able to raise it toward her. He stumbled back and again she had to bite down the urge to laugh.

Quicker than she'd anticipated, he recovered and came at her with the sword. She blocked him several times and was again able to strike him, though this time the edge of his blade was able to make contact with her forearm. Pain blazed through her arm. She saw a flash a blood spray and settle on the ground beside her. All that existed to her now was Levi and her desire to kill him.

She let out a deep animalistic yell and exploded forward at him, though it seemed like each shot she made he deflected until they were caught in a sort of give and take dance. If anyone around them had noticed the singular battle, they made no indication. Back and forth she and Levi went as exhaustion set into her bones. For a fleeting moment, she wondered if this stupid boy, this man from another world would kill her. It did not make sense. In all of her dreams, she was always victorious. The signs were constantly there. They told her that she would prevail. This could not happen. He could not beat her.

It seemed as though these thoughts ran through Levi's head as well because he seemed to fight with new vigor as her defenses waned. Now it was his turn to have the slight smile on his face, his turn to envision what life would be like when he defeated her. She would not give him the satisfaction.

He looked to his left as something caught his eye. For a moment, she followed his gaze. There at the edge of the line of trees they were in stood Emily. It would be fitting that her presence would bring the death of Levi. Lady Grustmiener was pleased to know this would be his downfall. She'd learned that it was Emily, all those years ago, who had thwarted her plans when Emily undid the great work Abaddon had accomplished and brought Levi back to his senses. This would be sweet retribution.

Lady Grustmiener turned and plunged her spear deep into his chest. The shock registered on his face a second later as he broke eye contact with Emily. Levi's heart tried desperately to beat around the foreign object which now resided in his body. Time seemed to slow. His shallow breaths sounded wet and weak in her ears. Lady Grustmiener smiled broadly. This was it. His end would be the beginning of everything for her. She turned away from him and took her spear, still wet from his blood, with her. He deserved no more of her attention. She now had other things to occupy her thoughts and time. She no longer had just a kingdom, but an entire world to rule. She laughed as she strode away.

ৰৰ

Levi fell back upon the ground and was thankful for the softened Earth. It felt so comfortable, and he thought it a nice place to rest for a few moments. He was so tired. His arms ached from fighting. *Just a second.* He told himself. He would rest for just a second and then get up and would continue to fight.

He wondered where Aura was. He hoped she was far away. She'd be so worried if she saw him like this. He would rest for a moment then walk back to the castle to get cleaned up before she saw him. He'd tell her about seeing Lady Grustmiener, he'd point to where she went, and together they'd defeat her, once and for all.

Just a moment. He would rest for just a moment more.

He took several more gasping breaths and then, for the last time, as his eyes drank in what was left of the afternoon sun, he exhaled in one final push. Levi died as a distant scream, mingled with a far off laugh, pulled him out of the world.

Chapter 47

Life and Death

It was as if Emily's world had opened up in a chasm around her—as if her soul was the Earth itself and was now being split in two. She strangled a scream as she watched Lady Grustmiener walk away. The woman laughed, a high-pitched cackle. As she disappeared out of sight, Emily ran as fast as she could to the fallen figure.

Levi was crumpled on the ground. Blood dripped from his partially opened lips, but no movement came. She could not take her eyes away from his fallen body and willed it to do something. Anything. She ignored the blood as it pooled all around him, his shirt soaked with the thick liquid.

'*Move!*' She screamed in her head. '*Don't be dead.*'

A boy, no more than a teenager, darted past her. His look was dazed, yet determined somehow.

"Help him," Emily heard herself say, though she felt disconnected from her body, as if she floated above it. As if she was back in that chamber from hell, trying to find any way to just live. Any way to make it back to those she loved, one of whom lay motionless in front of her.

The boy placed his hands on Levi's chest and a soft

light seemed to pass between them. The boy shook un-controllably and broke away several times, panting for air. Emily was transfixed.

"If anyone can save him, Adam can. I know he can," another boy said.

It was as if he'd appeared out of nowhere. The pair seemed like apparitions. Maybe they were angels? Maybe she was losing her mind once and for all. Though she wished so badly that they would be able to help, she didn't question them. She just wanted the boy to be tell-ing the truth.

A pulse ran through the ground like a sonic boom. Something shifted in Emily. She looked at the dirt be-neath her feet and couldn't quite place where the sensa-tion had come from.

The boy tugged on her arm and dragged her forward. "We have to help them. We have to get Levi and Adam out of here. They are both too weak to stay."

Emily couldn't compute what just happened. In front of her, the other boy, the one named Adam, was slumped on the ground and, for a moment, she thought that he might also be dead. But she saw a small movement, shal-low breaths that assured her he was not. She looked over at Levi and he had the same shaken movement. The blood that previously pumped so freely from his neck, chest, and arm had stopped, the wounds glued back to-gether somehow. She didn't understand.

"Here, help me lift them. I need your help," the boy next to her pleaded. "You help Adam, I'll get Levi. Here, take my hand."

Before she even knew what her body was doing, she had Adam around her shoulders and took the other boy's hand. The boy carried Levi but she still was unable to make sense of what had occurred. A cold sensation passed over her at his touch. She looked around as they walked forward and noticed that no one met their eyes or glanced in their direction as they moved through the scattered fighters. Although she did not know exactly what had happened, she knew somehow that they had become invisible to those around them.

"Just keep holding on," the boy said.

Emily held on tighter than she ever had to anything in her life.

They picked their way through the woods and, while she knew the war was still going on and heard all the sounds of battle around her, it was as if she wore earplugs that softly muffed the noise. She was so tired. All she wanted to do was sit down and rest. The boy must have sensed her slowing down.

"Don't let go of my hand!" he yelled and the great noise of his voice shocked her into compliance. "We are almost there. You can't let go of my hand!"

It seemed to take a lifetime to get to the castle, but it mercifully appeared before them. Emily felt herself hesitate for a moment before she was pulled forward. Her heart tugged in three distinct directions. She knew she needed to stay where she was for Levi's sake, but she also knew that somewhere in that place held her son, and somewhere on the grounds held Milskar. She knew the latter would be fighting. Nothing would keep him from always trying to save the world, and her.

There had been a change in Milskar, in both Milskar and Nikolas actually. It was subtle. Emily could barely put her finger on it, but it was as if something were permanently out of reach for the both of them. As if they looked at her, but weren't prepared to accept that she was really back with them. She knew it must have been hard, impossibly hard, when she was away, but it was difficult for her, too. Her scars were more visible than theirs, but both sets were just as real, and she housed hidden scars as well. She would awake in the middle of the night in a cold sweat and trembling so violently she was afraid it would wake Milskar up. It would take her several moments to remember where she was. To remember that her husband slept next to her, and that she was safe. But was she really safe? The battle had been brought to her home. She'd had a chance to stop it, but she failed. She failed, and now people around her were dead and dying.

It was difficult not to conjure up the images of seven years ago. Of that first battle and the blood and lives lost there. She had been so young then, yet she had tried so hard to fight, to make Milskar proud of her. Now here she was, scared to even participate, a small part of her relieved that she now had this excuse to return to the castle and away from the fighting.

They brought Levi through the castle doors and into the first room they came to. It took Emily a second to realize this was her old office. There was a long table which stood in the middle of the room. Emily and the boy helped placed the two unresponsive bodies upon it.

"What happened? Are they going to be all right?" she asked, worry filling her mind and words.

Levi still hadn't moved and neither had Adam.

"I don't know," the boy answered, obviously scared. "I think something happened when Adam saved him. I— it's the first time I saw him try to save a person who was actually dead. At least, I think Levi was dead. He looked it."

As if to refute what the boy said, Levi let out a soft moan. Adam lay perfectly still.

Emily wasn't sure what the boy had said. She'd heard about the group Theirra brought with her, but hadn't spent any time with them. She had been so busy as she recovered, and tried to convince everyone to surrender, that she did not have much time to socialize. From what little she had gathered over the last several days, they had some type of powers, sort of like Levi, but she didn't know what they were. Obviously, Adam was able to bring people back from the dead or fix any wound, but she wasn't sure what the boy meant by his statement.

"What?" she said.

"Kalan," he answered her unformed question. "My name is Kalan"

"What do we do now?" she asked him.

"We can go back out, continue to fight. Hope these two come out of it on their own?"

They stared at each other. As if to make part of the decision for them, Levi sat bolt upright. He took wild, gasping breaths. His eyes flashed between Kalan, Emily, and came to rest on Adam. This seemed to explain something to him, and he began to slow his breath.

"What happened?" he asked in a halted tone.

"She killed you," Emily said as she fought back tears, moved closer to him, and took his hand. "I swear I saw Lady Grustmiener kill you with my own eyes, but then this boy, Adam, laid his hands on you and…and…I don't know. All of a sudden, you're here." She gingerly threw her arms around him, careful not to hurt him, in case he was still injured. "But now I don't know what is wrong with him. I think, I think he may be dying."

She released Levi and they looked over at Adam, who lay so still upon the table. Levi moved slowly, swinging his legs until his feet made contact with the floor, and shakily stood. Emily moved to help him, but he waved her away.

"No, I feel fine. A little short of breath and sore, but I really do feel okay."

They all moved closer to Adam. Levi placed his hands on the boy's neck and wrist. He looked up at Kalan and shook his head.

"He's gone?" Kalan asked.

"I think he gave his life for me. But how, why? I didn't think he could bring someone back."

"Maybe he never really tried, maybe he feared this would happen," Kalan said. Levi looked distraught. Kalan shook his head. "He believed in this cause. He didn't do anything he didn't want to do, I'm sure of it."

"I just talked to him about this yesterday," Levi said. "Adam was practicing on several small animals and had worked his way up to a more complicated creatures like erons, but he seemed out of it after the animal got up on shaky legs moments after I broke its neck. He said he got so weak raising something small, he didn't ever think he could do something large. He didn't know if he could handle it. I told him not to worry."

He lowered his face into this hands and spoke through his fingers. "I said 'When the time comes, you will be able to help exactly as needed, I'm sure of it.' What have I done?"

Emily placed a hand on him and he lifted his face. His look of anguish pained her.

"You thought you were helping him, supporting him," she said.

"Did I encourage Adam to risk his life? He couldn't have thought I meant that? I never, though, never thought this could happen."

"Of course not," Emily said. "I am sure he did what he thought was right."

"Adam wanted to help," Kalan said. "I know he did. Help however he could."

A large crash from outside brought the three back to the present. Though it sounded miles away, it still shook the glass in the windows.

"I need to go back out there," Levi said.

"That's insane," Emily said. "You were dead, Levi.

You died. Please do not go back out there. You can only be lucky so many times."

"I need to go back out there. Aura, Milskar, the rest of them. I can't leave them out there. I have to fight. I can't let Adam die in vain."

They stared at each other for what felt like an eternity.

"All right then," she said. "Let's go."

Levi smiled at her. The three looked at Adam one more time before walking out the door and back to the castle grounds, wherever their fates would lead them.

Chapter 48

Kolas

Theirra was exhausted yet exhilarated at the same time. She could hear her blood pump in her body like a river as it rushed past her ears. She felt more alive than she had in, what, months? Years? Perhaps even more? Her arms trembled from the weight of the spear she held as blood dripped from its sharpened point. She couldn't even remember how all of it got on there. Flashes came at her, men and women ran toward her in fits of rage and then crumbled easily to the ground just steps in front of her. It was as if she hadn't even caused the deaths, as if the spear acted of its own accord.

Busu flew above her as she walked deeper into the forest. She heard clashes around her but didn't see any new foes in her sight line. She was wondering how much longer the fighting would go on when a young woman crossed her path. For a second Theirra was struck by her sheer beauty. She looked so young! What was this pretty young girl doing here in the middle of the woods with a sword in her hand and vengeance in her eyes?

The girl took one look at Theirra and smiled so coldly, Theirra swore she felt hands wrap around her heart. Then just as quickly the girl disappeared behind a tree. Busu landed on Theirra's shoulder, and she had to adjust her weight to the heft of the bird. He stared at her and squawked loudly in her ear before flying off to where the girl went. Theirra sighed. She didn't want to have to kill this girl but, just like with the others, she found herself walking forward, spear outstretched in front of her.

A figure moved out from behind the tree, holding a limp form of brilliantly colored feathers. Theirra froze in mid-step. It was as if all the air had been removed from the world.

"My love," Kolas's sweet voice floated to her. He dropped Busu to the ground. The bird didn't move.

"Kolas?" The words were like snowflakes on her lips, so light and quickly melting into oblivion. "Kolas, I do not—" But words failed her as he moved toward her.

"My love," he repeated, his voice an octave higher than she remember it. Funny what time did to memories.

He walked so slowly toward her, as if he was almost afraid of her, afraid that her out-stretched spear was intended for him. She looked and, the next thing she knew, her weapon was on the ground, though she could not remember having put it there. Why did he walk so slowly? She wanted to scream at him to hurry up and kiss her and hug her. Forget the war going on around them. Damn it all, damn everything else in the world except for the two of them. She could not move and cursed her rooted feet.

He finally reached her, and it took all of Theirra's resolve not to throw herself at him. She reached her arm out and touch his face lightly with her hand.

"I thought," she began, "I thought I would never see you again. I thought I would have to go through the rest of existence and never lay my eyes upon yours again."

Tears poured out of her, and it was difficult to see him clearly. An almost pained expression filled his eyes. Remorse? Regret? For what, for leaving her? She forgave him. She forgave him a million times over.

He could do anything to her, and she would forgive him, just to have him back. Nothing else mattered. He opened his arms a little farther and she was sure the long awaited embrace was about to come. She opened her arms too and clung to him as she sobbed and clawed at his back and neck in an attempt to bring him even closer to her.

He backed away from her and she saw her own hurt reflected in his eyes. Why did he back away? Why did it seem like he was about to leave?

"Don't go!" She wanted to yell, but was surprised when she realized that she couldn't talk.

She tried to step forward, but found she somehow now sat on the forest floor.

He had tears in his eyes. She looked down at her hands and found them covered in the brightest red paint she had even seen.

That sent another round of confusion through her, which ebbed once the pain registered fast and hard.

She looked down again and saw that it was not red paint covering her hands, and her chest, and the ground around her. It was her life, her blood, which surrounded her. Theirra looked up at Kolas, the pain in his eyes enough to break the hearts of every human and creature on the planet.

"I am sorry, my love," Kolas said, as his form slowly started to shift and change before her.

Theirra tried to focus, tried to understand how the pretty girl was in front of her once more.

"I am sorry, my love." The girl now repeated the same lines, her voice the same deepness as Kolas's had been.

Theirra opened her mouth once more, but was only able to take one last breath. The same air that had filled her lungs when she was born and took her first, shaky breaths escorted her out of her life just as easily.

෬ාො

Unna collapsed on the ground when the woman in front of her slumped to the side. Her eyes stared unblinking in Unna's direction. What had she just done? She had looked into that woman's heart and had seen only pain, anger, and darkness, but buried somewhere deep inside was this light. This warm place of love with a single image enclosed in it.

When the woman caught sight of her in her transformed state, Unna received a look she had never seen before, pure and unadulterated happiness. This stranger who had stood before her loved this person so much that all the darkness, all the hurt that had surrounded her whole being evaporated. It took everything in Unna to kill the woman, to use the instrument of this person she loved against her. Unna knew this was the price of war, but as she looked around, she realized she didn't want to pay it anymore. She couldn't even remember how she got to this place, how she wound up fighting in some war, literally a world away from her own home.

Unna got up slowly. She left her sword, still stained crimson, on the ground. She was turning to leave when a guttural scream reverberated behind her. A woman with long red hair ran up on her.

Unna was dead before she even fully comprehended what had happened. She didn't even put a hand up to shield herself when the fatal blow crashed down upon her.

Chapter 49

Regrouping

L evi, Emily, and Kalan exited the castle and walked toward the woods and the sounds of the battle. It reverberated around them and made it difficult to pinpoint exactly where it was located. A few yards away, they saw a small figure as it moved toward them. Out of the dusk walked Jada. It was hard to make him out at first. his skin almost blended into the background. He reminded Levi of paintings he had seen of Native Americans at the history museum he visited on class trips. Jada looked so strong and stoic, but as he got closer, Levi could see the fear on his face.

"I saw you here, I thought, I thought maybe we were done fighting," he said with hope in his voice as he reached them.

"I'm afraid this is far from being over," Levi said apologetically, "though really, if you don't want to do this anymore, just go back to the castle. I think you will be safe there."

Jada's shoulders sagged slightly, but he shook his head.

"I know what you can do to help us," Levi said. Jada

brightened at the prospect of usefulness. "We need to know where everyone is," Levi continued. "Can you see them?"

Jada seemed to zone out momentarily. When he spoke, he sounded far away. "Kiya, she's with a griffin. It appears she has met one that knows of this place. She is trying to convince it to make the others switch to our side."

Could it be? Levi wondered.

"Galina." Jada smiled slightly. "She just washed away a group that was trying to cross the river. But wait—" He frowned in concentration. "I think she's heading here as well. I think she saw me walking this way. Yes, she's coming here. Tab and Riagan are close to one another, and they are with Milskar."

Emily made a catching sound deep in her throat, but did not say anything, clearly afraid that she would break Jada's concentration.

"Calanthe is fighting on the other side of the river. She is strong, but there are so many of them." Jada closed his eyes tight. "I don't think I can watch her anymore."

Galina broke through the woods just as Jada said Adam's name.

"What are you guys doing here?" she asked. "You're missing all the fun."

"We're trying to keep tabs on everyone," Kalan said.

"All right, on with it, you were saying, Jada?" Galina looked casually over at them but didn't seem to take notice of the pale faces of Levi and Kalan as they stared back at her.

Emily looked from one to the other too, but she didn't know the extent of how this information was going to be received.

"I don't see Adam," Jada said in a panic and wheeled to look over at Kalan then Galina. "I don't see him."

"He—" Kalan swallowed.

"He died," Levi finished. "He died saving my life."

Galina looked like someone had punched her in the gut. She took big, gulping breaths, as if she couldn't get enough oxygen. "He can't be dead. He fixes broken things. How can he be dead? Where?" She looked up at them with eyes that begged a different truth to appear.

"He's inside," Kalan said.

Before he even finished talking, she had sprinted toward the castle. Kalan looked at Levi who nodded, the boy ran after her.

Now it was Jada's turn to look questioningly at them. Levi started to feel that contraction in his brain again, but he pushed back.

"I can just tell you." The way Emily shuddered next to him he could tell Jada had tried the same thing on her. "Lady Grustmiener found me and she killed me. Adam brought me back to life, and we think that maybe the effort of it killed him, but I'm not sure. There wasn't anything we could do. He saved me before anyone could stop him." Levi sounded as if this was an attempt to convince himself as much as he tried to convince her.

"Where is Aura?" Emily asked.

"She is kneeling in the woods. There is blood all over her."

Now it was Levi's turn to have his heart fall out through his feet. He thought he could have vomited or passed out. He felt even worse than he had when he'd been killed. He wanted Jada to stop. He didn't want to hear any more.

When Jada saw the look on Levi's face, he rushed on. "She isn't dead. I don't even think she's hurt," he said. He concentrated harder. "There is someone lying in front of her. No, two people lying in front of her. A girl, I don't recognize her. And next to her—" His voice caught and his eyes widened.

"Who?" Emily whispered.

"Theirra. She's dead. Theirra's dead."

Mixed emotions coursed through Levi. He was so relieved to hear that Aura was all right. His heart popped back into place and swelled with the beauty of the news, but the terribleness of their loss encapsulated it. If he had to be perfectly honest with himself, he felt like they'd lost Theirra weeks before, Aura possibly years ago, but there was always a hope that Theirra would come back. That the sadness would be lifted from her like a shawl that she would be able to leave behind. Now all that hung in the air was unfulfilled dreams. It almost crushed him in an entirely different way.

Galina appeared out of nowhere and flew at Levi. She landed several blows before he was able to regain his composure and push her back. It was as if a bubble had formed around him and she was unable to get any closer to him. She growled in frustration as Kalan held her back.

"Because of you, he's dead," she groaned as she sank to her knees.

It was true. If Levi had not been killed, Adam would not have saved him and possibly would still be here, but Levi couldn't dwell on such thoughts. Life was a complicated web, and he'd learned that one turn, one unexpected twist, sent ripples that sometimes could never be fully understood. He hoped that whatever sacrifice Adam had made would not be in vain, and that one day, Galina would be able to see that and forgive what that had happened.

A crack of lightning brought heavy rain to the area where they stood. As Levi looked around, he saw how defeated they all were. They had lost so much. Emily was right. They were going to lose everything. They should have surrendered when they had the chance.

"Emily," he said as he turned to her, tears mixed with the rain drops.

"No, Aura was right. Lady Grustmiener would have killed us all. I see that now. There was no way she would have let any of us live."

"Julia, can you send a bird to get Aura and bring her here? Kalan, can you gather the rest of them? Milskar, Amaline, Kiya, and Riagan? Do you think you have the strength to cover them?" Levi asked. A need to have them safe, to have them in one place, burned in him. "And Calanthe," he added. She was part of them now, too, he supposed.

"Yes."

"Jada, please go with him, show him where each of them are."

Jade nodded and the two disappeared.

"What do we do now?" Emily asked.

"If I had a dollar for every time I've been asked that…" Levi said quietly to himself.

Chapter 50

The Beginning

It took them the better part of an hour, but Kalan and Jada brought everyone back. By the time they stood in front of the castle doors, it was dark outside, the woods illuminated by patches of light, some magical, some from fires. There were still some sounds of fighting, but for the most part it seemed both sides had retreated back to safe places, to lick their wounds and regroup for the evening.

While the lightning had subsided, a steady drizzle continued. Galina still sat on the ground while tears dripped from her unfocused eyes.

When the others appeared in front of them, Levi went immediately to Aura who was covered in patches of blood on her arms, face, and chest. He hugged her and she responded, but it was mechanical and without emotion. He wondered if she was in shock. She stared miles off into the distance and barely acknowledged them as they stood there. He looked her over and checked each exposed part of her for wounds, but Jada was right, she was unhurt. The blood wasn't hers.

"I am so glad you're safe," Emily repeated over and

over into Milskar's neck as he spoke softly back to her.

"Theirra is dead," Aura said. Her eyes appeared blank as he pulled back to look into them.

"We know," Levi said gently.

"Adam," Aura brightened and looked around. "Where is he? He can help, he can save her!"

"Aura—" Emily started with pain in her voice.

"No. No, he will help her. You—" She pointed at Jada who had tears in his eyes. "Find him."

"Aura, he's dead," Levi whispered.

"No," she said with finality in her voice as she broke away from Levi's hold. "Find him, bring him to me."

"It's true," Emily continued. "He died saving Levi."

Aura looked around the group before her eyes rested on his. He nodded his head.

"You—you died?" she stuttered.

"I did, but Adam saved me."

They stared at one another. Levi's heart felt squeezed so tight in his chest it rooted him in place. *What if she wished Adam had saved Theirra instead?* he wondered. *Will she ever be able to see me and know my life and her friend's death are forever connected?*

Levi let go of Aura's gaze.

"Where's Julia?" Riagan asked.

They looked around, taken aback by the fact that she wasn't with them. Little Julia. So often forgotten.

Jada gasped.

"What is it?" Aura's voice sounded dry and cracked.

"She's not here."

"What do you mean she is not here?" Milskar said as he untangled himself from Emily's hold.

"Where is she?" Calanthe asked.

"I see."

What *did* he see? In front of him, as if he was there himself, was a street. A real street, pavement and everything. There was even a white line down the middle of it. Where in this land was something like that?

He looked out of Julia's eyes as she followed some-one. Images popped into Julia's head but they happened so quickly Jada wasn't able to focus on any of them.

It was light out, so bright, so much brighter than the place she had just come from, and Julia found it difficult for her eyes to adjust. And the noise! There was so much noise. Cars! How strange to not know the last time she had heard a car. And a dog as it barked. A siren went off in the distance. Brick surrounded her and, as she rounded a corner, the street turned to cobblestone underneath her.

Where was she? Jada tried to will Julia to look around, to give him clues, but he felt her put up a fight. She was aware Jada was there—surely she had to feel it—but it was clear he was merely allowed to be along for the ride. Julia ran the show and dictated what happened. She passed a sign and looked up. It was red and blue with white lettering. Jada had to concentrate to read it. The shock of what it said almost pulled him away, but he fought to stay present with Julia.

In the distance, maybe a block or two ahead, a woman walked. She stood out, not only for the way she dressed, but the way she moved. There was no one else on the street with them, and she moved with such determination. She turned down an even narrower alleyway. Julia knew if she followed, the woman would see her, so she crouched down at the corner and was able to see down the street from a cracked piece of mirror resting on a trash can opposite her.

The woman knocked on a door, which creaked in pro-test at being opened.

"Who is there?" a deep voice asked.

"She is waiting for me," the woman answered.

"Who is there?" the voice repeated.

"Oh, let her in, she has come from far away and worked hard enough to get here, Listrel," another woman's voice answered. This one was much older and sounded almost brittle.

Just before the first woman went inside, she looked back and forth along the street to make sure no one had followed her. At the last moment, her reflection caught in the mirror. Jada recognized it from visions he'd seen in Emily, Aura, and Levi's minds.

"Lady Grustmiener!" he shouted as he found himself plunged back into the darkness that surrounded them.

"What," Aura asked. It was as if some of the life was breathed back into her.

"Julia is with Lady Grustmiener. But I don't understand, I don't understand how it's possible." Jada was looked wildly around at them.

"You don't understand how what's possible?" Levi asked.

The image of the red, white, and blue sign burned in Jada's memory. "She's in Philadelphia."

For the second time in as many hours Levi's heart stopped.

About the Author

Kristin Durfee grew up outside of Philadelphia where an initial struggle with reading blossomed into a love and passion for the written word.

She has also been an author, since a very young age, writing short stories and poems, though she is now focusing on longer works. She is currently working on the final book in the Four Corners Trilogy.

Durfee resides outside of Orlando, FL, and when not enjoying the theme parks or Florida sun, she spends most of her time with her husband and their quirky dogs.

She is a member of the Florida Writers Association. Her first two books in the Four Corners Trilogy are published by Black Opal Books.

CPSIA information can be obtained
at www.ICGtesting.com
Printed in the USA
LVOW04s0534300816

502359LV00010B/41/P

9 781626 945173